FOCUS ON THE FARMER

LILLIANA ROSE

For Aunty Julie

BLURB

I capture moments for a living, hiding behind my camera. The Royal Adelaide Show was just another assignment, until Jackson Pearce, a ruggedly handsome farmer with a quiet strength and haunting blue eyes, forces me into the frame. After his bull introduces us headfirst, my job transforms into a dizzying, heart-pounding complication.

He sees past my city-girl defenses, stirring feelings I thought were buried. But his life is dirt roads and wide-open spaces, and mine is deadlines and duty to my dad. Jackson represents a future I never imagined, one that terrifies and tempts me in equal measure. The connection is real, the chemistry explosive, but can a love sparked in the heat of the show survive the distance? Or will choosing him mean losing myself?

FOCUS ON THE FARMER

CHAPTER 1

Megan

Click. Click. Click.

I scrambled back, clutching my Canon close. The sheer size of the cow lumbering toward me sent a shiver down my spine, even through the denim of my jeans.

Had I gotten the shot? I hoped so. Another step back, just to be safe.

The air buzzed, thick with the earthy smell of livestock, hot dogs, and cotton candy. A chaotic river of cattle, horses, goats, alpacas, and the odd bewildered-looking sheep flowed past me, heading toward the main arena of the Royal Adelaide Show. Grand Parade time. It was only Day Three, Sunday afternoon, but the grounds were packed, families soaking up the early spring sunshine.

Father's Day. Always the first Sunday in September here.

A familiar pang twisted low in my gut. Dad had been great about it, all 'Don't worry, love, work's important,' but I pictured his face, that slight droop at the corners of his mouth he tried to hide when he was disappointed.

Last year, we'd had a barbecue, just the two of us, trying to make new traditions after Mom…

No, focus. Work. I watched the cream-colored cows being funneled toward the arena gate, lifted my camera again, determined to capture something iconic for the *Stock Journal*.

Where could I position myself safely? Where was the *best* angle? I wasn't sure.

These weren't petting zoo animals, they were prize winners, enormous and unpredictable. I edged closer to the arena entrance, camera ready, but my focus wavered.

My gaze snagged on one man in particular, leading a massive cream bull. Moleskins, yeah, tight like the others, but there was an effortless competence in the way he handled the hulking beast beside him. A quiet focus in his eyes under the shadow of his Akubra, a solid presence amidst the chaos. He moved with the easy strength of someone completely at home in their skin, a world away from the city guys I knew.

Get the shot, Megan. I crouched down, aiming for a lower perspective of the oncoming cattle, definitely not the men leading them, despite the distraction. I peered through the lens, trying to focus quickly as hooves pounded closer.

Click. Click. Click.

"Look out!"

A blur of cream filled my viewfinder. I started to lower the camera, but before I could react, something connected hard with the side of my skull.

I screamed, a raw, involuntary sound ripped from my throat. An explosion went off behind my eyes. The world fractured into glittering shards against black velvet, tiny lights creeping in from the edges, pulsing. It was strangely beautiful, distracting me from the dull throb that had started behind my temples.

Then I thudded onto the concrete, backside first. A fresh wave of agony shot through me. Air punched from my lungs in a gasp. I'd been hit in the head. That much I knew. By what, exactly? I had no idea.

Faces swam above me, voices blurring. People rushed toward me.

Heat flooded my cheeks in mortification. The absolute last thing I wanted was to be the center of attention, especially for doing something stupid. That's why I hid behind the camera. My camera! My hand scrabbled on the concrete beside me, fingers closing around the familiar shape. Relief washed through me, sharp and sudden. My SLR digital Canon. It looked okay, mostly. Hard to tell with the pounding symphony starting up in my head.

More shards glittered at the edge of my vision, pulsing in time with the sickening thud in my head.

"They don't have points," I heard myself say. My voice sounded distant, wrong.

"Are you okay?" A man knelt beside me. The one I'd noticed earlier. The owner of the cream blur. I tried to focus on him, but the glittering lights were retreating, leaving a thick fog rolling into my mind. My thoughts felt thick, sluggish, like wading through treacle. Cotton wool seemed to be stuffed in my ears.

"No points," I repeated, vaguely disappointed. I'd never broken a bone, never had stitches, never experienced anything like this. So *this* was seeing stars. The phrase didn't do it justice at all. I touched the side of my head gingerly. Still there. Good. Hadn't blacked out either. Another tick.

"What are you talking about?" His hand touched my shoulder, surprisingly gentle for its size.

"The stars I can see," I mumbled, the connection between his question and my answer feeling tenuous. I forced myself to look at him properly. Youngish, mid-twenties, my age. His broad-brimmed hat hid most of his blond hair, but his blue eyes cut through the fog, sharp and startlingly clear. A dusting of stubble shadowed a strong jawline. Okay, even with my bell rung, I could register, he was definitely hot. The thought felt absurdly out of place.

"Shit." The word was low, intense. His hand tightened slightly on my shoulder. "My Bruce hit your head. More like grazed it along the side from the looks of the mark, but still, I'm sorry he was such a shit." He sounded genuinely appalled, guilty.

"Bruce?" I looked at him, trying to make the connection. "Is that your name?"

"No. My bull. His hoof struck your head. Lucky it was only a half jump he made, not a full-on blow."

"Oh. So that's what happened." Half kick? It felt pretty full-on from where I was sitting. The adrenaline was definitely fading now, replaced by a heavy, rhythmic thudding inside my skull. I tried to smile.

Now was *not* the time to flirt, but some automatic pilot seemed to have taken over. God, I must look like a complete idiot. I squeezed my eyes shut as a particularly vicious throb hit.

"Shit. We'd better get you to a hospital." There was urgency in his voice now, overriding the guilt.

Hospital. The word slammed into me. Suddenly, I wasn't just smelling dust and animals, but the sharp, sterile tang of antiseptic, and the underlying scent of sickness and bleach. Images of Mom's frail hand in mine, the beep, beep, beep fading. Cold dread clamped around my chest, stealing my breath.

"Oh no, I'm fine," I choked out, my voice thin and reedy. My returning awareness battled the drumbeat in my head. I became conscious of the circle of concerned faces around me, the rising murmur of voices. Mortification burned my cheeks again. Get away. Just get away.

I tried to stand. The world tilted violently, sliding sideways like a badly projected image. I gasped, flailing, my balance gone. Strong hands clamped around my waist, hauling me upright, pulling me close against a solid, warm chest. His chest.

"You are not all right," he insisted, his deep voice thick with conviction, a flicker of something, fear perhaps, in those sharp blue eyes, before concern smoothed it over. "A knock to the head is serious."

"I'll be fine." I ignored the nauseating sway, focusing on breathing evenly. Don't throw up. Not in front of the hot guy. Not in front of everyone. "Just give me a minute."

"You've had long enough."

"No doctors." The words were a panicked whisper. "It's only a little bump." I reached up tentatively, my fingers brushing against a rapidly swelling lump on my forehead that felt like a bloody goose egg. I swallowed hard, pushing down the bile rising in my throat. "No emergency clinic either."

My fingers came away warm. Sticky. A sickening chill iced through me. Blood. I wasn't good with blood. My vision tunneled.

"You're bleeding." His voice softened, but it sounded as if it were miles away.

The ground rushed up to meet me. My knees gave way.

He caught me again, his reaction instantaneous. "I'm taking you to the first aid room. Head injuries are serious." No arguing with that tone.

"Hey, Dad, take care of Bruce will you," he called out.

Before I could even form a protest, he scooped

me up with one arm securely under my knees, the other supporting my back. I instinctively tried to lean forward, away from him, but he simply tilted me back until my head had no choice but to rest against his shoulder. His heartbeat, steady and slow beneath my ear, was a surprisingly calming rhythm against the chaos in my head. His warmth seeped into me, soothing. He smelled real. Earthy, a hint of spice, maybe sweat. Not unpleasant. I sighed, relaxing into his hold despite myself. I could probably stay like this all day.

The first aid room was depressingly close. Disappointment pricked me as he gently deposited me onto a hard plastic chair in a small, basic room that reeked of Dettol. The sterile smell instantly brought back the hospital, and Mom. I pushed the thought away. I wanted his arms around me again, that solid warmth. Now he just stood beside me, a concerned stranger, and practical worries crashed back in.

How was I going to keep my job? Helen, my editor, needed Grand Parade shots. They'd be happening *now*. I couldn't afford this. Contract work meant no photos, no pay. And I'd ditched Dad on Father's Day for *this*. Everything was going spectacularly wrong. Hot guy or not, this wasn't the plan.

My head spun again. I dropped it into my hands, closing my eyes against the wave of dizziness.

"What happened?" A nurse appeared. She was short and slender, with an air of no-nonsense competence. Short black hair, practical blue uniform.

"She got struck in the head by a bull," the guy, my rescuer, supplied.

My head just pounded. Thinking hurt.

"You might be concussed." The nurse peered at my face. "Can you tell me your name?"

"Megan Lyall."

"Age?"

"Twenty-three." I risked a glance at him. He knew my name and my age. I didn't even know his. Weirdly intimate for strangers.

"Do you know this lady?" the nurse asked him, looking over her shoulder.

"Um... no... just, it was my bull who did the damage." He shoved his hands deep into his pockets, looking uncomfortable.

"How about you wait outside for a while?" Her voice was firm but polite.

"I just want to make sure she'll be all right."

I risked opening my eyes again. The worry etched on his face was undeniable. He looked torn when the nurse asked him to leave, glancing back at me, his jaw tight. It sent a different kind of flutter through me, unrelated to the head injury.

"Let me help her first," the nurse said, her tone brooking no argument.

Even though it was his bull, I knew it was my own stupid fault for getting too close. I didn't want him scared off by the nurse. Besides, he was, well, he was hot. I didn't want him to vanish before I could thank him properly. Or get his name.

"I won't go without seeing you." I forced my eyes open again, meeting his gaze. The apprehension there warmed something inside me. He looked tough, capable, but those blue eyes held a genuine kindness. A sweetie.

"I promise." I managed a smile. It hurt my head, but I held it. Having him watch while I was examined felt too exposed. He was still a stranger, albeit a ridiculously good-looking one who'd just carried me like a sack of potatoes. I needed to know I was okay, needed to get back to work. Then I needed his name. And I needed him to know he wasn't indebted. He'd done enough.

"Okay." He hesitated. "But if you need me to help you... hospital, doctors, anything... you make sure you let me know. I want to help you." The words carried a weight that felt like more than just polite concern. He backed out slowly.

"Right, let's clean up this cut," the nurse said briskly. "Good news is, it won't need stitches."

Relief washed over me, immediately followed by another wave of dizziness at the mention of stitches.

The nurse steadied me with a hand on my shoulder. "You might still need to see a doctor."

"No. I'll be fine." My voice was firmer now. "I just need a moment. I'm not good with blood."

"I'll clean the cut first, then we'll see. Can you walk to the back room?"

I nodded, instantly regretting the movement. *I can do this.* A bump on the head wasn't stopping me. *Cute guy waiting outside.* I used the thought as fuel, pushing myself carefully to my feet, I walked slowly toward the back room, acutely aware of the nurse hovering beside me, ready to catch me.

She helped me onto the examination bed. Despite her slight build, her grip was strong, reassuring. Lying flat eased the relentless throb in my head. She worked quickly, cleaning the abrasion above my temple.

My mind drifted back to the guy outside. What *was* his name? Where was he from? Did he have a girlfriend? Probably. Someone that striking couldn't possibly be single. Right? *Just thank him and go.* The thought landed with a dull thud in my foggy brain. Definitely not what I wanted to do.

The longer I lay there, the clearer my head became. The painkillers were kicking in, dulling the worst of the ache. I could actually sit up without the world tilting or stars exploding.

The nurse peeled off her gloves, dropping them in the bin before washing her hands. "I still recommend you visit a doctor."

"No." My response was short and final. "It's just a bump. The blood... it rattled me."

"Well, if you get overly sleepy, or the pain gets worse, promise me you will?" Her tone had that 'naughty schoolgirl' edge again.

"Okay." I swung my legs over the side of the bed and paused. No nausea. Good. I eased my feet onto the floor. So far, so good. The stars had faded, and the throb was manageable.

"There's one more thing," the nurse said, raising her dark eyebrows.

I looked at her, wary. I just wanted out of this sterile-smelling room.

"You shouldn't be alone for the next few hours. Just a precaution, if you are concussed."

"Fine." Easy. Say goodbye to the guy, process my

photos, and head home. Dad would be, oh, no. He was going out tonight.

"Is there someone I can ring?" The nurse read my expression like a book.

Damn. Thinking was still a challenge.

"A parent? A friend?"

I sighed. Dad deserved his night out. It would be hard for him without Mom. My friends all had their own lives. I hated causing a fuss, hated people fussing over me, even when maybe it was warranted. Then I remembered Kristie! My old boarding school mate. She was here, exhibiting sheep. But could I really ask her to babysit me? We mostly kept in touch via Facebook these days.

"I'll be around people at the show," I mumbled, not meaning to say it aloud. Thousands of people. If I collapsed, someone would notice, right?

"Not the same thing." The nurse was implacable.

I sighed again. "Okay, I'll call a friend." I pulled out my phone, fingers fumbling slightly, and sent Kristie a quick text: *Hey, you at the show yet? Can I swing by for some pics?* Vague enough. It satisfied the nurse, and maybe Kristie would actually reply soon. Anything to get out of this first-aid room.

The door swung open, and *he* ducked back inside. Tall, concerned expression wrinkling his forehead, still looking ridiculously good despite everything.

He hovered awkwardly by the door. "How's it going?"

An idea sparked through the headache haze, reckless but compelling. "You'll keep me company this afternoon, won't you?" It came out less like a question, more like a demand. I needed to get out, needed those photos, and needed to keep my job. Mom's voice echoed in my head, *Unnecessary risks, Megan,* but he seemed nice.

Unlike my ex, Mark, who'd also seemed nice until he turned out to be a prize-winning tosser. This felt different. And he *had* offered to help.

"Ummm..." He pursed his lips, considering. He shoved his hands back in his moleskin pockets, a casual shrug that somehow sent a jolt of heat through me. His rolled-up sleeves revealed tanned, strong forearms. My heart gave an unsteady thump.

"My job depends on it," I added, deploying my best pleading eyes. Just for a few hours, I promised myself. Then I'd go home and forget about this disaster of a day. But as my gaze locked with his intense blue eyes, I felt that invisible pull again. A low twist in my belly warned me that forgetting him wouldn't be easy.

"Okay, then." He smiled, a slow curve of his lips that spread warmth through me like sunshine.

"Anything to make up for what happened," he added quickly.

"First, you need to tell me your name." Saying it out loud felt slightly ridiculous, like knowing his name made wandering off with a stranger safer. But he didn't feel like a stranger. I'd already felt the steady beat of his heart against my ear.

"Jackson Pearce." He grinned, a wide, cheeky smile that stole the breath from my throat.

"And I'm twenty-five, by the way." He winked. "Guess I'll be a perfect escort for you for the day."

My mouth fell open. "Escort?" Lustful thoughts, yes. Plenty of those were buzzing around. But acting on them? Not usually my style. And 'escort' conjured up entirely different, less appealing images. I wanted a boyfriend eventually, not a transaction.

"Ah, no! Didn't mean it like that." He backpedaled furiously, color flooding his neck and face. He took a deep breath. "Meant... I'll keep an eye on you. Make sure there are no side effects from the knock." He put his right hand over his heart. "Honestly. I'll be a gentleman. Promise."

The raw sincerity in his eyes convinced me. Looking into them felt like seeing a glimpse of something real, something steady. A surprising calm settled over me, a peace I hadn't felt with my previous boyfriends, all three of them. Cautious, that was me. Usually.

But Jackson Pearce. The name felt right. Decent name, devastatingly good looks. Okay, the meet-cute was more of a meet-hoof-to-the-head, which was hardly ideal. Maybe that was enough to stop anything serious? I'd just enjoy the company. For a few hours.

"Good," I said, finding my voice. "Because I'll have you know I'm not that sort of girl."

"I know you're not," he replied, his gaze steady.

I smiled then, a real smile, ignoring the dull throb in my head and the ridiculous goose egg blooming on my forehead. I was getting out of here, getting photos, and I had a hot guy, a gentlemanly hot guy, by my side. Considering how the afternoon started, that felt like a definite win.

"If it gets worse, see a doctor." The nurse stepped forward, addressing Jackson. He towered over her, but she held her ground. "Have you had experience with potential concussion?"

"I have," Jackson confirmed, his voice serious again. "I'll keep an eye on her. And I'll take her kicking and screaming to the hospital if there are any signs. Or anything else requiring medical attention."

"Good. Thank you." The nurse actually looked relieved. "You're in good hands now."

"Thanks for your help," I said to her as we left. Kicking and screaming? I wasn't so sure about that part, but the fact that he cared enough to say it, even as a stranger, resonated deep inside. *He's just feeling guilty,* a cynical voice whispered. Maybe. But maybe it was more than that.

CHAPTER 2

Jackson

I held the first aid room door open, the scent of antiseptic hitting me like a physical blow, sharp, clean, but underneath, the ghost of something else, sickness, waiting rooms. Erin. I pushed the thought down, hard. Megan stepped out into the chaotic symphony of the show, the lowing of cattle, the distant screams from the rides, the sweet, greasy smell of donuts and hot dogs. She looked pale, fragile under the bright spring sun, and the slight tremor in her legs wasn't just my imagination.

She'd been bloody stubborn in there, refusing doctors and hospitals. I got it, especially after she mentioned her mom's passing. Hospitals weren't happy places. But a knock to the head from a bull wasn't something to shrug off. My gut clenched. I'd promised the nurse, promised *myself*, I wouldn't let her out of my sight. Guilt gnawed at me. It was my bull, my responsibility. But looking at her now, blinking in the sunlight, a strand of dark hair escaping her ponytail to curl against her cheek, damn, it wasn't just guilt keeping me glued to her side.

"Where to first, Megan?" I asked, keeping my voice soft. No need to spook her further.

She flinched almost imperceptibly at her name, the color rising in her cheeks as she looked away, scanning the crowd. Lost. The bravado she'd shown the nurse had evaporated. "The Grand Parade is well and truly over," she murmured, mostly to herself. "Now... I don't know..." Her voice trailed off, thick with a sudden, raw emotion that caught me off-guard. Failure edged her words.

"When was the last time you ate?" I asked gently, trying to anchor her. Low blood sugar wouldn't be helping that head knock.

She just shrugged, her gaze fixed on a family walking past, parents wrangling kids who were clutching showbags. Her shoulders slumped, and I saw the telltale shimmer in her eyes before she blinked furiously. Something about the families, the Father's Day atmosphere maybe, had hit a nerve. That sterile room had stirred something up in her, something deeper than the bump on her head.

"Let's get something to eat," I said, putting a light hand on the center of her back to guide her gently through the throng toward the food tents. She moved almost automatically, her focus inward. I could feel the tension radiating from her.

"I'm not hungry," she mumbled, her voice tight, tears dangerously close now. Her stomach probably felt like mine did whenever I thought too hard about Erin falling and the silence afterward.

I kept my hand steady on her back, a silent offer of support. Pushing her wouldn't help. "Are you sure about that?" I kept my voice low, close to her ear.

She shook her head, a lump clearly visible in her throat. *Get a grip*, I could almost hear her thinking.

Okay, change tack. "Something tells me you're a coffee girl." I kept walking, letting the crowd flow around us.

Silence for a few steps, then a tiny, almost imperceptible nod. The tension under my hand eased slightly. Good. Give her space, don't push. Coffee. Coffee fixed most things, temporarily at least.

"Right, then I know where to get a great coffee," I

said, letting my voice lighten, though the worry still coiled in my gut.

She finally turned her head, looking up at me, suspicion warring with need in her dark eyes. "Here at the show? You have to be joking." Show coffee was usually dishwater.

I laughed softly. "You just have to know where to go." The faint curve of her lips was progress.

"Really?"

"Yes, really. My shout. It's the least I can do." I steered her toward the Taste SA pavilion near the entrance, the aroma of proper, double-roasted coffee cutting through the general showground fug. "There's a free table over there." I nudged her gently forward. She squeezed between chairs and pushed prams to the corner table and sank down, looking exhausted.

"You sure you don't want any food?"

"I'm sure." She sounded like she meant it. Her stomach was probably still churning.

"I'll be back shortly." I gave her what I hoped was a reassuring smile and headed to the counter. Waiting for the coffees, I leaned against the counter, trying to look casual, but my gaze kept drifting back to her. She looked so small and vulnerable sitting there, the purplish lump on her forehead stark against her pale skin. She'd lifted her camera, fiddling with it, her brow furrowed in concentration. Or distraction. Probably distraction.

I caught sight of her reflection in the polished counter. She glanced up, her gaze flicking toward me, then quickly down again, color rising in her cheeks. Interesting. Then her expression froze, her breath catching. She was looking at a photo on her camera, her face paling slightly. It must have been one she took right before Bruce spooked. Seeing the bull again, even in a picture, yeah, that would rattle anyone.

"Here's your coffee." I placed the cup down carefully, along with a couple of sugar packets. "Didn't know if you needed sugar or not."

"Thanks, I don't." She looked up, startled, quickly closing the photo folder on her camera. She was definitely rattled.

"I know you said you weren't hungry, but I got some muffins." I put the paper bag on the table. "Chocolate chip or banana chip? I'll eat what you don't want." Mom always said food helped shock.

"Thanks, you didn't have to."

"Least I can do, considering." I sat down beside her, my leg brushing hers. A jolt, like static electricity, shot up my leg, surprising the hell out of me.

Megan jumped slightly, too, her head spinning, judging by the way her eyes widened. I put a hand on her shoulder instinctively. "You all right?" My voice came out rougher than I intended.

She blushed again, a fascinating wave of pink that spread down her neck. "Yes."

"You sure?"

"Yes," she insisted, reaching for the bag. "Now, I'm going to go for the choc chip muffin." Good. Getting some sugar into her was vital. She looked like she might faint again.

"Thought you might like the chocolate," I said, pulling out the muffins. They were still warm. "Banana chip's my favorite." I broke mine in half, steam snaking out. "Reminds me of being a kid."

"Good. Chocolate chip is my childhood and adult favorite." She took a cautious sip of coffee, holding the cup near her nose first, inhaling the aroma like it was medicine. After a few more sips, some color returned to her face, the lines of pain around her eyes softening slightly.

"Do you come to the show every year?" she asked, starting on the muffin. The sugar seemed to be working as she looked more alert.

I nodded, swallowing a mouthful. "Yeah. We show Murray Greys."

"I thought his name was Bruce." She frowned, rubbing her temple, and a fresh wave of guilt washed over me.

I managed a grin. "That's Bruce's *breed*."

"Oh." She stuffed more muffin in her mouth, looking perplexed. Sitting this close, I could feel the warmth radiating from her and smell the faint floral scent of her shampoo underneath the showground smells. It was distracting. Very distracting.

"He can be a little bad-tempered around crowds," I explained, trying to focus.

She automatically touched the lump on her head. "Sort of got that impression clearly."

"Hey, I'm really sorry about what happened." I reached out, resting my hand over hers on the table. Her skin was soft, cool beneath my rough fingers.

"It's not your fault," she answered, but her gaze unfocused slightly, her mind seeming to drift. That fog again.

"No, but I still feel responsible."

"You're not." Her voice was distant. Damn it, she was fading again. I stroked my thumb over the back of her hand, trying to ground her. Her focus blurred completely for a second, then she blinked, sighing softly as I pulled my hand away, leaving a tingling warmth where we'd touched. She looked, disappointed?

"Are you all right?" I asked again, leaning closer.

Her eyes snapped back into focus, a blush rising again. "Thanks for asking." She took a deliberate, deep breath. "I'm fine." She sat up straighter, pushing thoughts of me away, I guessed. Trying to focus on work. But I could see the effort it cost her. There was something about her, a vulnerability beneath the sass and determination that pulled at me.

She wanted to know me better, she'd said. The thought sent a surprising jolt of pleasure through me. Keep it light, Sunny. Don't scare her off. But then she asked the question.

"You mentioned to the nurse that you knew about concussions."

The air thickened. Erin. The memory slammed into me of the frantic phone call, the sterile white hospital room, the relentless beep of the machines, the awful silence when they stopped. My sister, lying there, broken, because I hadn't stopped her. Because I hadn't found her damn helmet. Because I was more interested in chasing girls than looking out for my little sister. The coffee cup crumpled slightly in my grip.

"You don't have to tell me," Megan said quickly, her voice soft, her eyes wide with instant understanding. She knew that look. She knew grief.

I drained the last of my coffee, buying time, turning the flimsy cup over and over in my hands. The silence stretched.

"It was my sister, Erin," I finally said, the name scraping my throat.

I saw her flinch, just slightly. Her own breath hitched. Her gaze didn't waver, though, instead it held mine, filled with a quiet empathy that went deeper than words. "I'm sorry," she whispered.

"It was a few years ago now." I forced the words out. "She was fifteen. Thrown from her horse after it had been spooked by a snake. Head injury." The clinical words felt inadequate, obscene. "Coma for a week. Then..." I couldn't finish. "The horse, Nanny... had to be put down." My voice faded.

Her eyes didn't leave mine. The sorrow reflected there felt fresh, raw, like it had only happened yesterday. "I'm so sorry," she repeated, her voice barely audible.

"It's not your fault," I mumbled, shrugging, trying to shake off the heavy cloak of memory.

"I know." Her voice was gentle, but firm. "I've caused you to remember, when you've only shown me kindness." She hesitated, then added softly, "My mom died of cancer about a year or so ago. I know what it's like to lose someone you love." She didn't reach out, but her gaze was a touch in itself, strong and steady.

My breath caught. She *did* know. That shared understanding hung between us, heavy but strangely comforting.

"You know what it's like, don't you?" I asked, the question redundant. "Losing someone you love?"

"Yes." Tears welled in her eyes, but she blinked them back fiercely. Then, her expression shifted, a deliberate attempt at lightness. "And now I'm going to change the subject, abruptly, without any subtlety, because we've gone too serious, too soon."

A weak smile touched my lips. Relief washed through me. "Okay. Now, I promised to help you keep your job. What do you need to do?"

"Pee." The word popped out, followed by a horrified clap of her hand over her mouth, her eyes wide.

I couldn't help it, I laughed, a genuine chuckle this time.

"I mean, I need to go to the bathroom," she corrected, her face flaming scarlet. That delightful lack of filter again. Combined with the lingering fog, it was endearing.

"Right. There's one around the corner." I stood up.

"I can go by myself."

I held out my hand. "I promised I'd keep an eye on you. Means I wait outside like a perv, so please don't be too long." I winked, but the words were serious. No way was I letting her wander off alone yet.

She hesitated, then took my hand. Her fingers were cold, but the spark was still there. She swayed as she stood, and I tightened my grip instinctively, steadying her.

"Careful."

"I'm all right." She pulled her hand away quickly, her motivation clearly being to avoid any further suggestion of hospitals. She picked up her camera bag. I pursed my lips but didn't argue. She wouldn't thank me for treating her like an invalid, even if the cold fear in my gut screamed that she needed wrapping in cotton wool.

We navigated the crowded tent exit. I pointed toward the ladies'. "That way." I let go of her hand reluctantly.

"I'll be waiting here," I called after her. "So don't do a runner on me." Her slight hesitation before she turned away told me the thought *had* crossed her mind. Stubborn, determined, and utterly captivating.

I leaned against the wall in the shade, crossing my arms, trying to look patient. Inside, I was anything but. Was she okay? Was she dizzy again? Was she going to climb out a window to escape me and my overbearing concern?

I scanned the crowd, my gaze snagging on anyone with dark hair before dismissing them. Waiting felt like an eternity. My promise to the nurse felt flimsy against the weight of my promise to myself—never again. Never let someone get hurt on my watch again.

Finally, she emerged, walking toward me with a determined smile, though she still looked pale. She was trying to show me she was fine.

"Where to?" I asked, straightening up.

"I need some photos of animals." She sounded tired, the earlier confidence wavering.

"What sort of animals?"

She looked at me blankly, the fog clearly rolling back in. She sighed. "Any."

Right. Distraction needed. And maybe a gentle confrontation with the source of the problem. "How about if I show you mine?" I saw the flicker of alarm cross her face before I quickly added, "The cattle, I mean. Don't worry. Bruce won't hurt you. I'll make sure you don't get that close to him."

She inclined her head, considering my offer. Maybe getting some photos, fulfilling her job requirement, would help settle her. And maybe seeing Bruce calmly tied up would ease some of the fear. Plus, selfishly, it kept her close. It gave me a reason to stay with her, to share a bit of my world.

"My parents' cattle are this way." I placed my hand lightly on her back again, guiding her toward the sheds, trying to ignore the jolt the simple contact sent through me. This city girl was getting under my skin in a way no one else had.

CHAPTER 3

Megan

His explanation about the bull's breed still echoed as he turned and walked down the aisle. My gaze lingered, maybe a beat too long, on the way those moleskins hugged his backside. I took a few steadying breaths, trying to pull my thoughts together, then forced my legs to move. My new Rossi boots, definitely more suited to city pavements than this minefield, required careful navigation. I didn't fancy scraping manure off them later, so I kept my eyes peeled, stepping cautiously.

Still, I managed to take in the scene, sticking to the center of the wide aisle to give the cattle tethered on either side a wide berth. The sheer bulk of the animals made my palms sweat. Owners were tending to them, some combing short, coarse hair with surprising gentleness, others lounging on hay bales or fold-up chairs, sipping coffee, a few even watching footy on tiny portable televisions. It was a whole different world tucked away back here. Some cows stood swishing their tails impatiently, others lay placidly on beds of straw, chewing their cud with unnerving calmness. They were huge. Intimidating. Especially after my run-in—or rather, head-butt—with Bruce.

But then, something shifted inside me. The ever-present photographer's eye clicked on. The light filtering through the high shed roof, the textures, the quiet intimacy between the farmers and their animals, and my fingers itched for the shutter. This wasn't just a line of beasts, it was a community, a way of life temporarily transplanted into the city.

I paused, lifting my camera. I framed a wide-angle shot down the aisle, deliberately placing Jackson's back slightly off-center. He wasn't the focus, not technically, though the temptation to zoom right in on him was strong. This shot was about capturing the atmosphere, the dedication of these farmers. I took a few more, varying the perspective, wondering how I could get higher for a bird's-eye view.

Then I saw her. A little girl, maybe five or six, fast

asleep, curled up against the massive black-and-white flank of a cow. A pink bow perched jauntily in her brown hair. The cow itself seemed almost protective, its sheer size a startling contrast to the child's innocent vulnerability. My breath caught. Fear warred with the undeniable pull of the image. Swallowing hard, I stepped closer, moving softly. I squatted down, the world narrowing to just the viewfinder. My professional instincts took over completely.

Click. Click. Click.

I needed permission to take photos of a minor. I scanned nearby and spotted a woman in her thirties watching me from a green fold-up chair, coffee cup in hand. I held up my camera questioningly. She gave a small nod. Perfect. I refocused, capturing a series of shots, the gentle rise and fall of the cow's breathing, the peaceful expression on the child's face.

Lowering the camera, I knew I had it. *The* shot. The one that might just make up for missing the Grand Parade chaos. I stood up, walked over to the woman, and showed her the image on the display.

"Can I have a copy?" she asked, her eyes lighting up.

"Of course." I fumbled in my handbag, pulling

out a consent form, notepad, and pen. The familiar routine grounded me. "I also need you to sign a release for the photo to be used in the paper, if that's all right? May I please have your name?"

"I'm Rachael Fields, and my daughter is Katie. We're from up north near Clare. Our stud is called Cloverfield."

Clare. Wasn't that near where Jackson was from? I scribbled quickly on the tiny lines, my handwriting messy, taking down her email address too. "Thank you."

As Rachael signed, I suddenly remembered Jackson. Where had he gone? I looked around, a ridiculous pang of anxiety hitting me. I didn't want to lose him, despite my earlier thoughts of ditching him. He was nearby, leaning against a post, watching me patiently. The sight sent a ripple of unexpected calmness through me. I smiled as he walked over.

"Good picture," he said, nodding toward the sleeping girl.

"I don't know how she can sleep there," I admitted. "I'd be too scared."

"They get used to us. Treat them right, they're really peaceful animals."

I chewed my bottom lip. Now that the photographic adrenaline rush was fading, the throb in my head was making a comeback. "Well, except Bruce."

"He's a softie, really," Jackson insisted. "Just not keen on the crowds and noise here. It's a bit different to home."

"I bet."

"Come on. My cattle are this way." He motioned for me to follow. "That's if you still want to see them."

"Of course." More photos needed to be taken. You always needed backups, different angles. That perfect shot often hid amongst dozens of others.

We walked under a banner: *'Feature Breed ~ Murray Greys.'*

"What does that mean?" I pointed as he glanced back.

"Each year, the show selects a certain animal breed to be the feature for publicity."

"Oh." Sort of made sense. "Have you finished the judging?" Ribbons of blue, red, white, and some wider ones combining all three colors, adorned the walls near some stalls.

"Finished most of the competition today. Just got the wide ribbons tomorrow."

"Wide ribbons?" I took a slow breath against the returning pulse in my head. Thinking seemed to aggravate it, but I was genuinely curious about his world. It felt so different, so much more tangible than my city life.

"Champions," he explained, pointing to his right. "Like those ribbons over there for the Angus breed." Black cattle stood in a neat row, backsides facing us. The ribbons were indeed wider, stitched with gold lettering.

I kept watching my step, trying not to get too close to the massive animals flanking the aisle. My heart rate was definitely elevated. Even with Jackson beside me, the proximity felt risky. "Are these cows milked?" I asked, trying to sound casual.

Jackson turned, a broad smile spreading across his face. "You don't know much about cattle, do you?"

"Nope," I admitted freely. "City girl through and through."

"Angus are bred for beef, just like Murray Greys. Milkers are in the other shed, over to the east."

I clamped my mouth shut before I could ask which way east was. I followed him, taking in the earthy smells, the low hum of bovine contentment that seemed to fill the shed despite the distant show-ground noise filtering in. It felt grounding. Real. A welcome change from concrete and exhaust fumes.

He stopped abruptly at the end of a row near the middle of the shed, and I nearly walked straight into his back. My nose filled with the scent of his shirt, that same intriguing mix of spice, sun-warmed cotton, and something distinctly male and outdoorsy. My head swam pleasantly for a second before a hand grabbed my arm.

"You sure you're all right?" His voice, close and concerned, cut through the momentary haze.

"Yes."

"I'm going to take you to the hospital." His grip tightened, insistent.

Panic flared, cold and sharp. No. Not again. I pulled myself together, focusing, meeting his intense gaze directly. "No," I said firmly. "I don't need to be in a hospital. I was just... miles away. Thinking. It's what I do when I'm taking photos." Not a complete lie. Photography did consume me. Just not quite like *that*. I held his gaze, hoping he couldn't see the lie, or the real reason my thoughts had scattered.

I surreptitiously clenched my right hand, resisting the urge to rub my temple where the headache was escalating. I'd take more painkillers later. I just had to get through this. It was time to change the subject. "So, where are your cattle?"

"Here." He gestured to the animals in front of us.

Light grey, broad-shouldered, heavily muscled. "Those three girls are ours. Then the bull, Bruce." I instinctively took a step back. "Another bull, Jeremy. And behind us," he spun around, "these two young ladies."

"Okay, that's quite a few." I shivered slightly, looking at Bruce again. "And they are all Murray..." Blast it, what was the name again?

"Murray Greys."

I ignored the shadow of concern that flickered across his face. He still thought I should be in the hospital. I had to prove I was fine. Absolutely fine. Because the alternative of him slinging me over his shoulder like a sack of feed, was not appealing. Well, maybe the *position* had possibilities. A ridiculous smile tugged at my lips. I quickly suppressed it. Standing here grinning like an idiot wouldn't help my case.

"You doing your photography thing again?" he asked, one eyebrow raised.

I nearly choked. He was observant. Too observant. "Sort of," I mumbled, glancing away.

I looked back at the cattle, trying to think professionally. What shots could I get? The Murray Greys were impressive. Maybe if I got higher up, on top of the stalls for a better angle. I turned back to the row behind us. All standing. A line of grey backsides. A potentially cheeky shot for my personal collection, maybe.

The cow on the end swiveled her head, regarding me with large, dark, curious eyes. For a moment, the headache faded. How could I engage Jackson more? He'd mentioned bulls and cows, but they all looked vaguely the same to me. Clueless. That was me. Time to ask more questions.

"How do you... um..." I hesitated, searching for the right words. "How do you know the difference? Between the girls and the boys?"

Silence. I glanced at Jackson. He looked uncomfortable. A faint flush crept up his neck, and he shifted his weight, suddenly finding the concrete floor fascinating. Oh, brilliant, Megan. Did I really just ask that? Heat crawled up my *own* neck.

"Same as with us," he finally mumbled, still not meeting my eyes.

"What?" The headache definitely wasn't helping my concentration. "They can't be the same as us."

His flush deepened. He cleared his throat. "Well... um..." He ran a hand through his hair, looking distinctly flustered. It was actually quite sweet.

I probably should have let it drop, but his

awkwardness was intriguing. "How *can* you tell them apart?" I pressed, trying to sound purely practical.

"You know, it's like people," he rushed out, clearly wanting the conversation over. "Guys have... testicles, and..." He trailed off, his gaze darting anywhere but at me.

Oh dear. I bit the inside of my cheek to stop myself from laughing. "And...?" I prompted, maybe a little wickedly.

"Well, girls don't," he finished lamely, his eyes finally flicking up to meet mine for a split second before dropping back to the floor.

I swallowed hard, keeping my expression neutral despite the mortification burning my cheeks. "Right. And I assume the positioning is the same?" I couldn't resist raising an eyebrow.

He nodded mutely. "On the outside. Between the back legs." He lifted a hand, vaguely pointing toward Bruce. "You can see clearly there on Bruce. Unless they're a steer... they've had their balls cut off when young... but you can still see their... um... dick... toward the back, on their underbelly."

I nearly choked. Okay, that was *way* more information than I needed. My face felt like it was on fire. Any thought of photography, headaches, anything other than crawling into a hole, vanished.

"You asked," he said defensively, noticing my expression.

"I meant, how do you tell *individuals* apart?" I clarified hastily, trying desperately to salvage the situation and ignore the lingering heat in my cheeks. Had I really just had *that* conversation? The earthy atmosphere of the shed must be getting to me.

He seemed relieved to change tack. "Ah. Well, I saw them as young-uns, cared for them growing up. Guess I just *know* them."

"Yeah, they look the same to me." The blush lingered, a burning reminder to think before speaking.

"Look." He stepped closer to the first cow in the row. "See, Penny has larger eyes? And Jin here is taller, with a slightly deeper color. And there's a mark under Ninny's left eye."

I followed him cautiously as he moved along the line of cows, roped securely in their stalls. They swished their tails, munched hay, seemingly oblivious to the showground noise. As Jackson pointed out their subtle differences, the shape of a head, the set of the ears, a slight variation in color, I started to see them not just as generic cows, but as individuals. Penny. Jin. Ninny.

"You have to look at the smaller details," he said,

his voice softer now. "Becomes natural after a while." He stood beside Jin, casually resting a hand under her chin, completely at ease. The brim of his hat shadowed his face, but I could see the genuine fondness in his expression.

Impulse took over. I lifted my camera, focused quickly, and snapped the shot before he realized. Posed photos always felt stiff, this natural moment was what I wanted.

"Hey! I wasn't ready," he protested, straightening up. "Take it again."

"You were fine," I insisted.

He grinned then, a wide, infectious grin. "You've got to get my best side."

I sighed dramatically. "You're being a bit... girlish."

The mock surprise that flashed across his face was priceless. I quickly took several more shots, capturing his playful reaction. When he realized I was still shooting, he poked out his tongue and crossed his eyes, leaning his head close to Jin's. "Jin and me make a good pair, right?"

I lowered the camera, laughing too hard to continue. "Somehow, I don't think those pictures are going to make it into the paper."

"Let me see." He let go of Jin's lead rope and

stepped behind me, leaning over my shoulder to look at the camera screen. His warmth enveloped me, his chest brushing against my back. I resisted the overwhelming urge to lean back into him as I pressed the buttons, scrolling through the images. His soft chuckle vibrated pleasantly close to my ear, his breath tickling my neck. "They're great! I'd be very disappointed if they didn't make tomorrow's paper."

I could hear the amusement in his voice. "My editor has a good eye. I'm not sure your crossed-eyes shot will get past her."

"What a shame."

I laughed again, enjoying the easy banter. For a moment, everything else melted away—the deadline, the headache, my slightly fuzzy memory. Heat rushed back to my cheeks, and I quickly looked around, pretending to study the banner above the stalls to hide my blush. *Sunnydale Murray Greys ~ MT & KA Pearce.* An oval portrait of a Murray Grey head completed the sign.

"Sunnydale?" I asked, hyper-aware of him standing so close beside me, his presence fuzzing the edges of my thoughts. I didn't want to move. Ever. Well, maybe somewhere more private. I pushed the thought away.

"Name of our farm," he answered easily. "Underneath is the breed—Murray Greys, bred for beef. MT & KA are my folks, Matt and Kim. My great-grandfather came up with it back in the late 1800s when he settled the land."

My mouth fell open slightly. Farm life felt like another planet. "You *name* your farm?"

"Yeah. What's so odd about that?"

"My family hasn't named our house."

"Not quite the same," he said, smiling gently.

Relief washed over me, he wasn't taking my city ignorance personally. "No?" I raised an eyebrow.

He made a soft 'humph' noise that vibrated somewhere deep inside me, stirring feelings I wasn't ready to acknowledge. "No. Just tradition, I guess. Some houses in the city have names."

"Not the small ones," I retorted, then clamped my jaw shut, suddenly conscious of the vast difference between Dad's modest suburban home and what must be the sprawling acreage of Sunnydale. I shifted my feet, uneasy, putting a fraction more distance between us. "Like I said, I don't know anything about farms."

"There's not much to it."

I sensed him watching me, his gaze steady. I resisted the urge to look back, focusing instead on the line of cow backsides in front of us. Tails flicked rhythmically. One turned its head, big brown eyes regarding us placidly as it chewed.

"I don't know much about city life," he offered.

"There's not much to it," I echoed quickly.

The awkwardness broke. I glanced at him, catching that cheeky grin again. Seeing his features clearly, the sharp eyes, the strong jaw, reignited that spark of desire. I pushed it down. Reality check. Photos. Deadline. Pay cheque. My brief enjoyment evaporated.

"What's wrong?" He stepped closer again, his hand landing protectively on my arm. "Is it your head?"

I shook my head, avoiding his intense gaze. "No. Just... I need a few more shots, then I have to get these images to my editor. Otherwise, I won't get paid this week." The reality of freelance life.

Taking photos was my passion, but the pressure of contract work, needing to deliver specific shots on a deadline, could be brutal. Especially when dealing with head injuries and distracting farmers.

"Right." His expression turned serious, determined. "Tell me what you need. I'll help you meet your deadline." The sincerity in his voice warmed me again.

"I want to get up there." I pointed toward the wide top of the wooden stalls lining the aisle. "Over on that side, so I can look along the full length."

He shook his head immediately, his brow furrowing. "I don't know if that's such a good idea. After, you know. I'd hate for you to fall and hurt your head again. You need to be careful."

Suddenly, I didn't *want* to be careful. I had a bump, yes, but I wasn't an invalid. *I'm fine*, I wanted to snap. But I bit back the words. Instead, I moved toward the end of the row, reached up, and grasped the top edge of the stall. The wood felt rough, splintery beneath my palm. I pushed down, trying to heave myself up.

"Wait." He was there in an instant, his hands spanning my waist, taking my weight effortlessly, and boosting me up onto the wide wooden ledge.

I perched there, looking down at him. He was glaring up at me, genuine worry etched onto his face. A pang of guilt hit me. I was stressing him out. He shouldn't care this much, we barely knew each other. But in the last few hours, something *had* sparked between us. I wanted to explore it, but my recklessness wasn't helping.

"Don't worry about me so much," I said softly. "Please."

"I just know how serious head injuries can be." He swung himself up easily to stand beside me.

I sighed. He wasn't going to let it go. "Because of what happened to your sister?"

He just nodded curtly. "Yes."

Okay, topic closed for now. I stepped carefully onto the nearest hay bale. Instantly, vertigo slammed into me. The shed tilted, colors blurring at the edges. I swayed, nearly losing my footing.

"Careful!" His hand shot out, clamping onto my waist, pulling me back from the edge, and steadying me against his side. His touch was firm, grounding.

"Thank you." I took a deep, shaky breath. Having him standing so close was definitely helping anchor me. I glanced over the edge—it looked a long way down—then leaned slightly against his solid frame. A shudder ran through me. That could have been nasty.

"I just need to get close to the edge," I explained, the lingering dizziness making me cautious. I dropped to my knees, shuffling forward on the scratchy hay, grateful for the steadying pressure of his hand on my arm. Reaching the edge, I raised my camera. It wasn't quite the perspective I'd hoped for, but it would have to do. I took a few quick shots, suddenly just wanting to be back on solid ground.

"Done." I eased back toward the center. He helped me rise, his rough hand sending that now-familiar jolt up my arm, making me lightheaded in a completely different way. For a moment, we just stood there, close, caught in a silent pause. Then he released my hand, and the spell broke, reality returning with a disappointing thud in my stomach.

I can't like a man this quickly. It was absurd. But it wasn't just the tight jeans or the muscles. It was the kindness in his eyes, the honesty in his smile, the way he seemed both strong and gentle.

"Get down carefully," he instructed. "Sit on the edge here, and I'll help you." He jumped down lightly, turning immediately, and holding his hands out as if ready to catch me.

"I'm not jumping." No way could I replicate his easy descent. My five-foot-four frame felt decidedly less agile than his six-foot-plus. As much as I wanted to be down there, close to him again, I hesitated.

The ground looked even further away now. My earlier focus on the photos had overridden my caution. Now, dizzy and slightly nauseous, even his trusting eyes and strong arms weren't enough to make me launch myself into the void.

Nope. Can't do it. I shook my head, a wave of disappointment washing over me. Perfect opportunity to literally throw myself at him, and my legs had turned to Jell-O for all the wrong reasons.

"That's okay." His voice was calm, patient. "Just put your foot here on this drum. It's not far down. Then I'll help you the rest of the way." He stepped closer, patting the top of a large metal barrel nearby.

I sighed. Staying up here wasn't an option. "That's it. Nearly there. Just a little further," he encouraged as I clung to the splintery wood, easing my left foot down onto the drum. My head swam again, and I gripped the stall tighter, stopping myself from tumbling.

"There, you made it."

My boot found the drum's surface. I tested my weight, balanced, then lowered my right foot beside it. My expensive camera swung precariously from my neck, my handbag bumping against my hip. *Should have put them down first.* Too late now.

"Slowly, slowly," Jackson murmured. I felt his hands close around my left ankle, steadying me further, giving me the confidence to trust him. My right foot settled firmly on the drum. A nervous giggle escaped me.

"Now, jump." He reached up, his hands settling firmly on my hips.

I looked down and paused. It wasn't that far now.

His relaxed expression, the gentle reassurance in his voice, melted the last of my fear. I leaned forward.

"Rest your hands on my shoulders."

I did as he said, my palms pressing against the solid muscle of his chest through his shirt. I bent my knees slightly, pushed off the drum, and launched myself forward. His hands tightened on my waist mid-air, guiding my descent, slowing me so my feet landed softly on the concrete with minimal impact.

"Oomph."

He was right there. So close. My camera pressed against his chest, an awkward third wheel. My hands were still on his shoulders, his on my hips. Time seemed to stretch, freeze. Looking up into his eyes, the noise of the shed faded. All I could think was, *I want to kiss him.* The thought filled my head, thick and insistent, pushing aside the lingering fog from the head injury.

He leaned closer, his gaze dropping to my lips, reading my expression. I felt the warmth of his breath, saw his own lips part slightly. He moved slowly, deliberately, as if not wanting to startle me. Closer... closer...

Beep beep! Beep beep!

My phone. Blasting its obnoxious horn ringtone from my handbag. I jumped, startled. The moment shattered. Jackson's hands dropped from my waist. Disappointment, sharp and tight, constricted my throat. Damn it! I fumbled in my bag, silencing the infernal noise. I'd chosen the loudest tone deliberately because I usually missed calls. Right now, I wished I'd chosen silent.

"It's my friend," I managed, my voice breathless. "She's here at the show."

CHAPTER 4

Jackson

The interruption of Megan's phone blasting like a road train horn shattered the moment between us. One second, I was leaning in, lost in the softness of her lips, the next, she was jumping back, fumbling in her bag. Disappointment, sharp and unexpected, hit me as she pulled away.

She finished the call, or text, or whatever it was. "My friend finally texted back," she said, her voice still a little breathless. She glanced nervously toward Bruce, who was contentedly munching hay, and took an automatic step back. The fear was still there, simmering under the surface. "Will you go to the sheep pavilion with me so we can meet her?"

"Sure." I managed a smile, trying to project calm

I didn't entirely feel. Seeing her flinch at the sight of Bruce sent a fresh wave of guilt through me. "He won't hurt you," I reassured her, probably for the tenth time. "Might want to turn your phone to silent, though, so it doesn't upset him." I didn't want to risk spooking him again.

She fumbled with the phone, her eyes darting between the screen and the bull. I watched her closely. Was that a slight tremor in her hands? Or just nerves about Bruce? Her head still throbbed, I could see it in the tight line of her mouth. She looked pale under the shed's fluorescent lights.

She shoved the phone back in her bag. "I'll get a few shots of the sheep before I go to the office. Then, I'll go home, and you can be free of me."

Free of her? The thought landed with a thud. Was that what she thought? That I was just sticking around out of obligation? Maybe part of it started that way, but standing here, wanting nothing more than to close the distance her phone call had created, no, it wasn't just guilt anymore. I felt a pang of disappointment as I saw it mirrored, briefly, on her face before she masked it.

"All good things must come to an end," she murmured, echoing some saying, then added with surprise, "Spending a few hours with you was actually a good thing."

Relief washed through me. *Actually* a good thing. Okay. Maybe there was hope. We started walking toward the sheep pavilion, weaving through the crowds. I kept glancing at her. She walked with that determined photographer's focus, but her steps seemed slower somehow. Less steady than before. Or was I imagining it, projecting my worry onto her? The urge to take her hand, to steady her, was strong, but I held back. Too soon. Too much. She already thought I was just being dutiful.

"Megan, over here!" A woman with friendly brown eyes and a sheep on a lead waved from across the bustling aisle of the sheep pavilion. Kristie, the friend.

Megan waved back, her face lighting up with genuine warmth as she headed toward her friend. I followed a step behind, trying to gauge Megan's energy levels.

"Wait." Megan stopped abruptly, lifting her camera. Professional mode engaged. She snapped several photos of Kristie and the sheep, a White Suffolk, I noted idly. She looked focused, competent, the earlier fogginess seemingly gone. Maybe she *was* fine? Maybe I was overreacting because of Erin.

After the photos, the two friends hugged.

"My God, that is a hell of an egg on your head!" Kristie exclaimed, her dark eyes wide with the same concern I felt churning inside me.

"I'm fine," Megan insisted, touching her forehead gingerly, then quickly pulling her hand away as if the bump itself surprised her. She'd forgotten. Another tick on the mental checklist. Forgetfulness.

"Who's this?" Kristie looked over Megan's shoulder at me.

"Jackson Pearce," I said, stepping forward, offering my hand.

"Kristie Johnson," she replied, shaking it firmly. "Where you from?"

"Up north, near Clare."

"He's got Murray's," Megan piped up, a touch of pride in her voice that made me smile despite my unease.

"You mean Murray *Greys*," Kristie corrected gently, grinning.

Megan nodded, a faint blush coloring her cheeks. "Right. Murray Greys." Another slip. *Checklist.* "Can I take some pictures?" she asked Kristie, quickly changing the subject.

"Sure."

"Great. Talk to me about your sheep." Megan

launched back into photographer mode, snapping away, asking questions. She learned they were White Suffolks, which needed correcting a few times. Her concentration seemed intense, but was it forced? Was she running on fumes?

I waited patiently, leaning against a pen railing, watching her, trying not to hover, but ready to step in. She was glad I was there, she'd said. The thought warmed me more than it should have. A beer later sounded good, it would give us more time together.

Suddenly, a wave of tiredness seemed to wash over her. She lowered her camera with a sigh that spoke volumes. "I think that's enough." She checked her phone. "It's close to three p.m. I've got to get to the office." She pulled the SIM card from her camera, slipped it into her jeans pocket, and packed the camera away. "Want to come, Kristie? We can all go for a beer afterward."

"Good idea," Kristie agreed, closing the gate on her ram.

"Works for me," I said, trying to sound casual. A beer sounded bloody brilliant. But first, the office.

"Come on then. This way." Megan started off, leading the way back toward the main thoroughfare, her pace quickening again. Too quick.

"Whoa, slow down." I reached out, catching her

arm gently, pulling her back. "You have to be careful, you know, with that bump on your head. You've been overdoing it." The words came out sharper than I intended, fueled by a sudden spike of fear. She looked too pale, too driven.

She snorted, trying to pull away. "This is *not* overdoing it."

"Megan, I think he's right," Kristie interjected, her expression mirroring my own concern.

Megan sighed, frustrated, looking between us. The fight seemed to drain out of her slightly. The crowds were thicker here, harder to navigate. She reluctantly slowed her pace. I saw the internal battle, her stubborn independence versus the undeniable physical reality.

Her head *pained* her, I could see it in the slight wince, the way she held her jaw tight. Her legs looked unsteady. *Jelly-like.* Another warning sign.

"I am fine," she insisted, but the words lacked conviction.

"Good," I said, my tone leaving no room for argument this time. "But I just want to make sure." I moved closer, walking beside her, Kristie on her other side. We were practically flanking her. She didn't protest.

She kept her focus rigidly forward, ignoring the

twisting sensation I could almost *see* churning in her gut. A fine sheen of cold sweat broke out on her forehead and upper lip, despite the cool breeze.

"You look really white, Megan," Kristie murmured, leaning closer.

Megan didn't answer, couldn't answer. I saw her swallow hard, her knuckles white where she gripped her camera bag strap. She was fighting it, fighting nausea, dizziness, maybe worse. Fighting collapsing right here in the middle of the showgrounds. She pushed open the door to the temporary newspaper office behind the grandstand, her movements jerky.

"Megan, where have you...?" A woman inside, Helen, the editor, I presumed started, annoyance clear in her voice, then she stopped dead, her mouth gaping open as she took in Megan's appearance. "What happened?" Concern flooded her face as she scrambled up from behind her desk.

"Just a little bump." Megan waved a dismissive hand, the gesture weak. She fumbled in her pocket, pulling out the SIM card. "I've got some photos. Unfortunately, I missed most of the Grand Parade, but I tried to make it up." Her voice was thin, strained.

"She was at the first-aid room," I supplied, stepping closer behind her, ready. My heart was pounding now. *Please, just hold on.*

A visible wave of clamminess washed over Megan. Cold sweat slicked her back. I could almost feel the chill radiating from her. She took a shaky step away from me, suddenly wanting space, needing air.

"Megan, you should've let me know! I'd have excused you," Helen said, flustered.

Megan just shrugged, holding out the SIM card. "Have a look. I know it's late for Monday, but there might be some photos you can use." Helen took the card.

As the small piece of plastic left her fingers, it was like a final string was cut. The tension holding Megan upright snapped. Her knees buckled. The color drained completely from her face. I saw the flicker behind her eyes, the sudden blankness, she was seeing stars. Darkness seemed to pool around her, and with a soft sigh, she surrendered to it.

She crumpled.

CHAPTER 5

Jackson

It happened almost in slow motion, yet terrifyingly fast. One second, she was standing there, pale but upright, the next, her eyes went blank, her knees gave way, and she was falling.

Not again. Please, God, not like Erin. The thought screamed through my mind, cold dread mixing with a surge of pure adrenaline.

I lunged forward, instinct overriding thought. My hands shot out, catching her just before she hit the unforgiving floor, inches from the sharp corner of Helen's desk. Another head injury was the absolute last thing she needed.

"Oh my god, Megan!" Kristie's voice was a near-scream beside me. Helen gasped, her face paling further.

I pulled Megan's limp body tight against mine, bracing against her dead weight. She felt terrifyingly fragile in my arms. Gently, carefully, I lowered her to the ground, easing her handbag and camera case, bloody heavy things, off her shoulder.

"Ring for an ambulance!" The order came out sharp, clipped. My first aid training kicked in, pushing down the panic. Check airways. Clear. Recovery position. Move gently.

Kristie, bless her, didn't hesitate. She had her phone already out, dialing, even though she looked shaken. Helen, the editor, looked worse, but she grabbed the desk phone. "There's a protocol... showground control..." Good. They were handling it. I could focus on Megan.

I crouched beside her, my heart hammering against my ribs. Stubborn girl. So damn stubborn. The urge to lecture her warred with overwhelming concern. I understood, I really did, why she'd fought going to the hospital. Losing her mom like that left scars. But seeing her lying here, unconscious, along with the anomalies I'd noticed earlier. The forgetfulness, the fatigue, and the slight unsteadiness, clicked into place with sickening clarity. I should have pushed harder. Should have dragged her to first aid sooner.

Working with animals teaches you to read the subtle signs and shifts in behavior. A flicker in the eye before a cow bolts, the slight change in posture before a ram charges. It translates to people, too, sometimes. I'd seen the signs in Megan, but I'd let her stubbornness, and maybe my own reluctance to force the issue, override my gut feeling.

Kristie and Helen were talking rapidly on their phones, coordinating, getting help. Their voices were a low buzz in the background. I reached out, brushing a strand of dark hair, soft as silk, away from Megan's face. Her ponytail had come loose during the day, framing her face, making her look younger, more vulnerable. I carefully avoided the nasty purple lump swelling on her forehead.

You are a stubborn shit, I thought, but the words were laced with a tenderness that surprised me.

In just a few hours, this woman had burrowed under my skin. It wasn't just guilt over Bruce anymore, it hadn't been for a while. It was her sass, her determination, the way she'd faced down her fear to get the shot, the unexpected vulnerability she tried so hard to hide. The fierce way she'd wanted to keep working even after getting kicked in the head.

Yeah, she was my sort of woman. The thought settled deep inside me, solid and undeniable.

"Hmmm." A soft moan escaped her lips. Her eyelids fluttered.

Relief washed through me, potent and immediate. "Relax, you're safe," I murmured, leaning closer.

Her dark lashes lifted, her eyes unfocused and dazed. "Where am I? What happened? Oh crap!" Recognition dawned, and she tried to push herself up.

"Easy. Stay lying down." I gently pressed her shoulder. "Don't want to have to catch you again. Wasn't any good at cricket, remember?"

A faint smile touched her lips, followed by a soft laugh that quickly turned into a grimace. "Argh, it hurts." She sank back down, covering her eyes with her hand. "It's bright in here."

"Here." I carefully lifted her head, sliding my thigh underneath to cushion it. Better than the hard floor.

"Thanks." She kept her eyes closed, her breathing shallow. "I'll be better in a minute."

My jaw clenched. No, she wouldn't be. Not this time. There was no way I was letting her brush this off. Not after passing out. "Head injuries are serious,

Megan," I said, trying to keep my voice gentle but firm. "You need to be careful."

She sighed, her head pressing a little heavier against my leg. "I'm tired." The fight had gone out of her.

"Ambulance is on its way," Kristie announced quietly from the doorway.

"Good. Thanks." I braced myself for Megan's protest.

"I'm fine," she mumbled, but the words were weak, lacking their usual fire. Relief, again. She wasn't going to fight this.

"I'll ring her dad," Kristie said, already rummaging through Megan's bag for her phone.

"Good idea." I stayed still, not wanting to jostle Megan.

"No need... bother him..." Megan's words slurred slightly. Another bad sign.

Waiting. I hated this part. The helplessness. The silence stretched, filled only by Megan's shallow breathing and the distant sounds of the show. What could I say? I settled for stroking her arm gently, hoping the simple touch conveyed the reassurance I couldn't put into words.

"He's on his way," Kristie reported, tucking the

phone back into the bag. "I'll let him know what hospital when they get here."

"I'll wait outside, make sure they find us," Helen offered, slipping out the door.

"Can you let me know what the doctor says about Megan?" The words were out before I could stop them. I *needed* to know.

Kristie looked at me, her expression understanding. "Sure. What's your number?" She pulled out her own phone.

I rattled off my mobile number, my throat tight. This might be it. I might never see Megan Lyall again after that ambulance pulled away. But at least I'd know she was okay. That had to be enough.

Two EMTs in green overalls arrived then, with calm efficiency in their movements. They went straight to Megan.

"What's happened here?" one asked, kneeling, pulling out a blood pressure cuff.

I carefully eased Megan's head onto the floor and moved back, explaining everything. The kick from Bruce hours ago, her refusal to go to the hospital, the first aid visit, the increasing symptoms I'd noticed, and finally, the collapse. The paramedic took her pulse, blood pressure, and shone a bright light into her eyes, his expression unreadable.

"Best we take her to the hospital, just to be sure," he said finally after his assessment. They expertly maneuvered her onto a stretcher.

"I don't need to go to the hospital," Megan protested weakly. "Just need… sleep."

"You've got a nasty bump, love, and you passed out. We don't take chances with head injuries," the EMT replied gently but firmly.

"What hospital will you go to?" Kristie asked, hovering nearby. "I need to tell her dad."

"Royal Adelaide."

Kristie moved to follow the stretcher out. "Can I go in the ambulance with you?"

"Of course."

I stepped back, feeling useless, my hands shoved deep in my pockets. I touched Kristie's arm as she passed. "You'll let me know how she gets on?" I asked again, needing the reassurance.

She nodded, her gaze serious. "Of course." She tapped quickly on her phone screen. "I've sent you a text so you have my number. Text me later, all right?"

My phone vibrated against my leg. "Thanks."

I watched them load her into the back of the ambulance. She looked so small on the stretcher, pale and exhausted. Not like Erin. No, definitely not as bad as Erin looked that day. But the fear was still a cold knot in my stomach. *She'll be fine,* I told myself fiercely. *They caught it early.*

I stood rooted to the spot as the ambulance doors closed, the lights flashed, and it began to pull away, inching slowly through the oblivious afternoon crowd. Helplessness washed over me.

It was out of my hands now. All I could do was wait.

And worry.

And replay the moment Bruce's hoof connected, wondering if I could have, should have, done something different. Wondering if this strange, fierce connection I felt to the stubborn city photographer lying in the back of that ambulance was real or just a product of guilt and adrenaline.

CHAPTER 6

Megan

Darkness. A strange rocking motion stirred me, jostling fragmented pieces of memory like loose tiles in my mind. I groaned, the effort of trying to fit them back together sending a fresh wave of nausea through me.

The office... handing over the SIM card... Helen's shocked face... then... nothing? My eyes fluttered open. A man in green overalls crouched beside me, his face blurry in the dim, swaying light. Ambulance. The metallic tang of antiseptic mixed with something else, possibly diesel fumes.

"We're taking you to the hospital," the paramedic said, his voice calm but firm. "You're doing okay right now, just a precaution."

Hospital. The word landed like a physical blow, sharp and cold. *No.* "No, I don't want to go." Panic clawed at my throat. It was the last place on earth I wanted to be. I tried to sit up, pushing against the hard stretcher.

"Lie back down, please." A familiar hand pressed gently on my shoulder. Kristie. Her face swam into view, etched with worry. "I've called your dad. He's going to meet us there."

"No." My mouth felt dry, sticky. Dad shouldn't have to come here again. Not for me. Another face flickered behind my eyes with sharp blue eyes and a concerned frown under a wide-brimmed hat. "Jackson?" The name escaped my lips in a breathless question. I hadn't thanked him properly. Hadn't given him my number. Even through the fog of pain and panic, the thought of him was a surprisingly solid anchor.

"He had to stay at the show," Kristie explained softly. "But he gave me his number so I can let him know how you are. He's very concerned for you, Megan."

Concerned. The word echoed, a small spark of warmth against the encroaching dread. He hadn't just walked away. I let my head sink back onto the surprisingly firm pillow, the rhythmic sway of the ambulance lulling me despite my fear.

I wanted to ask Kristie more, wanted to hold onto the thought of Jackson, but the words scrambled, refusing to form. The darkness at the edges of my vision crept inwards again, thick and heavy, pulling me back under.

The next thing I knew, harsh fluorescent lights burned through my eyelids. Beeping sounds, muffled voices, the squeak of trolley wheels on linoleum were like a discordant symphony that scraped against my raw nerves. I lay on a narrow bed, thin curtains pulled around me on either side, offering the barest illusion of privacy. Emergency Department. The air hung thick with that same sharp, clean smell from the first aid room, but here it was heavier, laced with the faint, sour tang of vomit.

"I don't want to stay overnight." The words came out sounding petulant, childish, but the desperation behind them was real.

"It's not negotiable, Megs," Dad answered, his voice firm but weary. He stood beside the bed, his familiar frame a solid presence in the sterile chaos, but the lines around his eyes seemed deeper tonight.

I huffed, folding my arms across the thin cotton hospital gown they'd put me in. Over the past hour, or was it two? I'd been poked, prodded, lights shone in my eyes, and asked the same relentless questions.

What day is it? What's your name? Who's the Prime Minister? My head pounded with the effort of concentrating, each pulse echoing the throb behind my bruised temple.

Kristie sat perched on the end of the bed, looking exhausted but offering a small, reassuring smile whenever I caught her eye. Guilt twisted tight in my stomach. She'd abandoned her sheep, her responsibilities, stayed with me through all this, and hadn't complained once. And here I was, acting like a spoiled brat.

But I couldn't help it. Being here scraped open wounds I thought were beginning to scar over. The antiseptic smell wasn't just antiseptic, it was the smell of hushed waiting rooms, of bad news delivered softly, of holding Mom's hand until it grew cold. Every squeak of a wheel, every disembodied announcement over the PA system, echoed the long days and nights spent here just over a year ago.

My vision blurred as the pounding in my head intensified. I held my breath, fighting another wave of nausea. *Bugger.* I knew, deep down, I wasn't okay. Fainting like that, it wasn't normal. A cold sweat bloomed under my arms, unrelated to the stuffy air behind the curtain. The sinking feeling intensified.

"You need rest," Kristie said gently, placing her hand over mine. Her touch was warm, grounding. "And someone who knows what signs to look for, keeping an eye on you. It should only be overnight."

"I don't like being here either, love," Dad added, his voice barely above a whisper.

That broke me. Tears welled, hot and stinging. The memory flooded back, sharp and agonizingly clear—Dad's frantic call, the desperate drive from university, running down these same corridors, praying I wasn't too late. But I was. Mom was gone. The grief, raw and suffocating, rose in my chest, stealing my breath. Panic edged closer.

Don't cry. Don't cry here. I'd cried enough tears to fill an ocean back then.

Mom wouldn't want more tears, she'd want me to live. *'Meet a nice boy, Megan,'* she'd urged one quiet afternoon, her voice weak but her eyes sparkling with mischief as I sat studying beside her hospital bed. Jackson's face swam into focus again with his kind eyes and easy smile. A different kind of ache spread through my chest. But the grief was too strong, too immediate. A single tear escaped, tracing a hot path down my cheek.

Dad pulled me into a tight hug, his arms strong and protective around me. I felt the tremor of his own suppressed sob against my shoulder, felt his fierce love holding me together.

"I should've stayed home with you today," I mumbled against his familiar shirt, the words thick with tears. "This has been a terrible Father's Day for you."

He pulled back slightly, his expression stern. "No. Don't you dare think that. You have to live your life, Megs. Don't worry about me."

"But I do worry," I whispered, swallowing hard against the lump in my throat.

"Just like I worry about you," he countered gently. "Which is why you're staying here tonight. No arguments."

I looked up at him, really looked. The exhaustion was plain on his face, the worry lines etched deep. It was because of me. The fight drained out of me, leaving only weariness and a dull ache. Thinking clearly felt like wading through mud. But one thought remained, practical and necessary.

"Okay," I conceded, my voice small. I paused, gathering my thoughts. "Dad? Would you mind bringing me some clothes tomorrow? Clean ones? Everything I have stinks of... well, farm."

A small smile touched his lips. "Sure thing, love. Tomorrow morning. Or maybe later tonight if they let me back in." He kissed the top of my head, his touch gentle.

"And... you don't mind dropping Kristie back at the showgrounds?" I glanced at my friend, who was trying valiantly to stifle a yawn. "Thanks, Kris. For everything."

"No worries," she said immediately. "Wasn't going to leave you. A lift would be great, thanks, Mr. Lyall. Judging starts early tomorrow."

"All right then," Dad said, squeezing my hand one last time. "I'd better go before the nurses kick me out for good."

"Thank you," I managed, offering them both a weak smile as they turned to leave.

I sank back against the thin, stiff pillows that smelled faintly of bleach. Uncomfortable as it was, my mind, blessedly, drifted away from the sterile room, away from the grief. It drifted back to the showgrounds, to messy blond hair under a dusty hat, to startlingly blue eyes filled with concern, to strong arms holding me steady.

Jackson. Had I completely scared him off? Ruined any chance before it even began? *I hope I see him again.*

CHAPTER 7

Jackson

My skull felt two sizes too small, throbbing in grim rhythm with the distant thud of music from the showground's main stage kicking off for the day. Monday morning. Ugh.

I squinted against the harsh sunlight filtering through the shed roof, the smell of stale beer clung to my clothes, mixed with the ever-present aroma of cattle and hay, churning my already sour stomach. Definitely had more than a couple of beers last night after Kristie left with Megan in the ambulance. Drowning my guilt, maybe. Or just trying to numb the worry coiling tight in my gut.

I hope Megan will be all right. The thought was a constant hum beneath the hangover headache. Logically, Kristie's text last night said she was just under observation.

But logic didn't stand a chance against the icy grip of memory. Erin. Lying still in that hospital bed. It was all my fault.

I hadn't been worried enough then, hadn't pushed hard enough about the helmet. I wouldn't make that mistake again. I should've forced Megan to go to the hospital straight after Bruce clipped her. But damn, she wasn't the sort to be forced anywhere.

That stubborn streak, the fire in her eyes when she argued with the nurse, it was part of what drew me in. That, and her smile, the way her brow furrowed when she concentrated, the way she tilted her head just so.

My phone vibrated in my pocket. It was probably Mom checking if I was up. I fumbled it out, blinking at the screen. Kristie's message from late last night was still there: *She's staying for observation. Should be ok. Thanks for your help today.*

My reply underneath looked pathetic: *No probs. ta.*'What else could I have said? *It was my fault she's there.* Or, *Let me know the second anything changes.* Felt too intense. Too much. I scrolled idly through a few other notifications. I had missed calls from Mom, a reminder about the Murray Grey committee meeting later. Nothing from Megan, obviously. She was stuck in the hospital. The thought sent a fresh wave of guilt washing over me.

"Morning, Jackson! Rough night?"

Speak of the devil. Julie sauntered up, leading one of her prize-winning heifers, a smug, knowing smile playing on her lips. She looked annoyingly fresh, her blonde ponytail swinging.

"Morning, Julie," I mumbled, forcing myself to meet her gaze, trying to keep my expression neutral. I busied myself checking the water trough level, avoiding her eyes. I wasn't in the mood for small talk, especially not hers.

"Saw you drowning your sorrows last night," she said, her voice dropping slightly. "Everything okay? You seemed... preoccupied." She leaned against the railing, deliberately close.

My stomach churned. Preoccupied was an understatement. "Just tired," I mumbled, turning abruptly back to the water bucket, needing to put distance between us. "Long week."

"Right." Her smile didn't quite reach her eyes. She studied me for a moment, clearly fishing. "Anything to do with that little photographer girl you were playing hero for yesterday?"

My jaw clenched. "Megan's in the hospital

because my bull kicked her in the head," I said, my voice tight. "Nothing heroic about it."

"Oh. Right." Her smile faltered slightly. "Well... hope she's okay then." She didn't sound particularly sincere. "Anyway, see you around, Jackson." She clicked her tongue at her heifer and moved on down the aisle.

I leant heavily against the stall railing. Bloody hell. Even a simple conversation felt like navigating a minefield right now.

I picked up the heavy water bucket, the familiar weight grounding me slightly. Back to work. Fill the troughs. Feed the cattle. Routine. My parents were off schmoozing with other breeders, so these jobs were mine. As water sloshed into the trough, tumbling like my thoughts, Megan's face swam back into focus. Will I get to see her again? Will she even want to see me after my bull nearly took her head off? She hadn't blamed me, not really, but the guilt was still a lead weight in my gut.

Do I want to see her again? I stood up straight, pausing mid-chore. The answer hit me with surprising force, cutting through the hangover and the lingering irritation from Julie.

Yes.

Unequivocally, yes. The connection I felt, that spark, it wasn't just guilt or proximity. It was real.

Now, how could I make it happen? Today was packed. Final prep for the championship judging tomorrow morning with the two heifers, plus the usual feeding and watering. When could I possibly get away? And how? She was stuck in the hospital.

My mind churned as I went back for another bucket, the routine movements automatic. Fill, carry, tip. Fill, carry, tip. By the time the last trough was full, a plan that was risky and maybe a little crazy, began to form. I would see Megan again. Soon. I had to. Just to make sure she was all right. Yeah, that was it. Just to check on her. The excuse felt flimsy even to me.

CHAPTER 8

Megan

The harsh fluorescent lights were the first thing I registered, stabbing through my closed eyelids. Then the sounds. The rhythmic *beep, beep, beep* of a machine somewhere nearby, the squeak of rubber soles on linoleum, muffled voices, and, closer, a rhythmic, wet snore echoing from beyond my thin curtain. Hospital. The antiseptic smell, sharper here, clawed at my memory, dragging up unwelcome ghosts.

The night had dragged on, a blurry cycle of discomfort and fragmented sleep. The starched, papery sheets rustled every time I moved. The snoring down the hall continued its relentless cadence. My roommate, an elderly lady behind the opposite curtain, seemed to get up for the bathroom every hour, her walker scraping against the floor. When she finally turned on her television at around 3:00 a.m. without headphones, the flickering blue light painted shifting shadows on my ceiling.

Just as I'd drift off, exhaustion finally claiming me, a nurse would appear, a cheerful shadow in the dim light, shining another flashlight beam in my eyes. *'What day is it, Megan?'* For the fifth time. My head throbbed with the effort of dredging up 'Monday'. More poking, prodding, the cold cuff tightening on my arm. *'Vitals are stable. Just precautions.'*

Precautions my ass. Each interruption scraped my nerves raw, leaving me tense and aching. Drifting off again, only to be jolted awake by the memory of Mom's hand, frail and cool in mine, the scent of antiseptic sharp in my nostrils, the awful finality of the silence when the machines stopped. I surfaced with a gasp, heart pounding, the dull ache behind my eyes intensifying. It was, without doubt, the worst night's sleep I'd had in years.

When the nurse came in again around 6:00 a.m., chirpy despite the hour, I couldn't hold back. "This is ridiculous. I feel worse now than when I came in."

She just patted my arm sympathetically after

taking my blood pressure yet again. "It's standard procedure for head injuries, dear. Best to be safe."

I bit back a sharp retort. It wasn't her fault. Besides, I was awake now, despite the bone-deep weariness. My head still pulsed with a persistent, dull ache, but the nausea had subsided slightly. The thought of being stuck here all day, waiting for a doctor's rounds late this morning, made my frustration simmer. I was supposed to be at the show by 9:00 a.m.

"I'm going to take a shower," I announced, swinging my legs carefully over the side of the bed. The room remained blessedly stable. Progress.

The tiny ensuite bathroom steamed up quickly. The water started lukewarm, and I cranked the tap hotter, hoping the heat might wash away some of the tension, the lingering hospital smell, the frustration. *I'm fine,* I told myself fiercely, scrubbing soap onto my skin. *Just need to get out of here.*

Then my foot slipped on the slick, tiled floor. One second, I was standing, the next the world tilted sickeningly. A jolt of pure panic shot through me as I flailed, grabbing wildly. My hand clamped onto the cold metal grab rail bolted to the wall, my knuckles instantly white. I gasped, heart hammering against my ribs, clinging on as waves of dizziness washed over me. Suddenly, I understood that bone-deep fear Dad sometimes talked about, the fear of falling again, the loss of control. My head throbbed violently in protest.

"Are you all right in there?" The nurse's voice, sharp with concern, cut through the steam from just outside the door.

"Yes!" I called back, my voice tight, praying she wouldn't come in and witness this humiliating display of weakness. Slowly, slowly, the nausea receded and the world steadied. I loosened my death grip on the rail, my hand trembling slightly. Taking my time, moving with deliberate care, I finished my shower.

Dried and dressed in the clean jeans and T-shirt Dad had dropped-off late last night, I felt marginally more human. Bless him, Dad had wanted to stay, but I'd insisted he go home to get some sleep before work. The simple act of showering had left me feeling drained, the headache stubbornly persisted. Still, getting out of the hideous hospital gown was a victory.

I peeked out of the bathroom, relieved to see the nurse had gone. Shuffling back to bed, I sank down onto the edge with a sigh, admitting defeat for the moment. Rest first. Then escape. Looking for a distraction, anything but daytime television, my eyes landed on the folded copy of *The Advertiser* someone had left on the bedside table. Probably Dad. I picked it up idly, flipping it open.

My breath caught. There it was. Front page. Katie, the little girl, curled trustingly against the massive flank of the black-and-white cow, her pink bow askew. My photo. A wide grin split my face, ignoring the protest from my bruised cheek. And underneath, in small print read, *Photo by Megan Lyall.*

A surge of fierce pride, hot and sharp, cut through the headache fog. *It was worth it.* Worth the bump, the hospital stay, everything. This was why I did it. This connection, captured. This was fuel. I *had* to get back out there. If only my phone weren't nearly dead, I'd check the online galleries, see if any others made it. I needed to call Dad soon, let him know when the doctor finally sprung me.

A soft knock on the door startled me. Not the nurse again, please. Despite the shower incident, I *was* feeling better. Tired, yes, but the fog was lifting slightly. I glanced back at the newspaper photo, the motivation hardening into resolve.

I'd be back at the show later. Taking more

photos. I smoothed the newspaper, pretending to read the accompanying article.

The knock repeated, a little louder this time.

"Yes?" I called out, trying to sound stronger than I felt.

The door creaked open, and a head peeked tentatively around the edge. Jackson. My heart gave a ridiculous, totally inappropriate lurch. He wasn't wearing the Akubra today. His blond hair, slightly damp, was styled casually, a little longer on top than I'd realized. He wore a clean, checked shirt, sleeves rolled up high, revealing tanned forearms dusted with golden hair. Faded jeans accompanied by polished work boots. He looked good. Really good. Worryingly good.

A wave of self-consciousness washed over me. *I didn't want him to see me like this.* Stuck in a hospital bed, probably looking pale and washed out, hair scraped back damply. I instinctively pulled the thin blanket higher over my lap.

"Shouldn't you be at the show or something?" The words came out sounding slightly accusing, not welcoming like I'd intended. Nerves.

"Got a few hours free," he said, stepping fully into the room. He held one hand behind his back, his expression hesitant as if he wasn't entirely sure he should be here either. "Besides, it's still early."

I was glad I'd changed. The old band T-shirt wasn't exactly stylish, but it beat the hospital gown. I shifted back against the pillows, trying to look casual. Time still felt slightly out of sync, the lingering effects of the head knock making conversation feel like wading through treacle. Focus, Megan. String a sentence together.

"What about visiting hours?" I asked, grasping for something sensible to say, something to keep him here just a little longer.

"Sweet-talked the nurses." A grin spread across his face, crinkling the corners of his startlingly blue eyes. It did funny things to my insides. "Just wanted to see how you were. And give you this." He brought his hand forward, holding out a single, perfect pink rose, its petals just beginning to unfurl.

My breath caught again. Where did he...? It was barely 7:00 a.m. "You're resourceful," I managed, taking the flower. Its sweet, delicate scent cut through the stale hospital air, a breath of the real world, of sunshine and earth, of *him*. It felt incredibly special, nicked from a garden or not.

A wave of tiredness washed over me, sudden and

overwhelming. I sighed, the rose drooping in my hand as my arm fell to my side. The brief surge of energy had evaporated. The rounds weren't for hours, but I knew, with certainty, they *had* to let me out today. Even if the headache bordered on migraine territory.

Painkillers, I reminded myself. *Lots of painkillers.*

My logical brain screamed *inappropriate, too soon, head injury,* but another part of me, the part that felt strangely calm whenever he was near, just felt happy he was here. "I want to see you again," I heard myself say, the words tumbling out before I could stop them, fueled by exhaustion and the undeniable pull toward him.

He stepped closer to the bed, his smile softening. "Hey, I'm here till the end of the week. Murray Greys are the feature breed, remember?" He winked. "Plenty of time for me to see you again."

"Good." The word was a sigh of relief.

Without meaning to, my eyelids drifted closed. The effort to stay awake, of interacting, was suddenly too much. The last thing I saw before the darkness claimed me again was Jackson standing beside my bed, his concerned smile still lingering on his lips, the scent of the rose filling the sterile air.

CHAPTER 9

Jackson

I tugged gently on the lead rope, guiding Bruce down the familiar aisle toward the small outdoor arena. Grand Champion judging for the Murray Greys. The culmination of months of preparation, years of breeding.

"Good luck, love." Mom gave my arm a squeeze before slipping ahead to find a seat in the stands. Dad was stuck helping out with the Angus judging, after the steward called in sick from dodgy show food, apparently, leaving me to handle Bruce for the final showdown.

Bruce lumbered beside me easily enough, his massive head level with my shoulder, the halter ring clinking softly. He seemed calm, more interested in the possibility of stray grass than the impending scrutiny.

Me? Not so calm.

My stomach fluttered, a weird mix of nerves and the lingering effects of last night's beers. I'd rushed back from the hospital this morning, feeling torn about leaving Megan but knowing I had to get Bruce ready. I washed him down, dried him, and clipped his tail just so. Winning Grand Champion wasn't just about bragging rights, it was serious business, good marketing for Sunnydale.

We lined up on the fake grass under the marquee with the other five finalists. I nodded curtly at Julie Anderson, two spots down, leading her young bull. She offered a bright smile, expertly handling her bull as it tested the lead. Seeing her smile, confident and composed in this world we both knew so well, sparked an unexpected comparison. Megan wouldn't know the first thing about handling a bull, would probably ask a dozen questions Julie would find ridiculous, but there was an honesty about Megan, a lack of pretense, a spark Julie just didn't have.

I straightened my shoulders, trying to project confidence I didn't entirely feel in my clean moleskins, a freshly ironed shirt, thanks to Mom, and polished boots. I looked the part, one hundred percent country. Bruce fidgeted beside me, sensing my tension. "Easy, boy," I murmured, resting a hand on his solid neck, while keeping an eye on the judges to gauge their reactions, and making sure Bruce stood square. The familiar routine.

I spotted Mom in the stands, sitting with the other breeders' wives, all in smart country style, hair done, ready for trophy presentations. She gave me a small, encouraging smile. I smiled back, but my focus snapped back to Bruce as he shifted restlessly. I couldn't afford to lose focus now. Not like this morning when Megan's face kept floating into my thoughts while I was trying to muck out the stalls.

Bruce was one of the older bulls here with solid muscle and good conformation. But the competition was stiff. Heath's bull next to me was impressive. Julie's young bull had potential. It would be close.

The waiting began. The boring part. Walk the animals in a circle. Stand still while the judges poked and prodded, checking teeth, testicles, legs, and hooves. Assessing their potential to sire strong calves, to thrive out in the paddocks, not just look pretty in a show ring.

My mind, inevitably, wandered. Back to the hospital room this morning. Megan, looking pale and exhausted against the stark white pillows, but her eyes lit up when she saw the rose. That blush spreading across her cheeks. God, I'd wanted to kiss her right then. But she was so tired, so fragile. The memory of her trying to be brave, her determination to get back to work despite everything, that stubborn sassiness was incredibly appealing.

I hope I'll have time tonight to go back and see her again.

The thought slammed into the wall of show commitments. Catching up with breeders, industry meetings, Dad wanting me to step up on the Murray Grey committee. A list stretched out, demanding my time. And yet, cutting through it all was the image of Megan's dark, expressive eyes, the curve of her lips, the surprising vulnerability she tried so hard to hide. It wasn't just physical, this pull I felt toward her. It wasn't just guilt over Bruce, or the memory of Erin making me overprotective. It felt deeper. More significant than any show ring fling.

"Walk on."

The judge's sharp command snapped me back. Heat flooded my face. Had he said it more than once? Damn it. Focus, Jackson. I nodded curtly, tugging Bruce's lead. "Come on, boy."

Bruce moved willingly, but I could feel his impatience growing. He kept trying to snatch at the fake grass. "Just a little longer, boy," I muttered, keeping the lead taut, holding his head high. Judges hated a bull that wouldn't behave.

We circled and then returned to the line. I watched the others, assessing strengths and weaknesses, an ingrained habit from years of learning from Dad. This was my world, the only one I'd ever known, ever wanted. Breeding cattle, working the land, it was in my blood.

But Megan wasn't part of this world. She knew nothing about it, yet her curiosity felt genuine, not condescending. Her questions, even the awkward ones about telling bulls and cows apart, were endearing, not annoying. *I wonder how she's doing now.* Did the doctor let her out? Was she resting? The worry tangled with the memory of her smile.

Bruce shifted again, pulling me back. The judges were conferring, heads close together, murmuring. Nearly an hour this had taken. They weren't agreeing with one from New South Wales, one local, and one from Queensland, it was designed to prevent bias, but often just dragged things out. They broke apart, walking back down the line, expressions unreadable.

Hurry up. The impatience wasn't just Bruce's

now. I wanted this over. Needed to know the result, yes, but mostly I needed my brain clear to figure out how, when, and *if* I could see Megan again. Visiting this morning felt necessary, driven by worry. Going back again felt different. More deliberate. More risky. Was it too soon? Too forward?

The judges huddled again. I glanced down the line. It was hard to call. Often they favored the older, proven bulls for Grand Champion. Bruce had a chance, but Heath's bull looked strong.

Julie's younger bull was a contender too. She caught my eye and smiled again. I managed a quick grin back before looking away.

We'd known each other for years, circled each other at these shows. Maybe a few years ago, something might have happened, but the timing was never right. After Erin, girls were the last thing on my mind. And Julie, she didn't make me feel like Megan did. Nervous and excited and tongue-tied all at once.

Dad caught my eye from the gate, giving me an encouraging nod. Deep breath. Relax. Bruce would feel my tension.

Finally, the New South Wales judge motioned the steward over and more whispers ensued. Then Mrs. Colin, Julie's Mom, stepped down from the stands, ribbon in hand. Someone fumbled with the microphone, feedback screeching briefly.

"Pleasure to judge... stellar line up..." The Queensland judge began his speech.

My pulse hammered against my ribs. Mrs. Colin was walking toward our end of the line. Heath or me. Probably Heath. Reserve Grand Champion would still be decent and worth the trip.

"...Grand Champion goes to MT & KA Sunny of Sunnydale!"

My jaw literally dropped. Bruce snorted as Mrs. Colin draped the wide, tri-colored ribbon over his thick neck. "Congratulations, Jackson. A fine bull," she said, shaking my hand.

"Thank you, Mrs. Colin." My voice sounded distant.

"Quick photo?" A young guy with a camera materialized. I forced a broad smile, blinking against the flash.

Click. Click. Click.

A pang of disappointment hit me. It should have been Megan taking this photo. Her eye for a shot, her passion, but then I was swamped. Handshakes, congratulations, and questions about Bruce's breeding. Dad and Mom joined me for more photos, beaming with pride.

It was only later, leading Bruce back toward the quiet of the stalls, the heavy ribbon swinging against his neck, that the irony fully sank in. If Bruce hadn't spooked yesterday, Megan wouldn't be in the hospital. But if Bruce hadn't spooked, I never would have met her.

"Apparently, I've got a lot to thank you for, mate," I mumbled, scratching the bull behind his ears. Now I just had to figure out how to see her again. And hope like hell she actually wanted to see me.

CHAPTER 10

Megan

Relief washed over me, potent and immediate, when the doctor finally signed my discharge papers this afternoon. Freedom. But it came with conditions, Dad had to pick me up, take me straight home, and ensure I rested for the remainder of the day. He'd taken the day off work, another pang of guilt for me, and solemnly assured the doctor he'd enforce the medical advice like a prison warden.

Surprisingly, I didn't argue. After the near-fall in the shower this morning and the bone-deep exhaustion still weighing me down, the thought of my own bed felt like salvation. Twelve hours of uninterrupted sleep sounded like heaven. Mostly.

A small, traitorous part of me felt a sharp pang of

disappointment. If I weren't under house arrest, I would have headed straight back to the show-grounds. Straight back to *him*.

Jackson's visit this morning had lingered in my thoughts all day, a warm counterpoint to the sterile hospital environment and the throbbing headache. His showing up, looking all solid and handsome and genuinely concerned, holding that single pink rose had unnerved me, but in the best possible way. It felt like confirmation. That spark yesterday hadn't just been adrenaline or concussion-induced delusion. Something real was developing between us, something fragile and unexpected that I desperately wanted to nurture.

But how could I nurture it from my bedroom? He'd probably try the hospital again later, after his judging and chores were done. I pictured him arriving, maybe with another stolen flower, only to find my bed empty. He might think I'd just vanished, didn't want to see him. Panic, disproportionate but sharp, pricked at me. I needed to let him know.

My phone lay on the bedside table, displaying its pathetic single bar of battery life. I picked it up gingerly. Dozens of messages pinged, friends asking if I was okay, work emails I couldn't face yet. I didn't have his number. But Kristie did.

My fingers fumbled slightly on the screen, the lingering fog making even simple tasks feel like a chore.

Me: *Hey Kris! Doc sprung me. Dad's taking me home to rest. Can u pls let Jackson know I'm not here anymore? Don't want him wasting a trip. Thx again for yesterday! M x*

I hit send, chewing on my lip. It felt indirect. Cowardly, almost. Relying on Kristie felt safe, but it didn't feel right. Not after he'd come all the way here for me.

Almost instantly, my phone pinged back. Not from Kristie confirming, but a new message *from* her containing just a name and a number, *Jackson Pearce.*

My heart gave a sudden, frantic leap against my ribs, the speed almost dizzying. Kristie, the subtle matchmaker. Staring at his name on my screen felt entirely different from asking her to pass on a message. Texting him directly, that felt like a step. A deliberate move toward something. Taking a deep breath, ignoring the tremor in my fingers and the fresh wave of dizziness, I opened a new message, his number now saved.

Me: *Hi Jackson, it's Megan. Just leaving the hospital now, Dad's taking me home. Didn't want you trekking

back here for nothing! Thanks again for the rose &
checking on me this morning.

Simple. Casual. Hopefully not too eager. I pressed send before I could second-guess myself, the phone immediately dying in my hand.

Damn it. Well, it was sent. The ball was in his court now. Assuming my phone hadn't died *before* the message actually went through. Great.

CHAPTER 11

Jackson

Disappointment hit me like a cold shower when the text message lit up my phone screen later that evening. *Hi Jackson, it's Megan...*' My pulse had quickened just seeing her name pop up, a ridiculous surge of anticipation. But the message itself confirmed she was gone. *...leaving hospital now, Dad's taking me home.*

Damn. I'd been rushing through the evening chores—topping up water troughs, throwing out hay—mentally rehearsing what I'd say when I got back to the hospital. My plan had been simple: finish up, grab another flower, maybe buy one this time, and head over. It felt forward, maybe even a bit desperate after visiting this morning already, but the pull to see her again was stronger than my hesitation.

Seeing her smile, hearing her laugh, even seeing her looking tired and vulnerable, it all just solidified the feeling that had been growing since yesterday. This wasn't just about guilt anymore. Not even close.

The afternoon had been a blur of congratulations after Bruce's Grand Champion win. More photos, more handshakes, endless questions about breeding lines. Then the Supreme judging against all the other breeds, which unfortunately, we hadn't won, the Angus bull took it, but Grand Champion Murray Grey was still a hell of an achievement.

The win was good for business, and good for Dad's pride. It should have felt better than it did. Standing there, posing for photos, all I could think was that Megan should have been the one behind the camera, her dark eyes sharp with focus, maybe a small smile playing on her lips. The win felt slightly hollow without the possibility of sharing the news with her later.

And now she was home. Out of reach.

I typed back quickly, trying to keep the disappointment out of my mind.

Me: *That's great news. Glad you're doing better. Rest up. See you at the show soon?*

I added the last bit, hopefully. Maybe she'd come back tomorrow? Or the next day? Would it be creepy to hang around the newspaper office hoping to bump into her? Yeah, probably. Bloody hell. This was complicated.

I shoved the phone back into my pocket, frustration simmering. I finished filling Bruce's trough, adding an extra forkful of hay.

"Wanna head to the Jumbuck?" Heath clapped me on the shoulder, finished with his own animals. The on-site pub was buzzing every night during show week.

Part of me wanted to just go back to the caravan to brood. But what good would that do? Megan was home, resting. I couldn't see her tonight. Going for a beer with the other blokes, talking shop, and having a laugh was the next best thing. Better than stewing alone. Besides, being able to walk to the pub instead of worrying about the hour-long drive home like back on the farm was a definite perk of show week.

"Yeah, sure," I said, forcing a grin. "Sounds good." I gave Bruce a final pat. "First round's on me."

Heath laughed, slapping my back again. "You bet it is, mate! After you stole that ribbon from me today!"

Yeah. Stole the ribbon, maybe lost the girl. Or at least, lost the chance to see her tonight. I followed

Heath toward the noise and lights of the pub, trying to push down the disappointment and focus on the beer I was about to buy.

CHAPTER 12

Jackson

Lifting the heavy water bucket felt like trying to hoist a small tractor. My skull felt two sizes too small, each throb echoing the dull, relentless pounding behind my eyes. Bruce kicking me would have felt better than this.

The smell of stale beer clinging to my shirt, mixed with the ever-present aroma of cattle, hay, and manure churned my already sour stomach. Definitely had more than a couple last night. After Heath and I left the Jumbuck, we ended up across the road at the main pub, and things got blurry.

All fueled by the hollow disappointment of Megan going home, the worry gnawing at me, the conviction I'd probably blown any chance I had. Beer had seemed like a good way to numb it. Stupid.

I stumbled back to the shared sleeping quarters, a glorified box shared with Heath, Julie, and her friend Kelly, sometime in the early hours, definitely waking everyone up. Cheap accommodation, yeah, but right now, cramped and stuffy, it felt like a punishment cell designed specifically for hangovers.

"Watering up a bit late," Dad's voice cut through the fog. He walked past, disapproval radiating off him even without looking directly at me. "Don't forget the committee meeting at ten."

I groaned inwardly, leaning my forehead against the cool metal railing of a stall. The meeting. Right. And feeding, watering, and mucking out, I had four more days of this.

Stamina felt like a foreign concept right now. Adding insult to injury, I vaguely remembered Julie shifting her swag closer to mine in the dark, and woke up practically spooning her. Or maybe it was Heath? Either way, it was not ideal. Definitely not ideal when my head was full of someone else entirely.

"Reckon you'll be in for an early night tonight." Dad's grin was devoid of sympathy. "Oh, and can you muck out the soiled bedding in all our stalls? I've got a meeting with the Elders reps." He didn't wait for an answer, just strode off, leaving me with a pitchfork practically materializing in my hand.

I knew it was gentle punishment. It wasn't the work itself, that was just part of the job. It was the timing. I'd hoped to sneak down to the newspaper office, casually ask Helen if Megan was expected back today. Now I had no chance. Dad had me chained here.

I gritted my teeth, hoisting the bucket again. The last time I'd gotten this drunk was years ago, after Julie and me had a fight, over some other girl she thought I was interested in. Just like last night. Over Megan. Trying to drink her out of my head because I figured Julie got the message, but I guess she still liked me or something.

She'd been there at the pub, hadn't she? Sidling up close, laughing too loud, her hand lingering on my arm. Fragments of the night flickered, hazy and unwelcome. Things felt complicated.

A sudden, icy dread washed over me, colder than the water sloshing near my boots. *No.* I nearly dropped the bucket, fumbling for my phone with trembling hands. My password felt alien under my clumsy thumbs. *Please, God, tell me I didn't.*

My message history. I scrolled and scrolled, relief

flooding me when I saw that nothing stupid had been sent to Megan. Thank Christ. But then, my thumb froze. Sent messages. Timestamped well after midnight. To *Julie Anderson.*

My blood ran cold. Why the hell would I text Julie? My thumb hovered over the message, dread pooling heavy and sick in my gut. I tapped it, squinting at the screen, the words blurring then snapping into horrifying focus.

Me: *Can't stop thinking about you. That spark. Hope you're ok. J*

Fuck. Oh, holy shit. *Fuck. Fuck. Fuck.* It slammed back into me. The drunken haze, Julie leaning in, the noise of the pub, wanting to text *Megan*, wanting to say something about that jolt when our legs brushed in the coffee shop, that feeling before her phone rang, but sending it to the wrong damn person. To Julie. She must think... *Oh, crap.*

I shoved the phone back into my pocket, a useless attempt to make it disappear, to make it unsent. I picked up the bucket, poured water into the trough with shaking hands, breathing through the rising wave of dizziness and nausea. This hangover was biblical.

How the hell do I fix this? I wanted Megan. Not Julie. But I'd just sent Julie a text practically declaring undying devotion, while simultaneously having no idea if Megan ever wanted to see me again. And if she *did* come back, and Julie was hanging off my arm... I groaned aloud, the sound ripped from me by a fresh wave of despair and self-loathing.

"Enjoy last night?"

The feminine voice sliced through my misery. I looked up sharply, a wild, irrational hope flaring— *Megan?*

"Julie." My heart hammered against my ribs, pure panic mixing with the hangover's bile. She stood there, looking annoyingly fresh and put-together despite the late night. Blonde hair swinging, coy smile playing on her lips.

Not Megan. Definitely not Megan. My head and heart were, at least, in violent agreement on that point.

"You were certainly enjoying yourself," she said, stepping closer, lowering her voice conspiratorially. "Especially later."

A cold sweat broke out across my forehead. *Later?* What happened later? Nothing. I was too drunk. Surely? But her suggestive tone, the way she looked at me, I felt like a rabbit caught in headlights.

My mind scrambled for an escape route, something to say that wouldn't dig this hole deeper. I didn't want to lead her on, not after that text.

We'd grown up seeing each other here, year after year. Maybe there was a time I'd considered her potential, but not now. Megan had eclipsed everything else.

Julie moved closer still, close enough that I could smell the soap-and-shampoo freshness from her morning shower. It hit me then, the shared sleeping quarters. This year was the first time we'd done it, crammed into that tiny room. Two guys, two girls.

I'd agreed because it was cheap, thinking nothing of it. Mates hanging out. But Julie had organized it.

Of course, she had. And Kelly, her friend, clearly had a thing for Heath. It was obvious by the way she followed him around. Heath, bless him, went bright red whenever we teased him about it, but he was interested. That was the difference.

I squeezed my eyes shut, the blindingly obvious truth hitting me with the force of a physical blow even through the hangover fog. *I am not interested in Julie.* Not like that. Not anymore.

"Well," Julie murmured, her voice dropping lower, snapping my eyes open. "I'm sure we can continue getting closer later. Maybe when there's just us in the room?" She raised a perfectly sculpted blonde eyebrow, the suggestion hanging heavily in the air. Then she turned, gave a deliberate wink, and sauntered away, hips swaying pointedly.

Shit.

I didn't need a billboard. I was in deep trouble.

My silence, my inability to immediately shut her down, hadn't doused the flame, it had fanned it. And now she thought.... Bloody hell. This was worse. Much, much worse.

CHAPTER 13

Megan

The wall of noise and smells hit me as I walked through the showground gates, holding out my membership pass to be scanned. Animal, sugar, fried fat. Day six. I'd missed two whole days convalescing at home, mostly sleeping far more soundly than usual, the exhaustion deep in my bones. A bone-deep weariness still clung to me, but underneath that was a thrum of nervous energy, a knot tightening in my stomach. I was back.

I'd managed to convince Helen, my editor, that I was fit enough to work, despite oversleeping that morning. My assignment was more general show photos, kids having fun, animals.

And maybe try for the Grand Parade on Sunday.

Plenty of time. But that wasn't the *real* reason I'd dragged myself here, battling the lingering fatigue. The real reason had startlingly blue eyes and a dusty Akubra, though I hadn't seen the hat last time. Jackson.

My thumb had hovered over his name in my contacts countless times yesterday. What could I even say after practically collapsing in his arms and then vanishing into the hospital system?

Me: *Hey, thanks for the rose & not letting me die?* Delete.

Me: *Hope you're having a good show?* Too casual? Too distant? Delete.

Me: *Still thinking about you?*

Whoa, way too much, too soon! Delete. In the end, I'd sent nothing, chickening out completely. Maybe just walking past his stalls, a casual 'thanks for everything' was safer. Less vulnerable.

Kristie had texted a few times, checking in, mentioning how hectic the show was. She'd headed back to her farm on Monday.

Kristie: *Sorry I missed you. I'll be back Thursday*

Me: *Great, I can see you then*

Kristie: *How's things with Jackson?*

I hadn't answered that one. How were things? I had no idea. Did he even have a girlfriend? Probably.

A guy that good-looking, that decent? Surely not single. The thought sent a fresh wave of anxiety through me. I took a deep breath, trying to settle the frantic butterflies doing acrobatics in my stomach.

Walking toward the cattle sheds felt different this time. That whole world, previously just a backdrop, now felt significant. Because of him. Because of that photo of Katie sleeping against the cow. I was still getting congratulations messages about the front-page credit, tiny font or not. It felt like a validation.

I clutched my camera bag strap, the weight familiar on my shoulder. Program in hand, I noted the Merino judging was scheduled soon. I should head there. But first I needed to make a detour. Through the cattle pavilion. Just a quick walk-through.

It was still early, only 8:30 a.m., and the crowds were thin. Mostly exhibitors, getting ready. I warily skirted a group of agitated-looking Agriculture school teenagers and gave the large transport trucks, where cattle were being loaded, a wide berth. No more risks. Stay aware. Stay clear.

I ducked into the relatively quieter Murray Grey section, the strong, earthy smell hitting my nostrils, no longer entirely unpleasant. My eyes scanned ahead, searching. Watching my step, trying to appear casual, I walked down the central aisle toward where I remembered his stalls were. *What if he's not here?* Suddenly, this felt like a terrible, mortifyingly hopeful idea. My stomach tightened, breath shortening. I paused, heart pounding a frantic, off-beat rhythm.

Okay, breathe. I inhaled slowly, but it didn't work. *Just walk.* Lift your head. It doesn't matter if he's here or not. I had to *try*. A text wasn't enough. I needed to see his face, gauge his reaction, figure out if this *thing* I felt was real or just concussion-induced fantasy mixed with gratitude. *Can I really lay my heart on the line this early?*

I kept walking, forcing myself forward, past the rows of placidly munching grey cattle. The Sunnydale stalls came into view. Tails swished. Hay rustled. No Jackson. My heart sank with a heavy thud. *Oh well.* Disappointment, sharp and surprisingly painful, squeezed tight.

"Can I help you?"

I looked up, startled. An older woman, elegantly dressed in a flowing grey dress, a woolen jacket, and a vibrant turquoise scarf, approached me with a questioning look.

"Ummm..." My mind blanked. All my carefully constructed casualness evaporated. What could I say? *'Just looking for your ridiculously hot son, who I have a massive crush on?'* seemed inappropriate. I should just go to the sheep pavilion. Get photos. Work.

"Hey, Megan."

My head snapped around at the sound of his voice. Jackson. Walking toward me, Akubra-less again, face clear in the shed light. Clean-shaven jaw, those blue eyes, that easy country style in his checked shirt and tight jeans. Relief washed over me, so potent it almost buckled my knees, followed immediately by a fresh wave of panic.

"Mom, this is Megan. She's the girl I told you about." He reached us, smiling that slow, easy smile.

His Mom? Oh God. *Already?*

This was *not* how I'd pictured seeing him again. Not meeting his mother two minutes after deciding I was probably just imagining things.

Play it cool, Megan. Don't hyperventilate.

"Pleased to meet you," Jackson's mom held out her hand, her eyes as blue as his, full of genuine concern. "I'm Kim. The bump on your head from Bruce looks nasty."

I shook her hand, her grip firm and warm. "Oh, it looks worse than it is." The lie felt clumsy. A night in the hospital and two days resting said otherwise. "I'm better now."

"Good. I'd feel very responsible if you weren't." Kim let go, then beamed at Jackson. "I'm off to the ladies' lunch now."

"See you later, Mom."

"Good to meet you, Megan." She smiled warmly at both of us before turning away, leaving me standing beside Jackson, feeling flustered, awkward, and oddly welcomed. My cheeks burned.

"Bye," I managed, hoping I wasn't glowing like a traffic light.

"Hey," Jackson said softly, turning fully toward me once his mom was out of earshot. "It's really good to see you up and about."

"Thanks." My voice came out breathless. My mouth felt desert-dry. Looking up at him, closer now, the sheer force of his presence hit me again. He looked even better than I remembered. Hotter. Completely jumpable, right here, right now. My body reacted before my brain could censor it, muscles tightening low in my belly, breath catching, a physical ache blooming in my chest. I wanted to touch him, trace the line of his jaw, kiss those lips again, and feel the solid strength of him.

Get a grip, Megan! I forced myself to take slow,

deliberate breaths, trying to cool the heat flooding my face and neck. *I don't behave like this.* I wasn't some animal in heat. The mix of horror and fierce excitement churning inside me was completely unfamiliar.

"Sorry I didn't reply to your text," I blurted out, needing to say something, anything, to break the spell. "My phone died right after I sent it." Any minute now I'd break out in a sweat, and I hadn't even touched him. The thought of just reaching out, brushing my fingers against the tanned skin of his forearm where his sleeves were rolled up, was almost overwhelming.

"No worries. Figured something like that," he said easily. "I've nearly finished feeding. Got to look after the beasts, then we could go for a coffee? If you like?" He winked, that familiar spark back in his eyes. "I seem to remember you're a coffee and a choc-chip girl."

Heat exploded low in my belly, radiating outward, stealing my breath again. He remembered.

He walked calmly over to Bruce's stall, taking hold of the lead rope, and scratching the big bull behind the ears. "Come closer," he invited, his voice gentle. "He won't bite."

Just like that, the heat turned to ice. Fear, cold

and sharp, punched the air from my lungs. Bruce. Standing there, massive, solid, the source of the blinding pain, the hospital, the fear. The memory of that hoof connecting, the sheer *power* radiating from the animal, there was no way. Jackson or no Jackson, I wasn't getting close.

I shook my head, taking an involuntary step back.

"He's fine," Jackson insisted softly. "It'll help you. You know, getting back on the horse and all that."

He smiled at me, warm and steady, a beacon cutting through my fear. That smile, it fanned the embers of attraction inside me, making them glow hotter, making me want to trust him. It eased the doubt, making him feel worth the risk.

Slowly, hesitantly, I walked toward him, drawn by that smile, by the heat that seemed to envelope me the closer I got.

Bruce suddenly flicked his tail, a sharp, sudden movement.

I froze, heart leaping into my throat.

"Steady," Jackson murmured. Was he talking to me or the bull? Bruce shifted his weight, a low rumble in his chest. I instinctively stepped sideways, away from him, but found myself blocked by the cow in the next stall.

"I don't think he likes me." My head began to throb, a familiar ache I was happy to blame on Bruce. I touched the fading bruise near my temple.

"He likes you all right," Jackson said, his gaze holding mine.

Was he flirting? A soft blush colored his cheeks, and his blue eyes locked with mine. I felt myself falling into them, the world narrowing. Maybe he wasn't talking about Bruce. I didn't care. A sense of calm settled over me, my usual determination surfacing. I stepped forward again, right up beside Jackson, close to Bruce's massive head.

"See?" Jackson murmured. "He's not scared of you."

A ripple of nerves went through me, but this time, it wasn't just about the bull. It was about Jackson, standing so close, his shoulder brushing mine.

"He likes to be stroked behind the ear, then down the neck. Like this." Jackson demonstrated, his large hand moving gently.

Bruce leaned into the touch, his eyes half-closing. *I can't believe I'm standing next to a ton of beef on legs.* My head swam slightly, but I held my ground. Being this close to Jackson had an intense effect, a dizzying mix of excitement and nerves. I didn't want to be too excited or I'd lose all control. Too nervous, and I'd bolt.

Jackson reached for my hand. His touch sent a jolt of pure electricity through me, chasing away the last dregs of fear about Bruce. He gently placed my hand behind the bull's ear.

The hide felt coarse, thick, but surprisingly warm underneath. The spot behind the ear was softer, velvety. I started rubbing, mimicking Jackson's movement, like petting a giant, hairy dog. Bruce leaned into my touch, a low sigh rumbling in his chest. I nearly snatched my hand back, startled by the sheer weight shifting toward me.

"See? Told you. He's just a big softie really." Jackson's voice was a low vibration beside me, soothing, reminding me he was right there. With those kissable lips and that hot body.

The more I patted Bruce, the more the specific fear of *him* faded, replaced by the much more potent awareness of Jackson beside me. It was almost a relief to focus on the bull, stopping me from doing something impulsive, like grabbing Jackson's shirt and pulling him closer. I kept my eyes fixed on Bruce's ear, not trusting myself to look up.

I knew Jackson was watching me. I could feel his gaze, steady and warm. If I looked up, met those deep blue eyes, I knew I wouldn't be able to stop him if he decided to kiss me. And if he didn't, I might just kiss him myself.

My arm started to tire. I moved my hand down Bruce's neck, the short hair surprisingly harsh against my palm, the muscle beneath solid as rock. The simple sensation felt heightened, charged, because Jackson was so close. Lustful, inappropriate thoughts filled my mind.

"This is the first bull I've ever patted." The words tumbled out before I could stop them, sounding utterly lame even to my own ears. Horrified, I finally looked up, ready to babble some kind of correction.

But Jackson moved first. He leaned in, closing the small space between us, and pressed his lips to mine. Warmth exploded on contact, a pleasant, fiery heat that melted through my bones. His lips were soft yet firm, moving slowly against mine, and fusing, evoking a delicious, deepening heat.

My thoughts dissolved. There was only the taste of him, faintly of coffee, maybe mint, clean and male, the gentle pressure, the slide of his lips, the heat building low inside me. My hands found their way to his waist, gripping his shirt, pulling him closer without conscious thought. The shed, the noise, Bruce, everything faded into a warm, humming background.

Someone cleared their throat. Loudly.

We sprang apart, breathless, startled. I glanced over my shoulder. A girl, about my age, stood a few feet away. Blonde ponytail, arms crossed, typical country clothes, and a face like thunder.

My heart plummeted. *Of course.* I should've known he was taken. Why hadn't I asked? Would he have even told the truth? My first boyfriend certainly hadn't. It didn't matter how nice they seemed. Hurt and humiliation washed over me.

"Jackson, I've been looking for you," the girl said, her voice sharp, clipped.

"Julie, this is Megan." Jackson's voice sounded strained. "My friend."

Friend. Ouch. Julie's eyes narrowed, flicking over me with blatant assessment before returning to Jackson. I felt Jackson's arm come around my waist, pulling me slightly against his side. It felt protective. It felt good. But it felt wrong now, seeing the fury on Julie's face.

"But you messaged me last night, you wanted me more than just a friend," her voice tight.

"I mean," Jackson fumbled, his cheeks flushing,

"Julie is my friend. And Megan is..." He trailed off, looking utterly miserable.

Julie didn't wait for the clarification. Her stare darkened further, then she spun on her heel and stormed away down the aisle.

"Julie...!" Jackson gritted his teeth, watching her go. He let out a long, frustrated breath and turned back to me, his expression desperate. "Megan, I am so sorry. Julie's not my girlfriend. I swear."

I just looked at him, my arms wrapped tightly around myself, a useless shield against the wave of humiliation. "She certainly acts like she is."

"I know. I know how it looks. I... I messed up." He ran a hand through his hair, the picture of misery. "Last night, after the show, I was drunk. And I sent a text." He paused, his gaze dropping to the floor. "It was a stupid, drunken text. And I acciden-tally sent it to her."

He finally met my eyes, and the shame there was raw. "It said... something about a spark. About not being able to stop thinking about... you." He swallowed hard. "It was meant for you, Megan. Every word. And I sent it to her."

The pieces clicked into place with sickening clarity. The possessive anger on Julie's face. Jackson's panicked fumbling. He hadn't just been caught kissing me; he'd been caught after sending a text that made her believe she had a claim on him. The hurt was a sharp, ugly twist in my gut, but it was tangled with a sort of hope, that he had been thinking of me, even though he was drunk and needed alcohol for courage to message me.

I looked up at him, searching his eyes, trying to gauge the sincerity warring with the panic there. He *looked* like he was telling the truth. But the situation and Julie's possessive anger... "I believe you," I heard myself say, though a knot of doubt remained.

"Thank you," he breathed, relief flooding his face.

But it was too much. Too complicated. The kiss, meeting his mom, the angry girlfriend-or-not, my head was spinning again, the earlier calm completely shattered.

"Look," I said, stepping back, needing space. "I've got to get some photos. For work. I'll... I'll see you later."

I rushed the words, slipping out from under his arm before he could stop me. His hand slid over my hip as I moved away, the brief contact flaring heat through me again, awakening that ache, that hunger.

No. He's got Julie drama. She might be just a friend, but she was a country girl. Part of his world and I wasn't. I was a city girl, through and through. Hell, I could barely stand next to his bull without panicking.

"Megan, wait," he called after me, his voice urgent. "Please come and see me again. I want you."

I hurried away, pretending I hadn't heard the last part. *I bet he wants me.* But the hurt, the insecurity, twisted sharp and ugly inside. I wasn't stepping on another woman's territory, friend or not. My eyes stung, and I blinked furiously, focusing on navigating the aisle, getting out of there. I knew that look on Julie's face, even if she hadn't said a word. *I'd hardly make a good farmer's wife,* the thought mocked me. *I'm just a fling while he's in the city. We both know it.*

CHAPTER 14

Jackson

I watched her hurry away, disappearing into the thin morning crowd, and the urge to go after her, to grab her hand, to make her listen, was overwhelming. But I let her go. For now. Frustration and self-loathing boiled up inside me, hot and acidic. I turned and kicked the solid wood of the nearest stall. Pain shot up my leg, sharp and immediate, but it was nothing compared to the mess I'd made.

Idiot! Why didn't I just tell Julie to piss off last night? Why the hell did I send that stupid text?

I forced myself not to limp as I started pacing, the dull throb in my foot a fitting punishment. How could I have been so blind?

The shared accommodation had been Julie's idea, of course. Julie was hanging around the pub last night, painfully so. Maybe part of me had known, had seen the potential for something easy, something expected, with Julie. She knew farm life, knew the drill. It would have been comfortable. Predictable.

But then Megan Lyall crashed into my life—literally. Rocked my world in a way that was anything but comfortable or predictable. Made me feel things I hadn't felt since, well, maybe ever.

Protective, terrified, intrigued, completely captivated. Since Bruce knocked her down, she was the only woman I could think about. And getting drunk last night, letting my guard down, sending that text to the wrong damn person had created one hell of a situation. A situation that might have just cost me the one person I actually wanted.

No. I wouldn't let it. Megan was worth fighting for. This mess was mine to clean up.

First step was to clear things up with Julie. I couldn't face Megan again, couldn't even think about finding her until this was sorted. Properly sorted. No ambiguity. I scanned the shed, my gaze sharp now, fueled by adrenaline and regret. I spotted her near the back, lurking in the shadows by some hay bales, pretending to check her phone but radiating pure fury. Right. Get it done.

I strode over, ignoring the lingering ache in my foot. She looked up as I approached, her expression hardening, ready for round two.

"Julie, we need to talk," I started, keeping my voice low but firm. No hedging. No excuses. "That text last night... it was a mistake."

"A mistake?" She stood up, crossing her arms, trying for nonchalant anger, but her eyes glittered. "Seemed pretty clear to me, Jackson. 'Can't stop thinking about you', wasn't it?"

"Yeah, I was drunk," I cut her off, my anger flaring. Anger at myself for being stupid, anger at her for trying to twist this. "But that wasn't the mistake. The mistake was sending it to *you*. It wasn't meant for you, Julie. It was meant for Megan." The words hung there, brutal but necessary.

Her face paled, then flushed a furious red. "You bastard! You let me think..."

"I know. And I'm sorry for that part," I said, meeting her glare head-on. Protectiveness for Megan surged, overriding my guilt about hurting Julie. "I messed up. I shouldn't have sent it drunk, and I'm sorry it caused confusion. But there's nothing between us like that. Not anymore. Maybe there never really was, not really." I took a breath, needing to make this absolute. "I'm interested in Megan. Only Megan. This thing between us, whatever you thought it might be... it's not happening. It has to be over."

"Bastard!" she spat again, the word filled with venom. She didn't argue further, just turned and stormed away, disappearing quickly down the aisle. "You better get your stuff out of my room before I burn it."

I let out a long, slow breath, the tension easing slightly, replaced by a hollow ache. One fire was put out. Now for the inferno. Megan.

A knot of anxiety tightened in my gut. Where would Megan have gone? She'd mentioned needing photos from the sheep pavilion earlier. Was she still there? Or had she just left the showgrounds altogether? Did she hate me now? After seeing that scene, hearing me call her a 'friend' like some kind of coward, would she even believe me?

I have to find her. The thought was a desperate prayer. Looking for her in the sprawling showgrounds felt like searching for a needle in a haystack, but I had to try. I had to find her, make her understand, fix this mess I'd made. Even if, in the end, she told me to get lost. I owed her the truth. I owed myself the chance.

I started walking quickly toward the sheep pavilion, scanning faces, my heart pounding with a frantic mix of hope and dread. *Please still be here, Megan. Please.*

CHAPTER 15

Megan

I walked blindly, stumbling through the thickening crowd, dodging prams and ignoring the excited shrieks of kids high on sugar. Tears pricked behind my eyes, hot and angry.

What just happened?

The scene replayed in my head—the kiss, the heat, the sudden interruption, Julie's furious face, Jackson calling me a *friend*. Just like Julie was his *friend*. A heavy, sick feeling settled in my stomach, like I'd swallowed rocks.

He'd apologized, yes, insisted Julie wasn't his girlfriend, mumbled something about a mistaken text meant for me. But the image of Julie's possessive glare, the way she'd stormed off screamed complication. And his fumbling explanation hadn't exactly inspired confidence. *He let me believe...* The anger warred with the hurt. Was I just some city fling, a convenient distraction while he was away from his real life?

I know jack-all about farming, the familiar insecurity whispered. *Hardly makes for a good farmer's wife.*

Compared to Julie, who probably knew exactly how to handle bulls and awkward silences and everything else in his world, I felt hopelessly out of my depth.

My lips still tingled, a traitorous reminder of the kiss, of the connection that had felt so real just moments before. Despite everything—the city girl/country boy divide, the Julie drama—that spark was undeniable. It went beyond just attraction, beyond the way my body reacted whenever he was near.

I touched my lips, the memory vivid. I wanted more than just a kiss, more than just sex, though the thought of *that* sent another wave of heat through me. I wanted to know *him*. I wanted to hope, maybe foolishly, that this could be something real. Something with a future. And I definitely didn't want to be fighting off other women for his attention.

I was competitive in my career. But with guys? I

relied on chemistry, on that mutual pull. And the chemistry with Jackson was off the charts, stronger than anything I'd ever felt. His taste lingered, salty-sweet, making my head spin all over again.

I sighed, rubbing my temples as the dull throb behind my eyes threatened a comeback. My thoughts were a tangled mess. Needing somewhere to escape, to think, I walked numbly up the ramp into the relative calm of the sheep pavilion and sank onto a cool metal bleacher seat. Below, exhibitors in white coats were leading sheep from their pens, lining them up. An announcement crackled over the speakers advising that judging would start in five minutes.

Work. I needed to focus on work. I pulled out the show program, forcing myself to scan the schedule as a distraction. Dogs, cats, horse events, it was a busy day ahead. But the words blurred. Jackson's face superimposed itself over the print. His smile, the intensity in his eyes when he'd kissed me, the desperation when he'd tried to explain.

It was too soon to go back. He needed to sort out whatever was going on with Julie. And I needed space. Seeing him again now, knowing what I knew... I wanted to kiss him again, wanted to let it lead somewhere more intimate, feel that connection deepen. But the thought of Julie, the potential for drama, cast a shadow. He'd called me a friend. A *kissing* friend? That didn't sit right. Not at all.

Why did the start of a relationship have to be so damn difficult?

The word hung in my mind. *Relationship?* I froze, the program slipping from my fingers. Where had that come from? It was way too soon for that word. We barely knew each other. A blush crept up my neck, warming my cheeks, but underneath the surprise, the thought didn't feel entirely unwelcome. A tiny, hesitant smile touched my lips. The potential was there, wrapped up in all the confusion and jealousy.

Okay. Deep breath. I wasn't running away completely. He deserved a chance to explain properly, without his angry 'friend' breathing down his neck. But not right now. I needed time to process, to calm down. *I'll go see him later,* I decided, picking up the program again, feeling a flicker of my usual determination return. Let him wonder a little. Let him sweat. I wouldn't make it too easy for him.

CHAPTER 16

Jackson

My swag and bag were safely away from Julie's intentions of burning them and now in my mates locker here on the show and I was bunking with them. I somehow survived the committee meeting, dodging any new jobs for next year by keeping my head down and pretending to take copious notes. Mostly, I just doodled variations of Megan's name in the margins, her face swimming in my thoughts, the memory of that kiss, brief as it was, a warm counterpoint to the droning discussion about sponsorship tiers.

Every time my mind drifted, picturing her walking away, that hurt look in her eyes, *gutless*, I cursed myself. I hadn't even managed to text her, let alone find her. What if she'd already left? What if she thought I was a complete player?

Walking back toward the cattle sheds, I felt eyes on me. Word travelled fast in the tight-knit show community. The scene with Julie hadn't gone unnoticed. I saw Mom talking with Mrs. Peterson near the Angus stalls. She gave me her stern, disappointed look, but thankfully said nothing as I passed.

I didn't need a lecture right now. It wasn't my intention to juggle two women. Hell, I could barely handle the thought of one.

There was only Megan. But convincing *her* of that after this morning felt like climbing Everest in dress boots.

First things first, damage control. I headed straight for the shared sleeping locker. No way was I spending another night crammed in there with Julie. Even if nothing happened, and nothing *would* happen, the thought of Megan finding out I was still sharing sleeping quarters with the girl who'd stormed off after catching us kissing was unacceptable.

No. I had to move my gear. Now. Before I even tried to find Megan again. Show her, somehow, that I was serious.

I reached the small, green-painted shed we'd

been using, fumbling for my keys. The cheap padlock felt flimsy, but my swag wasn't cheap. Nearly five years I'd had it, worn in just right. Losing it would be more than inconvenient. My hand closed around the lock.

"What the hell did you do to Julie?"

I turned, suppressing a sigh. Heath. Sauntering up with that look on his face—half concerned mate, half enjoying the drama.

"Man, she is *pissed* at you." He shook his head, leaning against the locker door.

My jaw clenched. "Just a misunderstanding," I mumbled, hating how weak it sounded. It *was* a misunderstanding, mostly hers. Fueled by my drunken stupidity. If only I hadn't drunk so much, I could've shut her down properly last night and kept her at arm's length. Avoided this whole damn mess.

"Oh yeah?" Heath raised an eyebrow. "Sounded like more than that. Heard she plans to string you up by the balls."

"Sounds about right," I muttered, rattling the lock again. It wouldn't budge.

Heath shifted his weight, blocking the door. "By the way, mate," he said, almost casually, "she's moved your stuff."

I stopped struggling with the lock, a quiet groan escaping me. "Where?"

"Over there." He pointed. My swag, duffel bag, and boots were all piled unceremoniously on the dusty ground nearby. I stared at the heap, pursing my lips tight to stop the string of curses threatening to erupt.

"Never mind, mate." Heath clapped me on the back, oblivious to the fury simmering beneath my exhaustion. "You'll get over her. Or see the light and make up with her eventually."

"Not making up with her," I said, my voice hard, firm. I met his eyes, needing him to understand this wasn't some temporary spat. "Nothing happened between us, Heath. And it's never going to."

"Sure," he said, clearly not believing a word. He tapped the padlock I'd been wrestling with. "Got us a new lock, too."

Of course, she had. Shiny, new, and definitely not keyed for me. "Right," I said, stepping back from the door. "Guess I'll find somewhere else to set up then."

Heath just laughed. "Good luck with that, mate." He pushed off the door and wandered away, probably off to find Kelly.

I stared at the pile of my belongings. Bending down, I picked up the swag. The bottom edge felt damp. I sniffed it cautiously. Water, hopefully. Not piss. God, I hoped it wasn't piss. I was too bloody tired for this. Stuffed from lack of sleep, worn out from constantly being 'on' for breeders and judges, and now this crap with Julie. All I really wanted, the only thing that felt important right now, was finding Megan. Apologizing. Explaining. Seeing if there was even a sliver of a chance left.

I struggled to gather everything, my swag unrolling, boots tumbling. Where the hell was I going to sleep tonight? It didn't matter. I needed to find Megan first, that was the priority. Everything else could wait.

CHAPTER 17

Megan

Hundreds of photos later, the sharp sting of the morning's encounter had faded to a dull ache. Mostly. Clicking the shutter, framing shots, and losing myself in light and composition had worked. Photography was my anchor, the place I went to process, to ground myself.

I'd captured laughing kids smeared with cotton candy, intent faces watching the sheep judging, the blur of motion on the carnival rides I was too chicken to try myself. For hours, I'd managed to push Jackson and the whole messy Julie situation to the back of my mind.

Almost.

In the quieter moments, between shots, it crept

back in. *He said she was just a friend.* Logically, I knew that. He'd been clear, even flustered. But the doubt lingered, a persistent little niggle. That look on Julie's face, and the bigger picture—me, the city photographer who panicked near livestock, him, the capable country guy whose life revolved around them. Was I setting myself up for heartbreak? Was I just a temporary diversion?

I'd decided, somewhere between photographing prize-winning rams and daredevil motorbike riders, that I *would* talk to him. Properly. Hear him out. But deciding and *doing* were two different things. Every time I thought about texting him, finding him, my courage failed me. That little voice whispered doubts, reminding me of the potential complications, holding me back. So, I threw myself back into work, letting the camera be my shield.

Now, heading back toward the relative quiet of the newspaper office, the distant screams from the rides and the thumping bass of carnival music followed me. Despite the emotional rollercoaster, a sense of satisfaction settled over me. The photos were good. I felt alive, buzzing with the energy of the show and the quiet pride of finally carving out a space for myself in this tough industry.

My legs ached as I climbed the steps to the

office, a reminder of the nearly six hours I'd spent walking, crouching, and chasing the perfect shot. I slumped into the worn office chair, pulling the SD card from my camera and slotting it into the reader. The familiar whirring as the images transferred was usually soothing, but today, my mind wouldn't settle.

"You're feeling all right?" Helen asked, looking up from her screen. She had that perceptive gaze that missed nothing. Practical short hair, smart blouse, she was always professional, even in the chaotic show environment.

"Yeah," I mumbled, staring blankly as thumbnail images populated the folder. "Just tired from walking around." It was more than that, though. So much more. Jackson's face swam into focus behind my eyes with his dusty Akubra tilted back, that slow, easy smile crinkling the corners of his eyes, and the memory of his strong arms carrying me.

"I'm not sure I believe you," Helen said gently.

"What?" I sat up straighter, heat prickling my cheeks. I'd been caught daydreaming, about *him*. "I'm fine. Really."

Helen chuckled softly. "Did you get to see that guy again? The handsome farmer?"

The heat intensified, spreading down my neck.

"What guy?" I stalled, knowing exactly who she meant.

She raised a perfectly sculpted eyebrow, her expression a mixture of amusement and knowing sympathy. "Don't play innocent with me, Megan. The one who brought you coffee. The one whose bull nearly took you out."

I kept my eyes glued to the screen, watching the progress bar fill, willing the blush to subside. Jackson, leaning against the stall, scratching Bruce behind the ears. Jackson, his lips meeting mine.

"You should go and see him," Helen suggested quietly.

I squirmed in my seat. This was my boss, not my best friend, sharing relationship advice over wine. "I don't know about that..."

"I think you should."

"Why?" I risked a glance at her.

"Because," she said, leaning back in her chair, "it's either him who's making you stare blankly at a completed download screen for five minutes straight, or you need to go back to the hospital for another check-up. Either way, you need to figure it out." She paused, her tone softening. "Go see him. Maybe it works out, maybe it doesn't. But at least you'll *know*, and you can move forward. Or," she added with a gentle smile, "at least get back to focusing on the excellent work you're hired to do."

I knew she wasn't criticizing, just stating a fact. My focus *was* shot. "Okay, okay. I'll just pick a few photos for you first, then I'll..." My voice trailed off.

Because Jackson was walking past the office window.

My breath caught. I followed his movement, drinking him in. Jeans, a checked shirt, and that confident stride. He looked just as good, just as solid and real and overwhelmingly attractive as he had this morning. Maybe even more so, now that the initial shock had worn off and the memory of the kiss was a warm hum beneath my skin.

"Exactly," Helen murmured, following my gaze.

The office door pushed open, and he stepped inside. My heart hammered against my ribs. *What do I say?* All the carefully rehearsed lines, the calm explanations I'd planned, evaporated. My mind felt like mush.

"Hey, Megan." His voice was low, hesitant.

"Hi," I managed, the sound barely a squeak.

He stopped in front of my desk, looking awkward, twisting his hands together before shoving them deep into the pockets of his moleskin jeans. I forced my gaze up to meet his blue eyes, deliberately avoiding looking lower, despite the magnetic pull. Now was not the time. Talk first. But the words were stuck somewhere in my throat, choked by the heat surging through me just from having him stand so close.

"I'm sorry about before," he said, his voice rough with sincerity. He looked genuinely uncomfortable, vulnerable even. My mouth went dry.

"How about we go for a drink?" he asked, then glanced quickly at Helen. "I mean, a coffee."

"I've got photos to sort first," I blurted out, falling back on habit. Work first. Always work first.

"Oh. Okay then," he started, disappointment flickering in his eyes.

"Take a break, Megan," Helen interrupted smoothly. "The photos can wait an hour. Go."

Relief warred with nerves. "Thanks, Helen." I grabbed my bag, my hands slightly trembling, and followed Jackson back out into the noise and bustle of the showgrounds.

As we walked toward the familiar Agricultural Hall café, he spoke again, his gaze fixed ahead. "I wanted to apologize properly. For earlier." He stopped, turning to face me fully. "Julie... she's a friend. Grew up together. She wants more, I know that. But I don't.

Not like that." His eyes met mine, earnest and searching. "I know you've just met me, and you've got every reason to be wary—Bruce, then Julie, but please believe me. There's no one else. There hasn't been for a while." He hesitated, then reached out, his calloused fingers closing gently around my hand. Warmth flooded my skin, sending a jolt straight to my core. "I want to get to know you, Megan. Nothing more for now," he added quickly, perhaps sensing my internal panic. "Just... get to know you."

Disappointment warred with respect. Part of me, the part still buzzing from that kiss, wanted *more* right now. But the cautious part appreciated his gentlemanly approach. He wasn't pushing. He was offering space. Time. Even though every nerve ending screamed for connection, for closeness, I knew he was right. "Well," I said, trying to keep my voice steady despite the tremor his touch ignited, "I can only take your word for it." It sounded cooler, more detached than I felt.

Be smart, Megan, my mom's voice echoed in my head. *If he's worth it, he'll understand.*

Jackson nodded slowly, his thumb tracing feather-light circles on the back of my hand. The simple gesture sent shivers down my spine. "I know it looked bad," he admitted quietly. "I don't know how else to convince you."

He didn't need to. Not really. But I wasn't going to make it completely easy for him either. Not when my own feelings were this intense, this overwhelming. Not when just standing here holding his hand made me want things I barely understood. Heart and mind were aligning, but caution still held sway. "Let's have that coffee then," I said, forcing a small smile. "See how things go." I resisted the urge to lean in, to kiss him again. "No promises, though."

"Thanks," he breathed, relief washing over his face. "That's... really kind. Giving me another chance." He didn't let go of my hand.

I didn't pull away. The feel of his rough, working man's hand against my softer skin was grounding and electrifying all at once, stirring those deeper, lustful feelings I was trying so hard to keep in check. He didn't need to know I was already mostly convinced. If coffee went badly, if more red flags appeared, I trusted myself to walk away. My world had been shaken up enough by Jackson Pearce. He'd have to earn his place in it.

An hour later, sitting across from him in the bustling café, the last vestiges of my worry had melted away. He made me laugh, effortlessly drawing me out, sharing stories about farm life, the funny parts, thankfully, not the scary bull parts, asking about my photography, and listening intently. The awkwardness vanished, replaced by an easy camaraderie, a spark that crackled between us with every shared glance, every brush of hands as we reached for the sugar. The bumpy start felt miles away.

My phone buzzed on the table, startling me. I glanced at the screen. "Wow, is that the time already? I should get back, finish editing those photos for Helen."

Jackson leaned forward, his fingers brushing against my bare forearm as he reached across the small table. Little sparks ignited where he touched, travelling up my arm, making my breath catch. "Come and see me afterward?" he asked, a slight hesitation in his voice that somehow made my heart melt a little more. He was so polite, so endearingly unsure, despite the palpable tension humming between us. Didn't he feel it? This electric current that made me want to forget about photos and deadlines and just stay here with him.

"Sure," I heard myself agree, standing up and slinging my bag over my shoulder. "I'm not sure how long it will take, though."

"That's fine. No rush. I'll be around the cattle shed." He stood up, too, walking me toward the café exit.

I smiled, feeling ridiculously happy. "Okay then. I'll come by."

"Good." He stopped just outside the entrance, the noise of the show swirling around us. He stepped closer, his gaze dropping to my lips. My pulse spiked. I stood perfectly still, waiting. He leaned down, his lips finding mine again. It was softer this time, yet somehow more intense. His warmth seeped into me as he gently massaged his lips against mine, once, twice. Then, the barest, tentative touch of his tongue against my lips, testing, questioning. He pulled back slowly, a wide, infectious grin spreading across his face. "Maybe more of that later?"

Hell, yeah! My own smile mirrored his, wide and maybe a little breathless. *And more than that,* a wicked little voice whispered in my head. "I hope so," I managed, my voice huskier than intended. With the last shred of my self-control, I turned away before I did something impulsive. "See you later, Jackson."

CHAPTER 18

Megan

I found him eventually, tucked away near the back of the Sunnydale stalls. He was asleep, sprawled out, using one of his cows as a backrest. It was surprisingly endearing. The cow itself was huge, creamy white, with enormous, floppy ears and legs folded neatly beneath its bulk. It chewed its cud with placid indifference, seemingly content to be a living pillow for the farmer currently snoozing against its side. How could he sleep so soundly next to a creature that could easily crush him with one wrong move?

He looked utterly peaceful, his chin dipped toward his chest, the late afternoon light catching the light stubble that darkened his jawline, making him look ruggedly appealing. His hair was tousled, his Akubra resting on his stomach, rising and falling with each slow, deep breath.

Even in the dim light of the shed, his blue striped shirt looked crisp and clean, a stark contrast to the pervasive smell of, well, cow. Manure, damp hay, that earthy animal scent that clung to everything in here. It instantly transported me back to primary school and Mr. Wings, my ill-fated pet rabbit, whose cage always smelled faintly of rotting hay before he made his great escape. I'd cried for a week. That, and getting kicked in the head by Bruce, pretty much summed up my animal handling experience. Not exactly prime farmer's wife material.

But logic had little sway right now. A primal, animal instinct drew me toward him, overriding the practicalities, the city/country divide, the fact that this show—and likely, whatever *this* was between us —would end in four days. He'd go back to his farm, his world, and I'd stay in mine. Yet, watching him sleep, so at ease amidst the noise and the *filth,* nestled against the cow's warm bulk, my heart hammered a frantic rhythm against my ribs. Heat pooled low in my belly, a familiar ache blooming in my breasts.

I stepped closer, torn. Part of me wanted to just

watch him, memorize the peaceful lines of his face. Another part, the part buzzing from our earlier kiss, wanted to wake him up, claim the time he'd promised, see where things led. How did one even wake a sleeping farmer using his cow as a pillow? My first instinct, embarrassingly, was to kneel and kiss him awake. But even with the sparks flying between us, that felt too bold, too forward. We weren't quite there yet.

Suddenly, ridiculously, I felt a pang of jealousy toward the cow. It got to be close to him, feel his warmth, while I stood here awkwardly debating wake-up etiquette. Taking a breath, I settled for the conventional approach. I cleared my throat softly.

Bad move.

The cow, startled by the unexpected sound, lurched sideways. Jackson jolted awake, tumbling forward off his bovine pillow with a grunt. I jumped back, heart pounding, suddenly terrified the startled animal might lash out.

Jackson blinked rapidly, his blue eyes wide and momentarily confused as he took in his surroundings. Then his gaze landed on me, and a slow, sleepy smile spread across his face, instantly calming my fear. "Hey," he rasped, his voice thick with sleep.

"You found me." Not a hint of annoyance at the rude awakening.

"Sorry!" Heat flooded my face. "I didn't mean to startle... her."

He chuckled, pushing himself up slightly. He reached out, grabbing my hand, his grip warm and strong, sending that familiar jolt through me. "S'alright. Come sit here." He tugged gently.

The softness in his eyes and invitation in his touch made my pulse kick up another notch. Trusting him, trusting the moment, I knelt beside him on the thick layer of hay bedding.

"Not there," he warned, just as my backside made contact.

"Why?" I looked at him, confused by the mixed message. And then I felt it. A distinctly unpleasant dampness, soaking through the seat of my jeans. My eyes widened in horror. I twisted, craning my neck to see. Oh. My. God. Fresh. Green. *Manure.*

Jackson choked back a laugh.

"It's *not* funny!" Mortification burned hotter than the damp patch rapidly spreading across my thigh. I scrambled to my feet, desperate to assess the damage, acutely aware of the sudden, pungent smell clinging to me. A long, disgusting brown-green smear decorated the back of my favorite jeans.

"It is," he managed, grinning now. "Well, sort of. It's not that bad," he offered, though his eyes were still twinkling with amusement.

"Not bad? Jackson, I smell like poo! I have to go home *now*." Disappointment crashed over me, extinguishing the earlier spark. This was *so* not how I'd pictured our reunion unfolding.

"Here, turn around, let me see." He got to his knees in one smooth motion, placing his hands firmly on my hips, turning me before I could protest.

"Hey!" His touch, even in this mortifying situation, sent electric signals straight to my brain, heat thundering through me despite the embarrassment. Him, kneeling, hands on my hips, checking out my manure-covered backside. My cheeks felt incandescent.

"You haven't really looked at the shit I sat in, have you?" I tried to twist away, but he held me steady, his grip surprisingly firm.

"Now that you mention it," he said, his voice dropping slightly, his gaze definitely lingering, "your ass *is* pretty damn sexy. Even with the... decoration."

My jaw clamped shut. More heat flooded my face. "I stink, I'm covered in poo, and you think my ass is sexy?" I couldn't believe him.

"Yeah," he confirmed, his expression utterly serious now, his blue eyes locking with mine. "I do."

My breath caught. The unexpected, sincere compliment sliced right through my embarrassment. His hands relaxed slightly on my hips, and I turned back to face him. He was still kneeling, looking up at me, the angle somehow intimate, vulnerable.

A wicked impulse took over. "Well," I said, raising an eyebrow, enjoying the sudden shift in power dynamic. "I didn't think you'd be the type to get on your knees for a girl so quickly, Farmer Pearce."

A satisfying flush crept up his neck. He grinned, a slow, appreciative curve of his lips. "You're providing some pretty damn good motivation, City Girl." He squeezed my hips gently, the pressure sending a delicious ache radiating through my lower body.

"Well, sorry," I said, trying to regain control of the situation, even as my knees felt weak. "Motivation is gone. I'm a mess. I have to go home and clean up." I tried to step back, but his grip tightened, holding me in place.

"No, you're not." His voice was low, definite.

"You can't possibly want me like this..." The smell, the stain.

"I do."

"No..."

"Well," he conceded, a playful glint in his eyes as he rose smoothly to his feet, pulling me flush against his body in one fluid movement. "Maybe not *quite* like this." His arms wrapped around me, strong and secure. "You're wearing a few too many clothes," he murmured, his lips hovering just above mine. "And now I've got the perfect excuse to help you get them off." He closed the distance, pressing his lips to mine.

I melted into him, welcoming the soft pressure, the familiar heat. He kissed me gently at first, pulling back slightly before pressing forward again, soft, sweet, tentative, stoking the embers inside me.

I parted my lips slightly, inviting him in. His tongue met mine, a hesitant exploration, tasting, learning. Hot, sweet, a little salty. It made me want more, so much more.

His lips slid from mine, sucking softly on my lower lip before returning with a new urgency, a demanding pressure that I met eagerly, my own tongue tangling with his, exploring and tasting him back. I clung to him, letting the kiss deepen, letting it transport me, blocking out the shed, the smells, everything but him and the heat building between us. A soft sound of pleasure escaped my throat.

He pulled back slightly, breathing hard, his forehead resting against mine, his arms still tight around me. "Okay," he rasped. "Definitely need to get you cleaned up."

His kisses had completely undone me. My body hummed, quivering with anticipation. "Yes," I agreed breathlessly. "And for the record, you're wearing too many clothes yourself." I tilted my head back, stealing another quick, hard kiss.

He groaned, pressing himself against me, hard and undeniable. I arched into him, reveling in the solid feel of his body, my mind racing with images of what it would feel like to touch him, taste him, everywhere. My cheeks flushed again, this time with pure, unadulterated want. Forget cleaning up. I wanted him. Now. The electric current between us was almost visible, making my knees tremble. This was going to happen. Soon. Very soon. Muscles low in my belly clenched tight, sending a rush of heat and moisture between my thighs.

"Right," he muttered, his eyes closed for a second as if gathering his strength. He kissed me again, quick and deep. Then, visibly forcing himself, he pulled back slightly. "We'd better get somewhere quiet before I lose what little control I have left and take you right here against the hay bales." He opened his eyes, his gaze intense. "This way."

He took my hand, his rough fingers tangling with mine, the simple contact reigniting the fire. I let him lead me down the aisle, past the rows of placid cattle that no longer seemed frightening, only vaguely curious. Walking brought the damp patch on my jeans back into sharp focus. And the smell, although honestly, in here, it just blended with the general earthy aroma. I giggled suddenly.

"What's funny?" Jackson glanced down at me, puzzled.

"Just... I finally fit in," I explained. "I smell like the animals."

He stopped, pretending to look offended. "Hey! I take offense to that. *I* don't smell like animals."

"That's not what I meant!" I squeezed his hand. "I meant *I* don't smell out of place anymore because I blend in with the surroundings."

"Oh." He still looked slightly confused. "So... you *want* to smell like animals?"

"No!" Honestly, men. "I mean, I'm not as self-conscious about the poo-smell because *everything* smells like poo in here!"

He stopped walking again, turning to face me, his expression serious but with laughter dancing in his eyes. "So... you want to leave your jeans on then?"

"Hell, no," I said immediately, reaching up to kiss him again, hard, flicking my tongue against his lips.

"Good," he mumbled against my mouth, kissing me back with equal fervor.

I pulled back slightly, grinning. "And for the record, *you* smell like spice and sunshine, with only the faintest, most appealing hint of animal."

"What?" He pulled away fully, laughing now. "Sunshine? Okay, no more kisses for you."

I pouted dramatically. "No?"

"Well..." His gaze softened, travelling over my face. "Maybe just for a second. Can't seem to keep my hands off you." He leaned in, capturing my lips again, brief but potent. "But we're getting seriously distracted," he murmured against my skin, "and my primary objective right now is getting you naked and clean. Preferably in that order, but I'm flexible."

My words caught in my throat again. My abdomen gave another tight clench. Focusing enough to walk felt like a monumental effort, with anticipation making my legs shake.

"Just a sec." He let go of my hand, stopping near

the end of the aisle where a cluster of bags and fold-up chairs marked the Sunnydale camp. He started rummaging through a large canvas tote bag.

"What are you looking for, dear?"

My head snapped up. Kim, Jackson's mom was strolling over, looking relaxed and casual in blue jeans and a vibrant ruby-red top. Country chic. Oh God, not *now*. Heat rushed back into my cheeks with the force of a tidal wave. I tried to smooth my hair, hoping I didn't look as flustered, and manure-scented, as I felt.

"Where are those wipes you always have, Mom?" Jackson continued digging, oblivious to my internal panic.

"Stop making such a mess!" Kim gently pushed him aside. "Honestly, Jackson. They were right here on top." She held up a familiar white packet of baby wipes. "What do you need them for anyway?" Her gaze shifted curiously toward me.

I didn't think it was possible to blush any harder, but I felt the heat intensify. I wanted the ground to swallow me whole.

"Megan sat in some cow manure," Jackson stated, completely matter-of-factly.

Kim's eyes widened slightly as she looked me over, then her expression softened with sympathy.

"Oh, dear. Well, you'll probably need more than these then."

"They'll be a start, at least," I mumbled, desperately wishing I could disappear.

"Your head looks much better, dear," Kim commented kindly, peering at my forehead.

"Thanks," I managed, realizing I'd completely forgotten about the fading bruise. Jackson had that effect, erasing everything else.

"You know," Kim continued thoughtfully, "I think Julie is probably a similar size to you. I'm sure she'd have a spare pair of jeans you could borrow."

I nearly choked. Borrow jeans from *Julie*? Over my dead, manure-stained body. "Oh, uh, thanks, but..."

Kim's expression suddenly cleared with understanding. "Oh! Right. Sorry, dear. Well... perhaps I could just give yours a quick wash under the tap? I've got some dish soap here somewhere. It might get the worst of it out so you can get home without..." She started rummaging in another bag.

"Mom," Jackson interrupted, his own cheeks starting to color now. "Can I just have the wipes, please?"

I pressed my lips together, trying hard not to laugh. Seeing him flustered by his well-meaning mother was unexpectedly sweet. It reminded me of my own mom, always trying to fix things. I missed that. "Really, Kim, I'll be fine with the wipes," I assured her.

"Okay, okay, dear. Just trying to help." She handed the packet to Jackson.

"Thanks, Mom. See you later." Jackson grabbed the wipes and my hand in one swift motion, practically dragging me away.

"Thanks, Kim!" I called over my shoulder, not wanting to seem rude. She *was* his mom, after all. And despite the awkwardness, she seemed genuinely kind.

CHAPTER 19

Megan

"Where exactly are we going?" The question slipped out as a sudden wave of caution washed over the heat pooling inside me. This was the Royal Show. A very public place. As much as my blood was pumping, pushing boundaries was one thing, but getting arrested for indecent exposure was quite another.

"My sleeping new quarters," Jackson answered easily, still pulling me along.

I dug my heels in, pulling him to a stop. "*Here*?" I couldn't keep the disbelief from my voice.

"Yeah." He turned back, his brow furrowed slightly at my sudden reluctance. "You do want to... I mean, if you've changed your mind, that's cool... well..." He ran a hand through his hair, looking flustered. "I'll be disappointed, obviously... because, you know, I like you... God, I sound like an idiot."

His vulnerability was surprisingly endearing. "I haven't changed my mind," I reassured him quickly, placing a hand on his arm, feeling the solid muscle beneath his shirt. "I just... I didn't realize people actually *slept* here. At the show. Honestly? I kind of figured you guys just bunked down with the cattle."

He grinned, relief flooding his features. "Nah. It's nothing fancy, just down here." He gestured with the packet of wipes still clutched in his hand.

I followed his gesture, scanning the area. Trucks rumbled past, cattle lowed mournfully from nearby pens, and the distant, tinny music and screams from the carnival rides created a constant background buzz. All I saw were more stalls and a row of nondescript, green-painted doors. Nothing remotely resembling sleeping quarters.

"The green doors," he clarified.

"*There*?" My jaw might have actually dropped. They looked like glorified garden sheds. Hardly cozy, and definitely not private.

"Yeah." He tugged my hand gently. "Hey, come

have a look. If you don't like it, we can figure something else out, go somewhere else?"

Somewhere else? Where? I still lived at home, so bringing Jackson back for hot, potentially noisy sex while Dad might walk in wasn't an option.

A hotel maybe? But Jackson squeezed my hand then, stepping closer, lowering his head to mine.

His kiss was immediate, demanding, a fiery bolt that seared my lips and shot straight down my body. He sucked gently on my bottom lip as he pulled away, nipping playfully. Rational thought dissolved. I no longer cared where we were.

"Show me," I managed, my voice husky. "Quick." I opened my eyes to find him watching me, a curious, intense look in his eyes.

He groaned, a low sound of impatience, and pulled me forward again. We ducked down a narrow alleyway behind the main cattle sheds, where another row of identical green doors stood. He stopped at one where a simple padlock secured it. Tucking the wipes under his arm, he fished out his keys and unlocked it, pulling the door open.

I peered inside. It was small, maybe three meters by two, and dark. The air was thick with the smell of cattle, a scent that was now disturbingly familiar, mingled with dusty hay and sweat.

A couple of rolled-up swags lay on the floor, along with some duffel bags. There was barely enough space to stand, let alone lie down.

Suppose I don't have to lie down, a wicked thought whispered, sending a fresh clench low in my belly at the image of him inside me, right here, standing up. But still, how were we going to manage? And how was I supposed to clean my jeans? My mind, usually so organized, felt like a tangled mess.

"You want me to go in *there*?" I looked back at him, not appreciating the amusement dancing in his eyes.

"You don't have to," he said softly, leaning in to kiss me again.

His lips, his taste, the sheer wanting that radiated from him made my knees go weak. Doubts evaporated like mist on a hot day. There was only this. Him. Now. "I want to," I breathed against his mouth, stepping over the threshold into the dim, confined space. "Wait... you're not the only one sleeping here?"

"No. A couple of other blokes from up north. I *was* sleeping over..." He stopped abruptly, guilt shadowing his face.

I didn't need him to finish. "Let me guess. With

Julie." I pursed my lips, trying to keep the annoyance out of my voice.

He nodded, looking miserable. "And Heath and Kelly. But nothing happened, Megan. Honestly." The sincerity in his tone, the desperation in his eyes had me believing him.

"Well, at least you're not sharing with her *now*," I said, trying to lighten the mood.

His expression somehow worsened.

I rolled my eyes. "Okay, okay, she kicked you out. Good. Means I can have you all to myself." I turned to face him fully in the cramped space. He immediately closed the distance, pressing his body against mine. His hands framed my face, thumbs stroking my jawline as his lips brushed mine. I closed my eyes, letting his taste, his heat, seep into me. I groaned softly, melting against him, loving the feel of his rough, calloused farmer's hands, that were surprisingly gentle, firm but with an underlying softness that made my skin hum.

"Now," he murmured, breaking the kiss, his breath warm against my cheek. "About getting you cleaned up."

A mischievous impulse took over. "Don't you want me dirty?"

His answer was another kiss, hard, passionate,

leaving no doubt. I groaned again as he pushed himself against me, his tongue exploring my mouth with confident strokes while his hips ground against mine, letting me feel the ridge of his erection through his jeans.

"You taste so damn good," he muttered, his hands slipping under the hem of my shirt and sliding up my bare skin, leaving a trail of fire that made my head spin.

"So do you," I whispered back, circling my tongue against his, reveling in the heat, the taste of him—coffee, mint, pure male Jackson—exploding on my senses. No more doubts. I wanted him. All of him. Right here. Right now.

I pressed myself harder against him, needing to feel all of his solid, country-hotness, needing my hands on him. He groaned as my fingers moved over his chest, mapping the hard planes of muscle through the cotton of his shirt. Heat seeped into my palms, a promise of the pleasure to come.

My fingers found his buttons, fumbling slightly in my eagerness. I worked my way down, deliberately letting my fingertips brush against his warm skin with each button undone, exposing the flesh I was desperate to explore. Pushing the shirt aside, I drank in his smooth, tanned skin, stretched taut over well-defined muscles. A definite six-pack. Oh Lordy, I couldn't wait to touch him.

Leaning forward, I pressed my lips to his skin, starting low, just above the waistband of his moleskin jeans. I traced slow, deliberate paths upward with my tongue, tasting the saltiness of his skin, the faint scent of spice and sunshine I'd teased him about earlier. It tingled on my tongue, addictive, urging me on.

He moaned with each lick, his hands tightening on my hips. When I reached his neck, I sucked gently at the base, pulling the skin taut, then moved higher, nipping softly just under his jaw.

He shuddered, his subtle movements encouraging me, emboldening me. I explored his skin with playful sucks and nibbles before capturing his mouth again in an explosive kiss. I instinctively raised one leg, hooking it around the outside of his thigh, opening myself more fully to the pressure of his hardness against my core. He groaned into my mouth, the heat intensifying between us, threatening to combust.

His hands moved, sliding up my back, then around my ribs, settling just under the line of my bra. He cupped my breasts through the fabric, squeezing with an urgency that sent my abdominal muscles clenching as need coiled tight within me.

I arched back slightly, granting him better access. He caressed my nipples through the lace, his thumbs pushing the delicate fabric against the sensitive peaks, heightening the waves of pleasure washing over me.

My hands gripped his waist, holding on as he trailed hot, open-mouthed kisses down my neck, along the neckline of my shirt. He pushed the fabric lower, frustrated when it stopped him, settling for kissing my breasts through the thin cotton. A deep moan escaped my lips. Every touch, every kiss, intensified the wanting, the desperate need to have him inside me, raising my temperature to a fever pitch.

My hand slid down between his legs, pressing against the impressive bulge straining against his jeans. He groaned again, thrusting his hips forward instinctively. As I massaged my palm against him, feeling him harden even further beneath the thick material, he continued kissing my neck, holding me tight against him.

"Get a room!" a gruff voice yelled from somewhere outside, startlingly close.

My head snapped up, then I immediately buried

my face against Jackson's chest, my cheeks flaming. Strangely, though, the embarrassment wasn't as acute as I'd expected. Maybe I was past caring.

"We *have* a room," Jackson called back, pulling away slightly.

He reached for the wooden door, tugging it closed, plunging us into near darkness, broken only by thin slivers of light filtering through the cracks. I didn't like losing contact, the sudden separation.

I reached out blindly, finding his solid form, and wrapped my arms around him from behind, pressing my cheek against his warm back. The heady scent of him, testosterone, clean sweat, that underlying spice, filled my senses, making my head swim with need. A need I desperately wanted sated.

"There," he said, his voice muffled slightly. "Now we don't have an audience." I heard the metallic click as he swung an internal latch across and secured the padlock. "And we won't be disturbed."

"It's still not exactly private," I murmured against his back, acutely aware of the thin wooden walls.

"I don't care." He turned within my arms, wrapping his own around me. "I want you." One of his hands slid higher, brushing deliberately over my breasts as he drew me close again, his mouth finding mine in the darkness.

I opened to him instantly, his tongue circling mine, slow, firm, possessive. His other hand moved downward, sliding over the denim covering my hip, then moving to the front, pressing against the juncture of my thighs. I moaned into the kiss as his fingers traced my shape, even through the thick fabric. His touch sparked fire, making me instantly wet and ache for more.

A sudden thought pierced the haze of lust. "You do have condoms, right?" I pulled back from the kiss, breathless, suddenly panicked at the thought of having to stop. If things went much further, stopping wouldn't be an option.

"Yeah." Even in the dim light, I could see the outline of his smile. Relief washed over me. I surged back toward him, returning to his kiss. His hand continued its exploration, teasing me through my clothes. I pushed at his shirt, wanting it gone, needing skin on skin. He helped me ease it over his shoulders.

"Like what you feel?" he whispered, his voice husky in the dark.

"You feel even better than you look." My fingertips traced the hard lines of his arms, pausing to squeeze his biceps. He groaned softly. I slid my hands over his shoulders, down his chest, across the washboard ripples of his stomach, savoring the feel of him.

"You," he murmured, "are wearing way too much." His fingers fumbled with the buttons of my top. I stepped back slightly, giving him room, then took over myself, my fingers more nimble. Hands trembling slightly, I slipped the top button near my neck through its hole.

"Can't see much anyway," I teased softly, my voice shaky. "It's too dark." I undid the next button, then the next, slowly parting the fabric, revealing glimpses of skin in the slivers of light.

"I can see enough," he growled, cupping my head, kissing me deeply as I undid the last button. His hands moved down my neck, pushing the shirt back off my shoulders.

I shimmied slightly, letting the soft material slither down my arms, goose bumps rising despite the heat as his hands moved upward again, tracing the lace outline of my bra. My mind blurred, thoughts dissolved into pure sensation. I gripped his waist for support, giving him free rein to explore, to learn my body.

His fingers slipped beneath the upper edge of the lace, the light touch sending electric tingles through me. My nipples tightened instantly, aching for more direct contact. Muscles deep inside me clenched, wanting him, needing something solid to hold onto as pleasure threatened to overwhelm me.

He pressed his palms flat against my breasts, squeezing gently, before pinching my nipples sharply through the lace. I gasped, a bolt of sharp, exquisite pleasure shooting through me, making me dizzy. I reveled in the sensation as his hands continued their ministrations.

He reached behind me, his fingers finding the clasp of my bra. It sprang open, and he pushed the straps aside, freeing me completely. Leaning down, his mouth closed over one hardened peak. I groaned aloud, helpless against the waves of pleasure crashing through me. My fingers tangled in his messy hair, gripping tightly, tugging playfully as his tongue rolled and flicked.

"You like that," he murmured against my skin, turning his attention to my other breast, lavishing it with the same devastating attention.

"Uh-huh," I managed, tugging harder on his hair, pulling him closer. He responded with another flick of his tongue. I gasped again, losing myself completely for a moment.

His hands slid down, over the manure-stained denim of my jeans to fumble with the zip. Impatient, wanting skin on skin, wanting *him*, I reached down to help him. With renewed urgency, his hands slipped inside my jeans, under the waistband of my lacy knickers, his fingers mapping the curve of my hip, then moving lower, over my mound, searching. Seeking the entrance that promised oblivion. I instinctively widened my stance, lifting one leg slightly to guide him, opening myself to him.

"So wet," he whispered, his fingers sliding easily through the slick heat between my folds.

"Of course," I breathed, holding my breath as he began a slow, circular massage against my clit. "You turn me on."

He grunted, a sound of pure male satisfaction. "You definitely do it for me." He kissed me again, his tongue mimicking the rhythm of his fingers.

My own hand moved lower, finding the hard length of him straining against his trousers. "Yep," I confirmed breathlessly. "You are."

He felt thick, hot, and ready. I cupped him through the fabric, feeling the heat seep through to my palm. A surge of possessive desire washed over me, I needed to feel him, skin on skin. My fingers fumbled with his belt buckle, then the zip, rushing to free him before pushing his jeans and boxers down over his hips.

I glanced down in the dim light. He was magnificent. Thick, long, pulsing slightly. Gently, reverently, I closed my hand around him. He groaned, his fingers moving deeper between my folds, parting the slick flesh, releasing another gush of moisture.

I gasped softly, lost in the dual sensations of the pleasure he was giving me, the pleasure of touching him. His rhythm increased, his fingers working magic, and my answering sounds became louder, less inhibited. I clamped my jaw shut, trying to stifle the moans, suddenly remembering the thin walls and the people outside. But he didn't let up, and the sounds escaped me, involuntary gasps and whimpers.

Suddenly, he sank to his knees before me. My hand slid off him as he gripped my hips, steadying me. I trembled, knowing what was coming, barely able to wait for the scorching heat of his mouth.

He kissed my inner thighs, his lips moist and soft, pressing firmly against my skin. I whimpered, the anticipation almost unbearable. He was making me wait, prolonging the exquisite torture.

I surrendered, giving myself over completely to his control, letting him guide me toward release. I closed my eyes, panting harder, arching my hips slightly. Then, finally, I was rewarded.

A puff of hot breath against my most sensitive skin, followed by the glide of his tongue, pushing, licking, tasting me. My hands found his head, fingers gripping his hair, needing the anchor as he worked his magic, building the pressure within me higher and higher.

I didn't think I could take any more, but each flick, each suck, sent another wave of pleasure crashing over me. He persisted, relentless, until control shattered, and I cried out, my body convulsing in a blinding orgasm that went on and on.

Breathless and trembling, I leaned over him, still making small, involuntary sounds as awareness slowly returned. "I think," I gasped, "everyone out there probably knows *exactly* what we were doing."

Jackson stood up, pulling me upright and moving me gently to the side. I felt his erection, hard and insistent, pressing against my thigh. A little trickle of moisture escaped me as I reached down instinctively to squeeze the smooth crown.

"If they didn't know before," he growled, his voice thick with need, "they'll definitely know shortly. Because I am far from finished with you." He closed his eyes for a second, taking a deep breath, while my hand moved, stroking up and down his length. He gently pushed my hand away. "I need to be inside you."

"I need you inside me," I echoed, my voice shaky. I gripped him again, squeezing hard enough to make him gasp.

"Now." He kicked off his boots and shimmied out of his jeans. I quickly did the same, kicking my own jeans and boots aside. He grabbed his swag from the floor, unrolling it with one swift movement, then pulled me down onto the surprisingly soft mattress, landing half on top of me.

"Wait..." he murmured against my skin.

"I know," I whispered back, feeling the smooth head of his cock nudging against my entrance. "I want to feel you like this for a second too. Just... not for long." The thought of him inside me, bare, hot, and hard was dangerously tempting. But reality intruded. This was risky enough already.

"Promise," he breathed, pushing a stray strand of hair from my face before kissing my cheek gently. "No losing control. Yet."

"Okay." I'd already lost control. And I was more than ready to lose it again, this time with him buried deep inside me. "But seriously, Jackson. Not long. I *need* you in me."

"I'll go in you when I'm good and ready," he teased, kissing me hard on the lips.

"Will you now?" I mocked back, though my body was screaming for him. He shifted his hips slightly, pressing the head of his cock more firmly against my entrance. I held my breath, looking up into his eyes in the dim light. He winked, then moved his hips down again, rubbing himself against me. I smiled, despite the ache of wanting.

"Had you worried there for a second." He chuckled.

"Shut up," I gasped, "and get inside me. Now."

He groaned, a deep, guttural sound, and with a swift, powerful movement, flipped me onto my back, settling his weight between my legs. He captured my mouth again, his tongue tangling with mine, tasting me, claiming me.

I instinctively opened my legs wider, wrapping them around his waist, enjoying the feel of his hardness resting against my entrance, poised and ready. I whimpered softly, unsure how much longer I could wait. He had me primed, slick and ready, already having brought me to orgasm once, and now expertly guiding me toward another.

His mouth left mine, trailing down my neck, then lower, finding a nipple. He bit down gently, the sharp pinch sending a jolt of combined pain and pleasure through me that made me gasp aloud. His hands roamed my body, igniting sparks wherever they touched.

"I like your sounds," he murmured against my breast. He reached over to where his jeans lay crumpled, fumbled for a moment, then pulled out a small, foil packet. Kneeling back slightly between my legs, his erection pointed toward me, thick, pulsing, impossibly inviting.

I couldn't resist.

My hand reached out, closing around his shaft, stroking the velvety tip while he ripped open the condom packet with his teeth. My efforts were rewarded with a low groan ripped from his throat. He pushed my hand away gently, then quickly sheathed himself in the latex.

"Ready?" he asked, leaning over me again, bracing himself on his elbows with his eyes locked on mine.

I nodded. "Been ready for a while."

"Good." He positioned himself at my entrance, the blunt tip pressing against my slick folds.

I responded instinctively, lifting my hips to meet him. He lingered there for a torturous moment, kissing me deeply, his hands resuming their exploration, one finding my breast, the other sliding down to cup my hip. I surrendered completely, kissing him back with abandon, widening my legs further, lost in the moment, wanting to feel him inside of me.

He lifted himself slightly, bracing on his hands, his muscles taut, and then, slowly, deliberately, he pushed forward, easing into me.

I groaned, a long, low sound, my hips tilting upward automatically, welcoming him, taking him deeper. I looked up at him, mesmerized by the sight. His smooth chest gleamed faintly with sweat in the dim light, tanned skin stretched over hard muscle, his face taut with concentration and pleasure.

"You look," he gasped, "as good as you feel." He shifted his weight back onto his knees slightly, licked his fingers, then reached down, placing them against my clit.

I held my breath, bracing myself. His warm, wet fingers found their mark, moving with unerring purpose, rubbing, circling, building the tension inside me to an almost unbearable level. My inner muscles clenched tightly around him, heightening the sensation for both of us, and I groaned again, louder this time, completely unable to control the sounds escaping me. The familiar, unstoppable ride toward orgasm took hold, sweeping me away.

The desperate need to climax drove me, made me surrender completely to the feel of his fingers working their magic, the friction of him moving inside me until he tipped me over the edge again in a blinding burst of contractions and breathless gasps. I reached up blindly at the peak, clutching at his shoulders, before tumbling back down against the thin mattress of the swag, boneless and spent. I couldn't speak, could only lie there, in the after-shocks still gripping my body.

"My turn," he growled, and began to thrust with new urgency, a driving rhythm that reignited the embers within me. I groaned as another shot of pure pleasure coursed through me with each deep stroke, each withdrawal.

Incredibly, impossibly, I felt myself climbing again, completely under his control, my breath coming in short, heavy pants, my sounds growing louder, less inhibited. I didn't care who heard anymore. God, it felt so good, him moving inside me, his strength pressing down, his hardness filling me, letting me clench around him as he moved.

My hands slid under his arms, gripping the hard muscles of his back, and holding on tight as he guided me toward another peak, this time bringing himself along with me. We moved together, faster now, bodies slick with sweat, working as one until we both cried out, jerking and shuddering in the throes of a shared orgasm, one that lingered in wave after wave of pulsing pleasure. I gripped him tightly, anchoring myself until my body finally stopped convulsing and he stilled above me, collapsing onto his elbows.

He rested there for a long moment, his breathing ragged. I moved my hands gently over his back, feeling the fine sheen of sweat coating his skin, which mirrored my own.

"God," he finally breathed out. "That was… good." He nestled his face into the curve of my neck, placing soft, feather-light kisses against my damp skin.

"Yep," was all I could manage, still breathless.

He eased himself off me carefully. "Messy part," he murmured, reaching for the discarded wipes.

"But worth it." I sighed, lying back on the swag, enjoying the delicious languor, the pleasure still rippling through my muscles.

"Hell, yeah." He finished cleaning himself, then wrapped himself around me, pulling me close against his side. The swag was definitely a single, offering minimal space, but pressed together like this in the small, dark shed, it felt intimate, perfect.

I nestled back against his warmth, inhaling his scent, and enjoying the simple comfort of his skin against mine. *I could get used to this.* The thought surfaced unbidden. Then reality intruded, there were only a few days left of the show.

Then he'd be gone. Back to his farm. Back to his life.

I pushed the thoughts away. Later. I'd deal with that later.

"Reckon a quick rest," he murmured, his lips brushing against the back of my head, "and we could go again."

A delighted giggle escaped me. I was exhausted, blissfully so, but his suggestion sent a fresh wave of warmth pooling low in my belly. "I might just hold you to that, Farmer."

"Good. I want you to." He tightened his arm around my waist, holding me securely against him. I relaxed completely into his embrace, enjoying the quiet intimacy and closeness that followed the intensity. "You're okay, right?" he asked softly after a moment.

I tensed slightly, unsure what he meant. "Of course. You looked after me very well."

"No, I mean..." he shifted slightly, "you're not dizzy or anything? From the hit on the head?"

"Oh." Relief washed over me. "Right. No, I'm good. Really."

He kissed the back of my neck again. "Good."

My eyelids felt incredibly heavy. Content, warm, wrapped in Jackson's arms, I felt myself drifting off...

Bang! Bang! Bang!

A loud rattling, aggressive banging on the door jolted me awake, my heart leaping into my throat.

"Oi! Jackson! There are others supposed to room here, too, mate!" a muffled male voice yelled from outside.

"Bugger," I whispered, heat instantly flooding my cheeks. I was mortified. The last thing I wanted was a walk of shame past his disgruntled roommates. I was usually *so* much more discreet than this.

"Give us a minute, mate!" Jackson yelled back, his voice laced with annoyance.

"Oh no," I groaned, burying my face against his chest.

"Don't worry about them," Jackson murmured, stroking my hair. "They won't care."

"We *do* care!" yelled another voice, closer this time. "Come on, Jackson, get a bloody move on!"

My face burned hotter. I wished the swag would swallow me whole.

"Hey, keep that up, and I won't open the door at

all!" Jackson threatened, a hint of laughter in his voice now.

"You bastard! You'll regret it if you do that!" The door rattled again under a heavier assault.

Jackson actually chuckled. "We'll be out in a minute!"

We. Oh God. My mortification rose to level ten. I scrambled up, feeling around frantically for my clothes in the near-total darkness. The air felt suddenly cold where Jackson's body had been warming me. I found my bra, fumbled it on, then my knickers, nearly tripping in the confined space. I located my jeans and was awkwardly shimmying back into them when my head collided sharply with Jackson's.

"Ow!" I rubbed the sore spot.

"Shit, sorry!" He reached out, gently rubbing my head, then pulled me into a brief, protective hug.

"It's okay." Part of me wanted to stay right there, wrapped in his arms, ignoring the impatient banging. But reality beckoned. I needed to get out of here, away from his roommates, away from this intensely charged space. I needed to go home, shower, and try to process the hurricane of feelings swirling inside me. Feelings for a man whose life was worlds away from mine.

He's not staying here. I'm not moving there. Even after the mind-blowing sex, the fundamental problem remained.

"Hey," he said softly, tilting my chin up, forcing me to meet his eyes in the dimness. "You don't... you don't regret this, right?"

He'd done it again. Read my thoughts, or at least sensed the conflict. "No," I said firmly, buttoning my shirt with trembling fingers. "Absolutely not."

"Good." He kissed me again, slow and tender, melting my bones all over again. "Because I'd really like to see you again."

"I bet you would," I teased weakly, trying to regain some semblance of composure.

"Not just for the sex," he said seriously, his gaze holding mine. "Though... that was incredible. But really, Megan. I want to get to know you more."

"Okay," I whispered, the word barely audible over the renewed, angry rattling of the door. I took a deep breath. "Guess we should face the music."

"Ready?" He squeezed my hand.

I nodded, quickly running my fingers through my hair, attempting to tame it back into some semblance of a ponytail. Jackson unlocked the padlock and swung the door open.

"About bloody time!" a guy standing there immediately snapped. He was tall and wiry, arms crossed, glaring.

"Looking a bit jealous there, Tate," Jackson said easily, wrapping an arm around my waist, guiding me out into the slightly brighter alleyway. My legs felt like lead. My cheeks were surely scarlet.

"You two might want to get a hotel room next time." Tate sneered. "Could hear you halfway across the showgrounds."

"Yep, definitely jealous," Jackson shot back, unperturbed.

"About time!" another guy stomped up, stockier, looking furious. "Was about to go find a crowbar, Jackson!"

"Settle down, Aston," Jackson said calmly.

Aston ignored him, pushing past us toward the small shed. He stopped abruptly in the doorway, his face darkening further. "You bastard!" he roared, turning back toward Jackson.

Jackson instinctively pushed me slightly forward, shielding me.

"Couldn't wait, could you, Jackson?" Aston yelled, pointing an accusing finger.

I swallowed hard. Suddenly, my legs worked just fine. I hurried away down the alley, not wanting to hear another word, not wanting to see the looks on their faces. Embarrassment warred with a confusing flicker of amusement and defiance.

All I knew was that part of me, the part still humming from his touch, ridiculously wanted to turn back, grab Jackson's hand, pull him back into that tiny, dark shed, lock the door, and start all over again. I didn't care whose swag it was as long as Jackson was in it with me.

CHAPTER 20

Megan

I managed about a dozen hurried steps down the alleyway, the taunts of Jackson's roommates still echoing in my ears, before the mortifying reality hit me again. *The manure.* After everything, the passion, the intimacy, the frantic dressing in the dark, I was still walking around smelling faintly of cow poo with a giant green-brown stain on my backside. "Oh God," I muttered, stopping dead. "I've got to go home."

Jackson caught up easily, his warm and reassuring hand finding mine. "You don't have to."

I looked back at him, incredulous. "Um, yeah, I kind of do. My jeans? Remember?"

He slapped a hand dramatically to his forehead. "Shit. Sorry. Completely forgot."

A small laugh escaped me despite my embarrassment. "Guess we were a little... distracted." I looked up at him as we started walking again, his presence solid and comforting beside me.

"We certainly were." He wrapped an arm firmly around my shoulders, pulling me close against his side, a possessive gesture that sent a fresh wave of warmth through me and chased away the lingering mortification. "Walk you to your car."

"Thanks." I slipped my own arm around his lower back, fitting myself against his side as we emerged from the relative seclusion of the cattle sheds and back into the main thoroughfare of the showgrounds.

People bustled past, but wrapped in Jackson's arm, I felt cocooned, still caught in the afterglow of our time together. I smiled, leaning my head against his shoulder for a moment. I would have preferred a much longer, naked cuddle session back in that tiny shed, preferably on a cleaner swag, but this easy intimacy, walking together like this, felt surprisingly right. If only my jeans weren't broadcasting my recent adventure, I would have happily stayed glued to his side for hours.

Longer. The thought surprised me. Was I really thinking beyond this single, intense encounter? Did I want more? That undeniable pull toward him, the one I'd felt from the start, seemed to have solidified into something stronger, something that scared me a little.

"This is me." Reluctantly, I pulled away as we reached my little red Ford Hatchback, fumbling in my bag for my keys. The bubble popped, reality intruding.

Before I could unlock the door, he pulled me into another embrace, holding me tight. "You really have to leave me?" he murmured into my hair, his voice low and husky.

"Dad will be home soon," I said, pulling back just enough to look up at him, a teasing glint in my eye despite the ache of leaving. "You could come meet him, if you like?"

A slow smile spread across his face. "I'd like that."

"Really?" I raised an eyebrow.

"Yes," he confirmed, his smile widening. "But maybe not immediately after I've had incredibly satisfying sex with his daughter for the first time." He leaned down and kissed my forehead gently. The simple gesture felt amazingly tender. "First things first," he continued, his expression turning serious, his blue eyes searching mine. "Can I see you again?"

Relief washed over me, swift and potent. I nodded, unable to stop the answering smile. "Yes. And not just because you're ridiculously good between the sheets." I rose onto my toes, pulling his head down for another kiss, my hands gripping his waist as I pressed myself against his solid warmth.

He ended the kiss far too soon, resting his forehead against mine. "Tomorrow, then?" The question hung there, filled with hope but also a fragile uncertainty. How could we make this work? He was leaving soon. This feeling, this connection, how could I hold onto it?

"You bet." I gave him one last, quick kiss, then forced myself to pull away before things escalated. Another kiss like that and we'd be scrambling into the backseat, and I had a feeling the residents of the nearby houses wouldn't appreciate the show. Definitely not worth explaining to the police.

"I'll come find you?" Jackson asked, shoving his hands into his pockets, looking endearingly uncertain again.

I nodded. "I'll probably be in the newspaper office around nine. Unless that's too early for a hard-working farmer?"

He chuckled. "Not at all. But... will you have work to do? I don't want to get in your way."

"Yeah," I admitted. "Still got heaps of photos to take, and I need to cover the Grand Parade properly this time, get the shots I missed the other day."

"Right. So maybe... maybe I should catch you later then? Give you space to work?"

Disappointment pricked at me. The thought of going through the whole night and most of the next morning without seeing him felt like torture. Even after the intensity of what we'd just shared, the fire hadn't banked, it still simmered, making the thought of holding back difficult, almost impossible. If I couldn't have him all night, I wanted as much time as possible before he disappeared back to the bush, back to his world. My heart sank a little.

"Actually," I heard myself say, pushing past the uncertainty, "if you're up for it, you could... come with me? While I work?"

His face lit up. "Seriously? I'd love that. How about I come find you after I've fed up the cattle? Then I'm all yours for the day."

"All mine?" I grinned. "I like the sound of that." I leaned in for one final kiss, quick but potent, before sliding into the driver's seat and tossing my camera bag onto the passenger seat beside me. I tried not to think about the dried, crusty manure potentially transferring to the upholstery. Gross.

I pressed the button to lower the window. "Can't wait," I said, meaning it more than I probably should.

Jackson leaned in, stealing another kiss. "Me neither."

I started the car, pulling away from the curb, my eyes catching his in the rear-view mirror. He stood there, watching me go, raising a hand in farewell. His image stayed with me, a warm, vivid presence that kept the loneliness at bay all night.

CHAPTER 21

Megan

The next morning, I arrived back at the showgrounds well before nine, feeling surprisingly refreshed despite a slightly restless night filled with vivid replays of the previous afternoon.

Clean jeans, fresh shirt, and yes, as a precaution, I'd even tossed an overnight bag with a change of clothes into the boot. Just in case. Although I planned on meticulously inspecting every single surface before sitting down anywhere near hay or livestock today. Lesson learned.

I wandered toward the cattle sheds, drawn by an invisible thread. The air was cooler this morning, carrying the sounds of preparation—the hiss of water hoses, the buzz of clippers, and low voices murmuring to animals. I paused near the washing bays, pulling out my camera instinctively.

Cattle were lined up, tethered patiently while handlers, some of them surprisingly as young as school kids, maybe, washed them down, scrubbed coats, dried them with massive blowers, and brushed their hair into fluffy perfection. I snapped a few close-ups, fascinated by the intense focus and care they took.

Questions bubbled up. Why this meticulous grooming? What were they looking for? I wished Jackson were here already, wished I could pepper him with questions and hear his easy explanations. And then, the question I'd avoided asking him yesterday surfaced again, heavy and unwelcome, *When are you going back?*

Back to the farm, back to the life where I didn't fit. He filled my thoughts constantly, a warm hum beneath the surface, but the knowledge of his impending departure cast a shadow, tightening my chest.

Keeping a respectful distance, I took a few more shots, then turned toward the newspaper office by habit. But then I stopped. Helen had the photos I'd stayed up late emailing last night. There was no real reason to go there yet. And every reason to find Jackson.

I doubled back, heading down the now-familiar aisle toward the Sunnydale stalls, anticipation bubbling inside me. The thought of spending the day with him, even while working, felt like a gift. Yesterday's intimacy hadn't faded, if anything, the memory made me eager for more, for the easy connection we'd found over coffee, the spark that ignited whenever we touched.

I reached his section, scanning the stalls. The cattle were munching hay contentedly, water troughs full. Signs of life, but no Jackson. Maybe his parents were around? A sudden feeling of being adrift, of awkwardness, washed over me as I stood there alone.

"Can I help you?"

The voice, sharp and unwelcome, made me turn. Julie. Standing there with her arms crossed, a challenging look in her eyes. My skin prickled instinctively. "Doubt it," I replied coolly.

"Looking for Jackson, I suppose." Her lips curved into a smirk that set my teeth on edge.

"Do you know where he is?" I asked, trying to keep my tone neutral, though I suspected she wouldn't tell me even if she did.

"Nope." The smirk widened. Pure smugness.

A shiver traced its way down my spine. I wasn't playing this game. I turned away, intending to walk off.

"You know, farm life's tough," she called after me, her voice dripping with condescending sweetness. "Really tough."

I hesitated, glancing back over my shoulder against my better judgment.

"Don't think you'd be up for it," she continued, her eyes narrowed. "A little city slicker like you? Wouldn't last a day out there before you went running back to your mommy, crying." She raised a perfectly plucked eyebrow, the picture of derision.

My fists clenched at my sides. "My mom's dead," I snapped, the words tasting like ash in my mouth. Then I turned and walked away quickly, hurrying before the hot tears blurring my vision could spill over.

I would so last more than a day.

The childish retort echoed in my head, but it wasn't the insult about my resilience that cut deep. It was the casual cruelty about my mom, twisting the knife in a wound that never truly healed. I practically ran toward the sanctuary of the office, needing somewhere to hide, to compose myself.

"There you are," Helen said brightly as I burst through the door into the small, stuffy room. She was shuffling photos on her desk. "Good timing, I've got a new job for you today."

I quickly swiped at my eyes with the back of my hand, hoping she hadn't noticed.

"Are you all right, dear?" Her forehead wrinkled with concern. She noticed. Of course, she did.

"Fine," I lied, forcing a smile. "Just... damn dust in my eyes. Hay fever, maybe."

She didn't look convinced but let it go. "Well, I've signed you up for some extra work. Important stuff. You're to spend the day over in the sheep pavilion, taking photos of farmers with their prize-winning sheep."

Sheep. Okay. Better than bulls. "Sounds good," I said, trying to inject some enthusiasm into my voice.

"It's a bit more involved than just snapping candids," Helen elaborated. "It's proper portrait work. They set up a studio area with a backdrop and lights, the whole bit. You're basically doing studio portraits, just... in a sheep shed. With sheep."

"Really?" I put a hand on my hip. "People actually pose formally with their sheep?" The golden rule flashed through my mind: never work with children or animals. This sounded like a potential nightmare. Not exactly the fun day wandering around with Jackson I'd envisioned.

"Yes, dear. For promotional materials for next year's show, breed society journals, that sort of thing."

Okay, that made more sense, and it was important work. Good exposure for me, too, getting professional portrait credits, and building my portfolio for the business I hoped to launch eventually. Even if it involved potentially uncooperative sheep.

"Right," I said, nodding slowly. "Okay. Just... I haven't really done that specific kind of portraiture before, especially not with livestock."

"Don't worry, Frank's heading over there to get things set up. He'll help you get started, show you the ropes. You'll be fine." Helen gave me that smile, the one that was encouraging but also clearly meant 'stop fussing and go do the job.'

"Okay, then. I'm on it." I slung my camera bag over my shoulder. "And thanks, Helen. For thinking of me for the extra work."

"No problem. You'll still need to get some general show photos today as well, but you can hand those in tomorrow. The ones you sent last night were excellent, by the way. Really captured the atmosphere."

Great. Extra work on top of extra work. My earlier anticipation deflated further. Between the portrait assignment and the need for more candid shots, where would I find time for Jackson? My usual determination surfaced, battling the wave of overwhelm.

I can do this.

"Oh, and hurry!" Helen added as I reached the door. "You were meant to be there five minutes ago. Frank gets grumpy if he's kept waiting."

I rolled my eyes inwardly. "Right. Thanks." I rushed out, heading back toward the sheep pavilion. *I should text Jackson,* I thought, pulling out my phone, fumbling to type a quick message while weaving through the growing crowds.

Me: *Got pulled onto urgent job in sheep pavilion. Not sure when free. Will find you ASAP. M.*

My mind was already racing ahead. How long would this take? Would I even get a break? Would I miss him entirely?

The sheep pavilion loomed ahead, a long, low building. I wasn't sure exactly where the 'studio' would be but figured a large backdrop screen would be fairly obvious. Hopefully. I pushed through the nearest entrance, stuffing my phone back into my pocket. The smell hit me immediately. Sharper, more acidic than the earthy scent of the cattle sheds. Definitely sheep.

"About bloody time!" A familiar, grumpy voice greeted me. Frank, wrestling with a large grey backdrop screen that seemed determined to resist him. Close to retirement but still wiry and strong, he glared at me over the top of the recalcitrant fabric.

"Sorry," I mumbled, dropping my bag quickly. "I only just found out I had to be here." So much for being early. So much for a relaxed morning. And so much, it seemed, for seeing Jackson anytime soon. I stepped forward to help Frank wrestle the backdrop into submission.

CHAPTER 22

Megan

"His back hooves aren't standing quite square," I murmured, more to myself than the owner. Six hours. Six solid hours photographing sheep, and I was starting to sound like one of the breeders.

I stepped forward cautiously, mindful not to spook the animal, and gently nudged the offending hoof with the toe of my boot. The ram shifted, annoyed, planting its foot correctly.

There. Square. Ram, not ewe, I'd learned that distinction quickly after being corrected sharply early on. Frank had stressed before abandoning me to the relentless schedule, *every detail matters*.

I stepped back, raising the camera. "Chin just a fraction lower, please," I directed the middle-aged man holding the ram's head, trying to keep the weariness out of my voice. A large champion ribbon was draped, slightly askew, across the animal's woolly back.

Click. Click. Click.

I fired off a series, remembering Frank's other piece of advice: *Take heaps. Digital's free, and these breeders notice everything.* He'd added, with the air of sharing a profound secret, that it didn't matter the animal, breeders were universally fussy. He wasn't wrong. I'd quickly learned to be meticulous, not wanting to upset the owners, or the sheep themselves. They might be shorter than me, but getting stepped on by a sharp hoof *hurt.*

"Okay, got a few more there," I said, lowering the camera slightly. "Think we're good."

"Thanks," the man nodded, already looking impatient. "When will the photos be ready?"

"They'll be available for viewing tomorrow," I replied, reciting the line I'd repeated countless times today.

My initial estimate of late Friday had been met with such dismay of being told, 'But we leave Friday afternoon!' So I'd resigned myself to an all-nighter editing. Hopefully, the extra effort would pay off with future work. This was my first big solo gig, after all.

I picked up the clipboard, crossing off *PJ & TM Jamison, Woolshed Flats*. Five more names stared back at me. I suppressed a sigh. Five more sessions, then probably six hours glued to the computer, sorting, editing, and prepping proofs.

And still no word from Jackson. Not a text, not a call. My stomach gave a little anxious flip.

After yesterday, after the intensity, the connection that felt so real, silence felt jarring. I told myself he was busy, just like I was. But a small, persistent voice whispered doubts, fueled by Julie's spiteful words this morning.

City slicker... wouldn't last a day... Maybe she was right. Maybe this whole thing was just a temporary distraction for him.

"Ready for me?" An older man approached, firmly gripping a large Merino ram, while his adult daughter followed with an equally imposing ewe. Merinos were big. They'd made me nervous initially, but hours of proximity had bred a grudging familiarity, a basic understanding of how to move around them without causing chaos.

I forced a professional smile. "Absolutely." It was late afternoon and the light was beginning to fade outside the pavilion doors. My feet ached, my eyes felt gritty, and the only breaks I'd managed were a rushed toilet stop and wolfing down a sandwich while juggling equipment.

The lack of contact from Jackson gnawed at me. I resisted the urge to pull out my phone again, knowing the screen would likely still be blank, mocking my anxiety. *It was bloody good sex,* my mind traitorously supplied, flooding me with vivid, distracting images. *Focus, Megan.*

"Mr. Lang?" I checked the list.

"That's me. And this is my daughter, Danny."

"Pleased to meet you both. I'm Megan." The old-fashioned manners Mom had drilled into me were proving surprisingly useful, especially with the older generation of farmers. "If you'd like to stand over here in the center?" I guided them toward the grey backdrop. "Were you thinking headshots, or full body with the sheep?"

"Could we possibly do both?" Mr. Lang asked hopefully.

"Of course." I was surprising myself with my newfound flexibility. Anything to keep the clients happy. "Okay, if you stand on the right with the ram, Mr. Lang, and Danny on the left with the ewe, then point their heads slightly toward the main aisle."

They shuffled into position. Show-goers occasionally paused, watching the peculiar spectacle, sometimes even taking photos of me taking photos.

"Just a minute." Mr. Lang carefully removed a broad ribbon from his own shoulder and draped it over the ram's back. I stepped forward automatically to adjust it, making sure it hung straight and centered. My fingers brushed the oily lanolin in the wool.

If only Mom could see me now.

A familiar pang tightened my chest, quickly followed by a wave of determination. Mom would have been proud, not because I was handling sheep, but because I was chasing my dream, living my life, even the messy, unexpected parts. Even the parts involving manure-stained jeans and falling for a farmer.

Shaking off the thought and hands slightly greasy, I lifted the camera, checking the frame. "Good. Just need them to stand up a little straighter, please." The vague instruction worked as both father and daughter instinctively adjusted their sheep, squaring legs, lifting heads. I took the shots, capturing the pride on their faces, the impressive stature of the animals. The Langs left beaming, and seeing no one else immediately waiting, I seized the moment, pulling out my phone, determined to send Jackson that text.

Bugger.

The message I'd typed hours ago, the one telling him where I was, sat there, unsent. Network error. I quickly hit 'send' again. *Bugger!* A low battery warning flashed less than five percent.

Heart pounding, I frantically typed a new message.

Me: *Still stuck in sheep shed. Phone dying! Find me?*

But before I could hit send, the next farmer arrived, leading another prize specimen. Damn it.

Shoving the phone hastily back into my pocket, unwilling to look unprofessional, I plastered on a smile. This job mattered. It was a step toward building my own business. Jackson would have to wait.

I'll text him in a minute, I promised myself, turning my attention to positioning the sheep. My photographer brain kicked into gear and I pushed aside the rising panic about my dead phone and Jackson's silence.

The next two hours blurred into a succession of sheep, farmers, and forced smiles. A few extras showed up, people not on the list who wanted photos. Exhausted as I was, turning away potential future clients felt wrong.

Finally, the last sheep was photographed, and the last breeder thanked. My whole body ached from standing, from concentrating, from the sheer effort of being pleasant and professional for so long. With leaden arms, I packed away my camera, dismantled the lights, and wrestled the backdrop screen back into its box—all the equipment Frank had so conveniently left for me.

Struggling under the weight, I stumbled back to the newspaper office, which was empty obviously Helen had gone home. One thing was certain, I wasn't going back out to take candid shots tonight. That could wait. Right now, processing these sheep photos would take me well past midnight as it was. I reached for my phone utterly, completely dead.

My lips pressed into a thin line. Frustration warred with a deeper ache, the fear of missing him, of letting this fragile connection slip away because of a dead phone and a demanding job.

No. I wasn't letting that happen.

Locking up the office, grabbing my camera bag, I headed back out into the cool evening air. There was only one place he'd likely be. And I prayed to whatever forces governed farmers and photographers that he was still there, waiting among his cattle.

CHAPTER 23

Jackson

I stared at the blank screen of my phone for what felt like the hundredth time, willing a message to appear. Nothing. The only text I'd gotten from Megan all day was a garbled mess sent hours ago, something about sheep, being busy, phone dying maybe?

It hadn't made much sense, it looked like she'd typed it in a mad rush. I'd tried to decipher it, tried to figure out if she was telling me where she was or blowing me off. Sheep pavilion. Okay. But when I'd finally gotten free from stewarding duties at the Angus judging, a job I'd been roped into at the last minute, and swung by there, it was deserted. The newspaper office was dark too.

So now here I was, nursing the same lukewarm beer for the last hour at the Goody, the pub across the road from the showgrounds. It was packed, shoulder-to-shoulder with country folk letting off steam.

The music thumped, too loud, forcing everyone to shout over the pop drivel blasting from the speakers. The air was thick with the smell of stale beer and fried food. A sudden, sharp pang of homesickness hit me. God, I missed the quiet, the smell of turned earth and ripening wheat under an open sky. Anything but this noise, this crowd. Even the cattle shed smelled better than this place.

I took another sip of the flat beer. Definitely wasn't making the same mistake as the other night by getting drunk. I needed a clear head, especially with Megan playing radio silence.

Was yesterday just sex?

A fantastic, mind-blowing roll in the hay, literally, on Aston's swag, which I was still hearing about, but just sex, nonetheless? The thought soured the already bad beer in my mouth. It hadn't felt like just sex. Not to me. The way she'd looked at me afterward, the way she'd felt in my arms, that felt real. So why the silence?

"So, how's that new little city girlfriend of yours?"

Julie's voice was right beside me. I didn't have to look to know she'd slid onto the stool next to mine, probably flashing that smug little smile she wore like armor. I took a slow breath, trying to keep a lid on the irritation simmering just below the surface.

Here we go.

"What's it to you, Julie?" I kept my eyes fixed on my glass, swirling the dregs.

"Don't be like that, Jacks," she said in that falsely sweet tone she used when she was digging for information or trying to manipulate someone. She wrapped her perfectly manicured fingers around the stem of her wine glass.

My head snapped up, a sudden, cold suspicion hardening my gut. Megan's silence... Julie wouldn't... "What did you say to her?" The question came out sharper than I intended.

"Nothing!" She feigned innocence, widening her eyes.

I narrowed mine, pinning her with a hard stare. "Don't bullshit me, Julie. I know you. Kicking my gear out wasn't enough, was it?" Anger started bubbling, hot and fast. The thought of Julie interfering, saying something to Megan after I'd explicitly told her off made my blood boil.

"I just don't think she's cut out for farm life, that's

all." Her eyes turned cool, calculating. "Just giving her a little... reality check. For her own good. And yours."

Fury surged through me, hot and blinding. *Damn her.* Was that why Megan hadn't replied? Had Julie's poison actually worked? "A reality check?" I repeated, my voice dangerously low. "You had no right. Megan's got more grit and heart than you'll ever understand." I leaned closer, making sure she heard me over the din. "What happens between us is none of your damn business. I thought I made that clear."

Tears welled in her eyes, and her lower lip started to tremble. "Why?" she whispered, the tears finally spilling over. "Why couldn't it have been us, Jackson?"

I pushed my stool back, standing up abruptly. The noise, the heat, her tears—I couldn't stand being near her a second longer. My worry for Megan twisted with anger at Julie's interference.

"Because I'm not interested," I said, my voice flat, cold. "And this? This behavior right here? This is exactly why." I turned my back on her and pushed through the crowd toward the exit, ignoring her choked sob.

"Hey! Leaving already, mate?" Heath called out as I passed their table.

"Yeah, need some air," I called back over my shoulder, not breaking stride. I just needed to get out, I needed to try Megan again.

I took a deep breath, letting the chill night air seep into my lungs, trying to cool the anger still simmering in my veins. Pulling out my phone, I dialed Megan's number, my thumb hovering over the call button. It went straight to voicemail.

Of course it did. Her phone was probably dead, like her garbled text suggested. Or maybe Julie's words had hit their mark. Still...

"Megan, it's Jackson," I said into the phone, trying to keep the frustration out of my voice, trying not to sound as needy as I suddenly felt. "Look, I got your text... sort of. Been trying to find you. Heard Julie might have spoken to you. Hope whatever crap she fed you isn't why I haven't heard from you. Call me back when you get this. Please."

I hung up, shoving the phone back in my pocket before I did something stupid, like leaving another dozen messages, laying bare just how much her silence was messing with my head.

Maybe Julie was right. Maybe Megan had second

thoughts. Maybe yesterday was just a mistake, a moment of madness fueled by adrenaline and proximity. The uncertainty gnawed at me, colder and sharper than the night air.

CHAPTER 24

Megan

I lingered near the cattle stalls, the familiar earthy scent doing little to soothe the restless energy buzzing under my skin. Exhaustion pulled at me, my feet throbbed, my shoulders ached from the camera bag, and the thought of hours hunched over a laptop editing sheep photos was deeply unappealing.

But the desire to find Jackson, to see him, to simply *be* near him after yesterday, was a stronger current. I'd already circled the area twice, scanning faces, peering into the dim corners of the shed, my hope dwindling with each empty glance.

Where *was* he?

I looped around the Sunnydale stalls one last

time, my gaze falling on Bruce, placidly munching hay.

"Any idea where your owner is?" I asked the massive bull, my voice laced with weary frustration. He just swished his tail, blinked slowly, and went back to his dinner. "Right. Thanks for nothing."

My phone was still a dead weight in my pocket, and my work deadline loomed. Logic dictated I go home, charge the phone, tackle the editing marathon, and hope for tomorrow.

Resignation settled heavily in my chest, tangled with a thread of anxiety. What if he wasn't here tomorrow? What if he'd already packed up and left? The show was winding down. This fragile thing between us felt like it could vanish as quickly as it had appeared.

With a sigh that seemed to carry the weight of the entire showgrounds, I turned toward the exit, heading for the long walk back to my car parked streets away.

Home, then.

Charge the phone, send that message, reassure him. Finish the work. Sleep.

Then tomorrow. We could spend the day together tomorrow, surely?

The plan felt flimsy, vulnerable to a thousand

possibilities. And all the while, underneath the practicalities, vivid images from yesterday afternoon kept flickering behind my eyes of his hands on my skin, the taste of his kiss, the feeling of him moving inside me. Concentrating on editing sheep photos was going to be torture.

THE NEXT MORNING, sunlight streamed through my bedroom window, but my mood was decidedly gray. Curled up on the lounge in my pajamas, legs tucked beneath me, I frowned at my phone screen, finally charged and alive with text notifications. My stomach clenched with guilt.

I scrolled back, finding his text messages from last night.

Jackson: Tried finding you. Where'd you disappear to?

Jackson: *Hope you're okay. Worried about you.*

Then, the one that made my heart ache:

Jackson: Heard Julie might have spoken to you? Don't know what she said, but I told her straight to leave you alone. Hope she didn't upset you. Hate for her crap to get between us.

Relief washed over me, warm and sudden. He'd

defended me. He cared enough to confront her. But the relief was quickly chased by guilt for not replying, for letting him worry.

Then came this morning's text message, sent early.

Jackson: *Morning. Would really love to see you today. Coming into the show? If you haven't had enough of me yet 😊. I'll be around the cattle stalls pretty much all day. Hope to see you.*

A blush crept up my neck. The warmth of his words, the clear desire to see me, it was lovely, almost overwhelming. Poor guy, thinking I was ignoring him.

But then, the last message, sent about an hour ago, landed like a punch to the gut.

Jackson: *Okay, maybe I sound desperate. Look, if you're interested, come find me. If not, I get it. No hard feelings. Won't text again.*

Panic seized me.

No!

He thought I was blowing him off! After yesterday, he thought it meant nothing? Because my phone died and I got swamped with sheep portraits? This was *not* the message I wanted to send. Not at all.

My thumbs flew across the screen, desperate to fix this.

Me: *Jackson, SO sorry! Crazy busy day, then phone died! Just saw messages. Overslept. Definitely interested! On my way in now. See you soon! M x*

I hit send, holding my breath until the 'delivered' notification popped up. There. Problem solved. Hopefully. Hopefully, he'd understand.

Then I saw I had a new voicemail from Helen. I listened, a wave of relief washing over me as she praised the sheep photos I'd uploaded in the wee hours, mentioned happy clients, a happy editor-in-chief, and even a bonus coming my way. All I needed to do was drop off my tax forms.

Wow. Maybe I *was* cut out for this freelance life. Feeling slightly more grounded, I quickly replied to a few other messages, reassuring friends I hadn't fallen off the face of the earth.

I needed to shower and get dressed, but to my dismay, a quick laundry basket inspection revealed zero clean jeans. Checking the forecast, which was warm, sunny, I opted for a knee-length floral skirt and a loose top instead, with flat shoes, thankfully. Grabbing my camera bag, I headed out, the earlier panic replaced by a nervous, fluttering anticipation.

Parking was a nightmare, forcing me miles away. The thirty-minute walk gave me too much time to think. Jackson hadn't replied to my text yet. Should I go straight to the cattle sheds? Or check in at the office first, be professional? Doubts resurfaced.

Maybe missing each other yesterday *was* a sign. Maybe this city-girl-meets-country-guy thing was doomed from the start. Maybe I should just focus on work, protect my heart.

Lost in thought, I physically bumped into someone, stumbling slightly. "Oh, sorry!" I mumbled, looking up.

And froze. Julie. Standing right in front of me, arms crossed, a familiar challenging glint in her eyes. Here we go.

"You should watch where you're going," she snapped.

"So should you," I retorted, folding my own arms, refusing to be intimidated today. "Honestly, doesn't anything polite ever come out of your mouth?"

"How dare–" she started, then abruptly clamped her mouth shut, her expression hardening.

I held her gaze, challenging her right back. "You had no right," I said, my voice low but steady, the anger from yesterday resurfacing, cold and sharp. "No right to say what you did to me. Especially not about my mom. Just because you're jealous Jackson's looking at someone else." I took a deep, shaky breath, trying to keep the anger from boiling over.

Something shifted in her expression. The hardness wavered. "You're right," she said quietly, stunning me into silence.

"I know I am," I managed, watching her closely. Was this another manipulation?

"I shouldn't have said those things." Her eyes, usually so sharp, softened with what looked like genuine regret. "It was mean. Spiteful."

"It was," I agreed, still wary, thrown off-balance by this unexpected turn.

"I'm sorry," she continued, her voice thick with emotion. "Truly. I... I couldn't live without my mom, and... well, you're so young to be without yours. It was cruel of me. I was hurting, seeing you two together, realizing it was really over between him and me. It broke my heart a bit, seeing that kiss." She inhaled sharply, her eyes misting over.

I didn't know what to say. A flicker of empathy stirred within me, cautious but real. Her pain felt genuine.

"But seeing it... it was good for me, I think," she went on, seeming to gather herself. "Helped me see things clearly. Helped me accept it. Now I have some perspective, I... I can actually be happy for you both." She reached out unexpectedly, grabbing my hand.

I flinched instinctively but didn't pull away. My own eyes prickled. I still wasn't sure I trusted her, not completely. The things she'd said had cut deep. Especially the comment about Mom. Even if she hadn't known.

"And I really hope it works out for you two," she finished, her grip tightening slightly.

"Thanks," I mumbled, feeling overwhelmed. "It was... what you said about my mom. That's what hurt the most, you know." Voicing it felt important.

Julie nodded, shamefaced. "I know. And I didn't know she'd passed, but that's no excuse. I just... I want you to know I'm truly sorry. I wish I'd kept my mouth shut."

"Okay." The anger finally dissipated, leaving behind a weary sort of sadness. The raw hate I'd felt toward her faded. But forgetting wasn't easy. The wound felt less raw, but the scar remained. "Just... please don't ever treat me like that again," I said quietly.

"I promise." She squeezed my hand one last time before letting go. Then, a tentative smile touched her lips. "And hey, maybe I can even be a bridesmaid at your wedding one day?"

My eyes widened. "Whoa!" I laughed, startled. "That's... jumping the gun just a little bit, don't you think?"

Julie laughed, too, a genuine, relieved sound. "Maybe. But I've honestly never seen Jackson look at anyone the way he looks at you. Anyway, whatever happens between you two, I hope we can be... well, if not friends, then at least civil. No more ill feelings."

"That's good to know," I said, managing a sincere smile back. Clearing the air felt unexpectedly good, like shedding a heavy weight. Which reminded me... "Speaking of Jackson... do you happen to know where he is?"

"Yeah, actually. He's over at the main arena. Helping out with the junior judging today." Her smile turned conspiratorial. "Come on. I'll take you to him. He'll be stoked to see you." She started walking, weaving through the crowds.

I hesitated for only a second, then followed, a small voice whispering, *She'd better not be playing some kind of joke.* After the emotional rollercoaster of the last twenty-four hours, my nerves felt frayed. Seeing Jackson again, suddenly, a swarm of butterflies erupted in my stomach. Would it feel the same? Had the magic dissipated overnight? Sex changed things, added layers of expectation and vulnerability. What if...?

"This way." Julie's voice pulled me from my spiraling thoughts. I hurried to catch up as she led me toward the large, covered arena. We navigated down an aisle bustling with teenagers leading impeccably groomed cattle. I surprised myself by remaining calm, slipping past the large animals without the usual surge of panic. A fleeting memory of Bruce's hoof connecting with my head surfaced, a phantom throb, but it faded quickly, replaced by a surge of focused anticipation.

I'll know when I see him.

We reached a cordoned-off rectangular area covered in fake grass. Inside, four sleek black cows were being led in a tight circle by teenagers dressed smartly in cream moleskins, striped shirts, and polished boots. Judges observed intently.

"There he is." Julie stopped, pointing toward the edge of the ring. "Next to the Over-Judge."

My eyes found him instantly. Standing tall beside an older man, clipboard in hand, Jackson looked serious, focused on the judging. Then, as if sensing my gaze, he glanced up. His eyes met mine across the arena.

The serious expression melted away, replaced by

a slow, broad smile that crinkled the corners of his eyes, a smile just for me. In that instant, every doubt, every anxious flutter, vanished. Peace flooded through me, warm and certain.

Yes. I want him.

No question.

"Right, I'll catch you later then," Julie murmured, giving my arm a quick squeeze before disappearing back into the crowd.

I nodded, my gaze fixed on Jackson as he excused himself from the judge and started walking toward me, keeping to the edge of the ring.

"Hey, gorgeous." He reached the railing, his eyes sparkling with that familiar mischief, making my pulse quicken.

"Hi," I breathed, suddenly shy.

He leaned over the railing, his free hand coming up to gently cup my chin to tilt my face toward his. And then he kissed me.

Right there, in front of everyone. It wasn't tentative or questioning, it was a kiss full of fire and certainty, a claiming. Pleasure burst on my lips, warm and electric, chasing away the last lingering shadows of doubt.

This was real. This feeling, this connection was real. I rested my hand on his shoulder, grounding myself, inhaling his familiar masculine scent—sunshine, spice, and something uniquely Jackson—that fired up my senses all over again.

He pulled back reluctantly, his eyes searching mine. "I'm sorry about yesterday," I blurted out, my lips still tingling. The urge to pull him back for another kiss was almost overwhelming.

He grinned. "Glad you found me today. Was starting to think I'd have to put a missing person ad in the paper." He winked.

The easy banter settled over me, comfortable and familiar. "Wouldn't have helped. I don't read the paper."

"No? Then it's just as well you showed up." He leaned in again, pressing another brief, firm kiss to my lips. "Was that Julie I saw you with? She didn't give you any more trouble, did she?"

"No, yes... I mean..." It was hard to think straight with him so close. "It's fine. We're fine. Cleared the air."

"Good."

A pointed cough sounded from behind him in the arena. Jackson glanced back, a flush rising on his cheeks. "Right. Better get back to it." He looked genuinely disappointed. "Sorry, looks like I'm stuck here until after lunch at least." He lowered his voice.

"Honestly? I'd much rather be spending the day with you."

"Me too," I admitted, smiling despite the pang of disappointment. "Look, it's okay. I should probably go see Helen anyway. How about I meet you back here around two?"

He hesitated. "I'd like that. But judging... it takes as long as it takes. Hard to put an exact time on it."

"Okay." I hated the uncertainty, especially after yesterday's communication breakdown. "How about I just swing by around then and see how things are looking? We can play it by ear?"

"Yeah, okay. Text me." He paused, a slight frown creasing his brow. "Your phone *is* charged now, right?"

I patted my pocket. "Yep. All good. Yours?"

He nodded. "See you later, then." With one last lingering look, he hurried back to the waiting, slightly grumpy-looking judge.

A slow breath left my lips, carrying the lingering warmth of his kiss as I settled onto an empty spot on the tiered seating. It felt like second nature to pull out my camera, a familiar shield to hide behind while I waited. Though I aimed for shots of the arena and the young handlers with their animals, Jackson's easy competence kept drawing my focus, making him the unintentional star of every frame. The nuances of the event were a mystery, but the feeling of watching him in his element was perfectly clear. It just felt right.

"It's wonderful, isn't it? Helping the next generation learn about the cattle."

I turned, startled, to find Kim, Jackson's mom, settling into the seat beside me. "Oh, hi, Kim."

"They have to judge the confirmation of the cattle first," she continued conversationally, gesturing toward the ring, "then write up their reasoning. Then they're judged on how well they handle the animals *and* how well they articulate their judging decisions."

"Oh, right." I nodded, trying to follow along. To my untrained eye, the four black cows looked remarkably similar. Clearly, I had a lot to learn about this world.

"It teaches them what characteristics to look for," Kim explained patiently. "Vital experience for when they start breeding their own herds one day."

"On-the-job training, basically?" I cradled my camera, half-listening, half-watching Jackson as he spoke quietly to one of the teenagers, offering what looked like gentle encouragement. He belonged here. The thought brought a familiar mix of admiration and anxiety.

Kim laughed softly. "Yes, you could certainly call it that."

I smiled back, but the butterflies in my stomach hadn't quite settled. Meeting a potential boyfriend's mother this early felt strange, especially when 'boyfriend' wasn't even the right label yet.

What am I even doing here? I glanced back at Jackson, catching his eye again across the ring. He gave me a small, private smile.

Oh. That's why.

But where could it possibly lead? If I ever seriously considered leaving the city, leaving Dad, how would he cope on his own?

"You're deep in thought there, dear, for a Saturday morning," Kim's gentle voice broke through my spiraling thoughts.

"Just thinking," I admitted, deciding in that moment to offer a small piece of truth, prompted by her kind eyes and the lingering emotional vulnerability from the encounter with Julie. "About my mom, actually. She passed away from cancer last year. I worry about my dad being alone."

Sitting here, watching this slice of country life, thinking about Jackson, about futures felt complicated. And sitting next to his mom, who radiated warmth but also reminded me keenly of my own loss, wasn't exactly simplifying things.

Kim's expression softened with understanding. She placed a comforting hand gently on my arm. "I'm sure she'd be incredibly proud of you, Megan."

Unexpected emotion surged, hot and fast, prickling behind my eyes. I blinked furiously, trying to hold it back.

"Yes," Kim continued softly, her voice filled with quiet conviction. "And before you say I don't really know you, or your mom, and you're right, I don't, I do know what I saw the other day. And what I heard from some very impressed sheep exhibitors. You have a good heart, dear. And you're not afraid of hard work or learning new things." She smiled warmly, a genuine, encouraging smile.

Being talked about by the exhibitors felt strange, but was apparently positive. But those thoughts blurred as emotion choked my throat. Kim's simple words, her quiet empathy resonated deeply.

Most people stumbled, awkward and uncertain, when Mom's death came up. But Kim, Kim understood. It was there in her eyes, in the gentle pressure of her hand. Of course, she understood. She'd lost her own daughter.

"Thank you," I managed, to speak. "You... you seem to understand. Most people don't know what to say."

Kim's own eyes misted slightly. "I do understand, dear. And I know a mother's hopes for her daughter." She fumbled in her bag for a tissue, dabbing discreetly at the corner of her eye. "Now, I must apologize. Jackson would tell me off for being too forward, sticking my nose in. It's not the done thing in the city, I hear."

"It's okay," I whispered, inhaling deeply, fighting the tears. "It's... good. To be reminded what a mother thinks."

Despite my efforts, one tear escaped, tracing a slow path down my cheek. But it didn't burn like the tears I'd cried before. Something felt different. A fragile mix of sadness and a tentative, emerging hope.

Maybe I *was* moving on. And maybe, just maybe, Kim was right. Maybe Mom *would* want this for me —this adventure, this challenge, this unexpected connection. Maybe she'd want me to be brave enough to see where it led.

CHAPTER 25

Jackson

I had to physically force myself not to keep glancing over at Megan. Every time my eyes strayed to the stands, I got caught, soaking up the image of her sitting there, her attention seemingly fixed on the arena, a small smile playing on her lips. But then Mom sat down next to her, and my stress levels shot through the roof.

Shit. What are they talking about? Please don't scare her off, Mom.

I held my breath, watching them from the corner of my eye. Mom had a way of being blunt.

Honest to a fault. A country trait, maybe, but one that didn't always land well. My stint at boarding school in Adelaide had smoothed some of my own rough edges, taught me a bit of city diplomacy, how to hold your tongue and not just blurt out the first thing you think.

But back on the farm, back where I belonged, subtlety wasn't exactly prized. Had I forgotten how to navigate this?

Then I saw Mom dabbing her eyes with a tissue.

Oh no. Megan looked sad, too, her expression vulnerable. *Okay, I gotta intervene.*

Whatever was happening, I didn't want it to derail whatever this fragile thing with Megan was becoming. Mom wouldn't mean any harm, I knew that, but Megan wasn't country-tough. Not yet, anyway. And after whatever Julie had pulled, I couldn't risk losing her now.

The thought blindsided me. *Losing her.* When had she become someone I could *lose*?

The question of whether she could ever fit into farm life, truly be happy miles from anywhere, flickered through my mind, it was a genuine worry tangled up with a fierce, surprising hope. But that was cart-before-the-horse thinking. Way too soon. First things first: get to know her better. Build something real. And I had a few ideas about where to start *that*.

I started to move toward them, my eyes locked on

Megan, my pulse picking up speed just at the thought of being near her again. She had this effect on me, undeniable and potent. A grin spread across my face before I could stop it.

"Jackson! Over here!" the Over-Judge barked.

Damn it. I froze, turning back to see him beckoning impatiently. I glanced back at Megan and Mom. They were still talking, looking serious, maybe sad, but not angry.

Okay. Maybe it was okay. Megan knew I had duties. She'd said she'd wait. Reluctantly, hoping Mom wasn't accidentally sabotaging my entire future, I walked back to the judge.

"Help me tally these score sheets."

"Sure." I took the stack of papers and sat down, forcing myself to focus on the numbers, the adding up, the ranking. When we finally finished, maybe twenty minutes later, I looked eagerly back toward the stands.

She was gone.

A sharp pang of disappointment hit me, surprisingly strong. I missed seeing her there. More than missed it, I *ached* to see her, right now. To feel her lips under mine again, taste her, trace the curves of her body, I was only just beginning to learn. Heat pooled low in my belly, and I shifted uncomfortably, forcing my thoughts onto a different track.

Get a grip, Jackson. You're worse than Bruce with a paddock full of heifers.

It's okay. I'll see her later.

I clung to the hope. Yesterday's mess, the missed connections, the silence had planted seeds of doubt. Was she really interested?

Or was I just a convenient show fling? But seeing her today, watching her watch me, the easy smile she'd given me had felt real. Something had shifted. What started as maybe just a bit of fun felt like it was rapidly turning into something more. Something I didn't want to mess up. I just had to make damn sure she felt the same way.

CHAPTER 26

Megan

Finally. Photos were taken, edited through the night, and then uploaded. Clients were happy, my boss was happy, and a bonus secured. I finally had time. Time for Jackson.

Please let him be free.

Not wanting a repeat of yesterday's communication disaster, I leaned back in the office chair, pulled out my blessedly charged phone, and sent him a text.

Me: *Sheep duties officially DONE! Still around?*

My pulse hammered against my ribs while I waited for the three little dots to appear. The simple thought of seeing him again, after nearly twenty-four hours apart, sent my hormones into overdrive.

A reply pinged back almost immediately.

Jackson: *Definitely still here. Was starting to worry you'd run screaming back to the city! Where are you?*

A few quick messages later, we'd agreed to meet back at the cattle barn. My stomach did a nervous flip-flop as I walked over, the earlier exhaustion momentarily forgotten, replaced by buzzing anticipation.

Entering the familiar shed, I was surprised that the pungent, earthy smell barely registered anymore. Had I actually gotten used to it? I navigated the wide aisle confidently, easily sidestepping the drying cow pats on the concrete.

See? Getting the hang of this country life.

Still, I wasn't quite brave enough to perch on a hay bale near Bruce. Spotting a lone fold-up chair tucked in a corner near Jackson's stalls, I gratefully sank into it.

The adrenaline started to fade, and the exhaustion from the long day and short night crept back in. The lowing of cattle, the rustling of hay, the distant hum of the showgrounds created a surprisingly soothing white noise.

My eyelids grew heavy. Despite the noise, despite the anticipation, I started to doze.

A soft voice pulled me from the edge of sleep. "Hey, you."

I stirred, blinking my eyes open. Jackson. Kneeling in front of me, his hands resting lightly on the arms of the chair, trapping me in the best possible way. He looked tired, but his eyes were bright, focused entirely on me.

"Jackson," I murmured, sitting up straighter, instantly awake now.

"Finally." He smiled, the warmth reaching his eyes. He reached out, taking my hand, his calloused thumb stroking over my knuckles. The simple touch sent a jolt straight through me. "Managed to find each other again." He leaned closer. "Wish we had somewhere more private, though."

The memory of the cramped, dark shed flashed through my mind. It had been urgent, intense, but... "Finally," I echoed, smiling back, letting my gaze linger on his lips. My eyes felt heavy, inviting.

He didn't need a second invitation. He leaned forward, his lips brushing mine, soft and tentative. A question. He pulled back slightly, then pressed again, firmer this time.

My mouth opened under his, a silent welcome. His tongue dipped inside briefly, a taste, a promise, before his lips slid away, sucking gently on my lower lip, sending shivers down my spine. Then he was back, kissing me deeply, possessively, his tongue dancing with mine, tasting me, claiming me. Heat exploded low in my belly, the familiar ache intensifying.

Jackson pulled back, breathing a little heavier, his eyes dark with desire. "Can't stay here."

He tucked a stray strand of hair behind my ear, his fingers lingering against my cheek. "But... I might have an idea." He glanced up again, toward the hay stacked high in the loft area above the stalls. A slow, wicked grin spread across his face. "Come on."

He stood, pulling me up with him. "Let's go somewhere a little more... elevated." He guided me toward the sturdy wooden railings of the stall, the same ones I'd awkwardly climbed before.

"Up *there*?" I hesitated, leaning into him, the solid feel of his body against mine making my knees weak. "That doesn't seem much more private, Jackson."

"It will be," he promised, his voice husky. He took my camera bag, easily tossing it up onto the wide top ledge of the stall wall. "You'll see. Your turn."

"Okay." I sighed, mostly for show.

The truth was, the thought of being hidden away

up there with him, surrounded by hay, was ridiculously appealing.

"I'm wearing a skirt this time. Not exactly climbing attire." I placed my foot on the middle rail, trying to figure out the logistics without flashing everyone in the vicinity.

"You didn't seem to mind an audience the other night," he teased, his voice low and gravelly. "Weren't exactly quiet, were you?"

Heat flooded my face. "I'll be silent this time," I whispered conspiratorially, "*if* we do it up there."

The image his words conjured—him naked, hard, ready—sent another wave of heat pulsing through me. Moisture pooled between my thighs. I wasn't sure I *could* be silent.

He stepped closer behind me, wrapping his arms around my waist, pulling me back against his chest.

"Oh," he murmured, his breath hot against my neck, sending electric prickles down my spine. "But I *like* your noises." He punctuated the words with a soft kiss, then another, harder this time, sucking gently on the sensitive skin at the base of my neck.

A soft gasp escaped me. I tilted my head, granting him better access, reveling in the way he made my body hum. "And I like the way you kiss me," I whispered back, leaning into his strength, folding my arms over his.

He pressed himself against me, letting me feel the hard ridge of his hardness through his jeans.

"I know," he growled softly, planting a few more fiery kisses before reluctantly pulling away. "Right. Up you go. Quick, before I lose what little control I have left and take you right here against the rails."

"Hey, I'm not one of your cows," I retorted playfully, trying to regain some semblance of composure. "You can't just have me standing up like that."

He groaned, burying his face in my hair for a second. "Don't talk like that," he mumbled. "Turns me on way too much." He gave me a gentle nudge. "Up. Go."

His urgency was contagious. Fueled by a sudden surge of adrenaline and pure, unadulterated want, I reached for the top rail and hauled myself up. "Don't you dare look up my skirt!" I called down breathlessly.

"Wouldn't dream of it," he replied, his voice laced with laughter. "Thanks for the suggestion, though."

Glancing down halfway up, I saw his cheeky grin as he deliberately moved closer, angling for a peek. "Jackson!" I hissed but couldn't suppress the laugh bubbling up. It felt freeing. Liberating. Whatever happened next, whatever the future held, this moment felt exhilaratingly *alive.*

Driven by a primal need that overshadowed caution, I scrambled the rest of the way onto the wide platform above the stalls, landing on a bale of hay. The scratchy stalks pricked my bare legs, but I barely noticed. I already felt giddy, high up, buzzed with anticipation, and the heat Jackson stirred within me.

He clambered up easily behind me, landing lightly on the balls of his feet. His grin sent another pulse of desire contracting deep inside me. "See?" he said, gesturing around. "Up here. Private-ish."

"Not quite," I countered, looking around. We were higher, yes, but still relatively exposed if anyone bothered to look up.

"As long as no one looks up," he reasoned.

"And if they do, let's hope they don't call the police," I added wryly. Maybe taking him home wouldn't have been such a bad idea after all? But the thought felt distant, irrelevant now.

"Got an idea." He held out his hands. I took them trustingly. "Just stand over here for a sec."

He guided me toward the back, away from the edge, then started rearranging the heavy bales, his muscles flexing under his shirt. I watched him, appreciating the easy strength, the competence.

My earlier giddiness solidified into a focused ache, a deep longing to feel those arms around me again, to feel his skin against mine, to have him inside me. The sounds from the shed below—the rustle of cattle, a distant voice—seemed to fade.

Up here, surrounded by the sweet, dusty scent of hay, it felt like our own world. And honestly? The slight risk, the absurdity of it all, only intensified the electric current humming between us. My muscles clenched again.

Yep. Hot and horny, my brain supplied unhelpfully. *And ready.*

"There." He brushed his hands together, surveying his work. "That should do it."

He'd created a makeshift nest, walling off a central area with bales stacked two high. Reasonably hidden, unless someone came climbing up which was unlikely.

This was definitely the last place I'd ever expected to have sex. High above a cattle shed, on a pile of hay. I laughed suddenly, the sound echoing slightly in the cavernous space.

Jackson looked momentarily confused. "Can't

say I did anything funny." He pulled me close, my breasts crushing softly against his hard chest.

"Sorry." I smiled up at him. "Just... this is unexpected. You sure we'll be okay up here?"

"Don't worry. No one ever comes up here." He helped me step down into the hay-bale nest he'd created. It felt surprisingly cozy.

The air smelled warm, sweet, earthy, the scent of sunshine on dry grass. "Unless," he added, leaning closer, his eyes glinting, "you're too noisy." He winked.

"I won't be," I promised, though my body was already betraying me, humming with anticipation of this touch. I didn't want to be disturbed.

"Sounds like a challenge," he murmured, pulling me fully against him, his hands cupping my face as he kissed me.

I wrapped my arms around his waist, holding him tight, tilting my head back, ready. He met my mouth with a hard, passionate force that stole my breath, sending my head spinning, and my knees threatening to buckle. There was no challenge. No way I could control the sounds he dragged from me. Especially not when his hand slid down my chest, pausing to deliberately brush over my breasts before pinching a nipple, hard, through the fabric of my top and bra. I groaned, arching into the sensation.

"See?" he mumbled against my lips, his voice thick with satisfaction. "Not going to be quiet at all." He pinched again, just to prove his point. Pleasure shot through me, sharp and sweet, making my breasts ache, making me wetter between my legs.

"And *we*," I gasped, acutely aware that we were still partially visible from below, "better get properly out of sight before someone works out what we're doing."

"Chances are low," he murmured, but he knelt then, running his hands down my sides, his touch making my knees give way. He guided me down gently into the hay nest.

Lying back, looking up at him, the world narrowed to just this space, just him. He followed me down, stretching out beside me before kissing me again.

My mind blurred, melting under the heat of his mouth and the pressure of his body. But then... scratch. Itch. The stray stalks of hay poked insistently through the thin fabric of my skirt, digging into my bare legs. I squirmed, trying to find a comfortable position.

"What's wrong?" He pulled back, frowning slightly.

"This hay." I grimaced. "It's not exactly five-star bedding. It's really scratchy."

He laughed, a warm, rumbling sound. "Right. Forgot about that bit. Wait here." He scrambled up and disappeared over the hay wall for a moment, returning triumphantly with a familiar red tartan picnic blanket.

I wriggled aside as he unfolded it, spreading it carefully over the hay, smoothing out the creases to create a soft, inviting surface.

"Is this... your picnic rug?" I asked, recognizing it from the showgrounds.

"Yeah," he admitted, kneeling beside me again. "Well, technically it's Mom's."

"Mom's?" I grimaced again. "What's she going to say if she notices it's... uh... been borrowed?"

The thought of explaining hay fragments and potential bodily fluids to his mother was mortifying. A familiar pang hit me—*this week will end, he'll go home, this won't last.*

"What makes you think she'll find out?" he countered, amusement dancing in his eyes.

I shrugged, unable to voice the fleeting anxiety. Mothers just knew things.

He chuckled, seeming to read my mind. "Relax. I'll throw it in the wash later, silly. No evidence." He leaned closer, his voice dropping. "Now, come back down here where I can touch you properly."

I settled back onto the surprisingly soft blanket, kicking off my flat shoes. The annoying itchiness was gone, replaced by the soft crackle of straw beneath the rug as I moved.

"Better?" he asked, his eyes warm.

"Much. Thanks." I looked at him coyly. "Guess I'm not much of a farm girl if I can't even tolerate a quick romp in the hay."

"Nah," he dismissed, leaning over me. "Rom-coms lie. No one mentions how bloody itchy hay really is. It's bad enough handling it when you're feeding out, let alone when you're about to get naked." He kissed me then, deep and slow, his tongue sweeping into my mouth.

"Besides," he mumbled between kisses, his hand starting a slow journey up my side, "I want you to be comfortable. Very comfortable."

Soft sounds of encouragement were all I could manage as his exploration began in earnest. His hand skimmed over my waist and slipped under my loose top, his fingers splayed against the bare skin of my back. Heat radiated from his palm, sending a tremor through me, making my womb contract sharply.

He pulled me closer, then gently lowered me fully onto the blanket, his body partially covering mine. His hand slid down my side, tracing the curve of my hip, then moving lower, stroking the outside of my thigh through my skirt.

"You feel so good," he murmured, his voice thick.

A surge of boldness, fueled by his touch, made me grin. "Wait till you're inside me," I whispered cheekily. "I'll feel even better then." This sassy side of me seemed to emerge only around him.

He groaned, a low sound of mingled desire and impatience. His fingers found the hem of my skirt, gliding slowly up my bare leg beneath it. I sighed into his mouth, kissing him back eagerly.

Whatever the future held, right now, this moment, this feeling, was everything. My own hands slid under his shirt, rediscovering the hard planes of his chest, the ridges of his abdomen. Farm-strong muscles, honed by real work.

His hand continued its upward journey, brushing against the sensitive skin of my inner thigh. My pelvic muscles clenched hard. Moisture pooled, slick and ready, anticipating his touch, anticipating *him*.

But he steered his hand away slightly, tracing the curve of my hip instead. "I want to enjoy every exquisite inch of you first," he whispered, his fingers gliding back down my leg. "You're toned."

"Zumba," I managed breathlessly, pulling his shirt open, needing to see him. "Pretty sure *this*," I smoothed my hands over the defined bumps of his chest, "isn't the result of a gym membership." He inhaled sharply, flexing slightly, enhancing the view. I gasped softly.

The heat between us intensified, the urgency building. His tongue circled mine, mimicking the slow exploration of his hands. I sighed again, completely lost in the sensations.

His hand moved back up my leg, pulling the skirt higher, fingers tracing the delicate lace edge of my panties. He skimmed inward, toward my inner thighs, higher and higher.

I instinctively shifted, parting my legs slightly, wanting him to touch me *there*, needing the friction, the release. But he held back, teasing me, stroking the fabric just beside my damp heat, then moving back, over my hip, cupping my backside through the skirt, and squeezing firmly. I gasped sharply at the unexpected pressure.

He growled softly against my neck, nuzzling his lips down my skin toward my collarbone, stopping at the neckline of my top. He kissed his way back up to my mouth just as his fingers finally slipped beneath the lace edge of my knickers, finding the slick heat between my folds.

Soft sounds escaped me, encouraging him. His fingers slid through the moisture, exploring gently, then moving lower, toward my entrance, circling, teasing.

"My God, you're so wet," he murmured, his voice rough with need.

"Of course," I breathed. "You turn me on." I reached up, kissing along his jawline, sucking lightly at his skin until my arms trembled from holding myself up.

I collapsed back onto the rug with a low moan as his fingers began a relentless, circling rhythm against my clit. The familiar tension coiled tight and low in my belly. He knew exactly where to touch, how to move. I felt the orgasm building, a wave gathering force deep inside. I let go, surrendering to his touch, my body arching instinctively.

He switched pressure, light then firm, driving me higher, faster. Then, just as I neared the peak, he shifted, pulling my knickers aside, and dipped his head. His tongue slid through the slickness, hot and demanding. I nearly came right then, a choked cry escaping me. But he pulled back, denying me the release, leaving me trembling, suspended on the edge, and completely at his mercy.

"You," he growled, his eyes blazing down at me, "are wearing far too much." He hooked his fingers into the waistband of my panties, tugging them down.

I lifted my hips, helping him, pushing my skirt down at the same time.

"And *you*," I countered, my fingers fumbling with his belt buckle, then the button and zip of his jeans.

He kicked off his boots, sliding the denim down, along with his boxers, wriggling free in one fluid motion. He knelt beside me, magnificent, fully aroused.

"You definitely look ready," I whispered, admiring the sight of him, hard and pulsing, poised above me.

"But you're not... quite... naked yet," he murmured. Reaching for my top, he pulled it slowly over my head, and tossed it aside.

He cupped my breasts through the lace, massaging gently, drawing soft whimpers from me. Feeling my nipples harden against his palms, he pinched them, quickening my breath, intensifying the ache between my legs.

I need him. Now.

With deft fingers, he unhooked my bra, sliding the straps off my shoulders. Cool air hit my skin as my breasts were freed. I arched my back instinctively, offering myself to him. His mouth closed over one nipple, tongue flicking my hardened nub, sending shivers of intense pleasure through me. I groaned, loud this time, past caring who heard. The pleasure was too intense.

My fingers glided up and down his smooth, sweat-slicked back as he worshipped each breast in turn. Then my hand moved lower, finding his erection, closing around the thick, hot length of him, stroking rhythmically and squeezing the velvety tip until a drop of moisture pearled there.

He reached behind him, fumbling in the pocket of his discarded jeans until he pulled out a condom.

"Always prepared, Farmer?" I teased, continuing my ministrations.

"Wouldn't want to miss out on a second of this with you." He grunted, tearing open the packet with his teeth and quickly rolling the latex on.

Before I could react, he gently pushed me back against the blanket, settling himself between my legs. I wrapped my legs around his waist, pulling him closer, guiding him toward my entrance.

He paused there, poised, looking down at me, his eyes dark and intense. Then, slowly, deliberately, he pushed forward, entering me inch by glorious inch. My muscles stretched, clenched, and welcomed him. His answering groan was deep, guttural, and told me everything I needed to know.

He began to move, a slow, deep rhythm that had me gasping, my hips lifting instinctively to meet each thrust. The tension built again, coiling tighter and tighter, but different this time, deeper as I felt more connected to him.

He increased the pace, his thrusts becoming harder, faster, driving me toward the edge. A small, sharp orgasm rippled through me, making me cry out, clenching around him.

The sensation seemed to push him further, his control snapping. He groaned my name, his rhythm becoming frantic, powerful, driving us both toward the precipice. It hit simultaneously, a blinding, shattering release that pulsed between us, through us, leaving us clinging together, gasping, slick with sweat, lost in the echoing waves of pleasure.

I sighed heavily as the last tremors faded, my muscles slowly unclenching, my body boneless against the blanket. My hands rested limply on his back.

He shifted his weight slightly, kissing me softly, lingeringly. "You definitely didn't worry about who might hear you that time," he murmured against my lips, a satisfied smirk in his voice.

"Pretty sure it's only the cattle down there, right?" I whispered back, my voice husky.

"Hope so." He kept kissing me, gentle, lazy kisses that smoothed away any lingering embarrassment about how loud I might have been.

"It was entirely your fault," I accused playfully. "For being so damn hot."

"Right back at you, Ms. Sexy." He chuckled, running his hands slowly down my back, sending delicious shivers through my blissed-out body.

"Well." I sighed dreamily, snuggling closer, acutely aware of our nakedness in the intimacy of the moment. "Maybe we should just... stay up here for a while. Hide out. Not show our faces." All I cared about right now was being here, like this, with him, for as long as possible. It felt if I left him now, it might be over. And I didn't want that.

"Good idea," he whispered back, pulling the edge of the blanket over us. "And if we rest long enough, maybe I can take you on another ride. See if we can stir up the entire shed this time."

A thrill shot through me despite my exhaustion. "You're on," I murmured, kissing the side of his neck before letting my eyes drift closed, safe and utterly content in his arms.

CHAPTER 27

Megan

"Are you sure you're okay getting down?" Jackson asked, his voice still a little rough from our recent activities, his hand warm on my lower back.

"Of course," I replied, though a blush crept up my neck.

The only real hazard was flashing my knickers on the way down, but honestly? After the last hour, with only the drowsy cattle as witnesses, modesty felt like a distant concern.

My body still hummed with a pleasant, languid warmth, the afterglow settling deep in my bones. Thoughts swirled lazily of the scratch of hay against the soft blanket, the heat of his skin, and the intensity in his eyes.

I don't want to say goodbye.

Not tonight. Not after this.

This felt different from the first time, less frantic, more connected, and somehow deeper. I wanted more of this feeling, more of him. I wanted to see where this could actually go.

I eased myself into a sitting position on the edge of the hayloft, swinging my legs over. Turning carefully, I gripped the top rail, preparing to climb down ladder-style.

Maybe I won't have to say goodbye.

The thought sparked a frantic churn of possibilities. Could I make this work? Find a job near his farm? Clare wasn't exactly a bustling metropolis. Finding photography work might be tough. But the desire was there, startlingly strong.

I want to try.

I couldn't believe how quickly, how completely, I was falling for this farmer. Literally...

My foot, searching for the next rail down, slipped on a loose bit of hay. A sharp gasp escaped me as my hands scrabbled for purchase. For one heart-stopping moment, I dangled, suspended between the loft and the concrete floor below.

"Hang on! I've got you!" Jackson's voice was sharp

with alarm as he reached down, grabbing for my arm.

But it was too late. My grip failed and I let go.

It wasn't a huge drop, maybe five feet, but I landed awkwardly, my shoulder slamming against a heavy metal feed drum before my head connected with a dull thud. "Ow!" Stars didn't explode behind my eyes this time, but the impact jarred me. I sat there for a stunned second, rubbing the back of my head, assessing the damage.

Okay. Sore, definitely, but just a bump. Nothing serious. The adrenaline spike faded almost as quickly as it had hit, leaving me feeling slightly foolish.

Jackson landed beside me seemingly moments later, vaulting down from the loft with an agility that belied his size. He was kneeling beside me in an instant, his face pale, his eyes wide with a fear that seemed wildly disproportionate to my clumsy tumble.

"Megan? How bad is it? Are you hurt?"

"I'm okay," I reassured him, trying to inject some lightness into my voice. "No stars this time, promise." I became aware that my skirt had ridden up again in the fall. "God, Jackson, you've seen my knickers more than anyone else." I tugged the fabric down, attempting a teasing smile.

He didn't take the bait. His expression remained tight, almost frantic.

"Let me see. Move your hand." He gently but firmly pushed my hand aside, his fingers probing the back of my scalp. The intensity of his concern felt off. Too much.

"Seriously, Jackson, I'm fine. It was just a little knock."

"No. You're not fine." His voice was harsh, strained. "We need to get you to a hospital. Now."

I stared at him, bewildered. "What? No! Jackson, it's nothing like before. It barely even hurts."

But the fear in his eyes was thick, suffocating. It wasn't just concern, it was raw terror. His whole body was rigid with tension.

"Jackson," I said softly, reaching out, putting my hand on his arm.

He flinched away as if burned. "No! Don't argue. I'm not taking any risks. Not again."

Not again.

The words hung in the air, heavy and cold. And suddenly, I understood. This overwhelming panic, this refusal to listen wasn't about me. Not really. It was about Erin.

My minor fall had ripped open his old wound. The way he was looking at me, the frantic energy radiating from him, it screamed unresolved grief, unbearable guilt.

"I won't let anything happen to you," he choked out, holding out a hand to pull me up, his knuckles white.

I looked up at his tormented face and made a decision. Ignoring his outstretched hand, I stayed put.

"Jackson, please. Sit down. Just for a minute. Talk to me." My voice was quiet but firm. "I don't think this is about my head, is it?"

He stood frozen, his chest rising and falling rapidly, his jaw clenched tight. He looked trapped, cornered by his own fear.

"What really happened to your sister, Jackson?" I asked gently, keeping my gaze steady on his.

"I told you," he bit out, his voice rough.

"You told me you blame yourself," I clarified softly. "Why? Why is it your fault?"

"Because it *is!*" His voice cracked, rising sharply, startling the nearby cattle into restless movement.

My own nerves frayed. Was I pushing too hard? Was this the right thing to do?

This raw, wounded version of Jackson was unfamiliar, unsettling. But I recognized the shape of his pain. I knew the crushing weight of grief, the insidious tendrils of guilt.

That I triggered. Six months of grief counseling after Mom died had felt like torture at the time, but it had taught me things. How to sit with pain, both mine and others. And I knew how to listen.

He finally sank down onto the concrete floor in front of me, his posture defeated. "Fine," he muttered, staring at the ground between his boots. "I'll tell you."

I swallowed hard, bracing myself. I wasn't a therapist, but I could listen. That much I could do.

"Erin... she wanted to go riding," he began, his voice low and strained. "It had been raining all morning so the ground was slick. She couldn't find her helmet... not that she liked wearing it anyway. Stubborn." He paused, taking a ragged breath, fighting for control.

"I told her not to go. It was a bad idea. She just laughed, told me she'd be fine and to stop being such a bossy older brother." His eyes reddened, glistening with unshed tears. "I should have stopped her. Hidden the damn saddle. Tackled her. Something. Or at least... at least made her find the bloody helmet." He sighed, a heavy, broken sound, his shoulders slumping forward. "But we argued. She yelled at me... said she was sixteen, not a child, she didn't need my permission or my lectures." He stared down at his hands, twisting them together.

I waited, giving him space, letting the silence stretch. When he didn't continue, I leaned forward slightly, touching his arm again. This time, he didn't pull away. Instead, his hand closed over mine, gripping it tightly, his skin surprisingly cold despite the warmth of the shed. The contact seemed to ground him slightly, easing a fraction of the tension radiating from him.

"It's not your fault, Jackson," I said softly, firmly.

"But I feel like it is," he whispered, his voice thick. "I could have... I could have gone with her. We used to ride together all the time. But I was seventeen, more interested in..."

"Girls?" I finished for him gently. He nodded, a flicker of self-reproach crossing his face. "Jackson, you were seventeen. That's normal. And she was sixteen. Also normal to want independence, to push boundaries, to think she was invincible." I squeezed his hand. "Do you really think she would have thanked you for physically stopping her from doing something she loved? Wouldn't that have just driven a wedge between you?"

I searched his eyes, pleading with him to see it. "She was old enough to make her own choices, even if they were risky ones. It was a tragic accident, Jackson. Awful. But it wasn't your fault."

I drew on the words my own counselor had used, words that had slowly, painfully started to make sense over time.

"You'll always carry the grief," I said softly, running my thumb over his knuckles. "Losing someone you love... it changes you. But you can learn to manage it. You need to start making peace with what you could control and what you couldn't." I took a deep breath, meeting his gaze directly. "You couldn't control her choices, or the weather, or how horses react. You couldn't control the outcome. But you *can* control letting go of the blame. It wasn't your fault, Jackson. You missing her, loving her... that's forever. The guilt doesn't have to be."

He stared at me for a long moment, his expression unreadable. Then, with a choked sound, he pulled me into a hug, burying his face in my shoulder, his arms wrapping tightly around me.

I held him, feeling the tremors that ran through his body, the release of tension held for far too long. I felt the dampness seep through my shirt as silent tears finally fell. I just held him, offering silent comfort, understanding the catharsis of letting go, even just a little.

After a long time, he pulled back slightly, his eyes red-rimmed but clearer, the frantic terror replaced by a deep, weary sadness. "I'm still worried about you, though," he murmured, his voice rough.

"Then make sure I get to my car safely," I replied softly, resting my head against his shoulder and breathing in his familiar scent. The air between us felt different now, quieter, more fragile, but deeper too. I felt closer to him than ever, but also acutely aware of the weight of his past, the scars he carried.

"I don't want to leave you tonight," I admitted quietly.

The question hovered on the tip of my tongue: *When are you leaving? When do I have to say goodbye for real?*

But looking at his vulnerable face, feeling the fragile peace settling between us after the storm, I couldn't ask it. Not now. It felt too harsh, too demanding. I wanted to hold onto this moment, this connection, just a little longer, without the shadow of departure looming over us. I wanted to go to sleep remembering the warmth of the hayloft, not the ache of his leaving.

"Me either," he whispered back, tightening his arm around me.

I pulled back just enough to look into his eyes. "You'll see me tomorrow, then?" I needed that reassurance.

A flicker of the old Jackson returned, a hint of the cheeky glint in his eyes as the raw emotion receded. "Hell, yeah," he confirmed, his voice regaining some of its usual strength. "Count on it."

CHAPTER 28

Jackson

I whistled some nameless tune as I went about refilling the water troughs for the cattle, my mind miles away from the task at hand. Specifically, it was about ten feet directly *above* the task at hand, replaying vivid scenes from last night in the hayloft.

Megan beneath me, the feel of her skin, the sounds she made... *What the hell was I thinking?*

A blush crept up my neck despite the cool morning air. Remembering how tight she felt when I first pushed inside her, how wet and ready she was. I shifted uncomfortably, my jeans suddenly feeling too tight. Meeting her for breakfast in a few minutes was pretty much all I could focus on.

"Something interesting got your mind this morning, Jackson?"

"What?" I snapped back to reality, abruptly torn from my X-rated daydream. Heath stood there, leaning against Bruce's stall, grinning like he knew exactly what, or who, I'd been thinking about.

He just pointed. I followed his gaze. "Bugger." Water sloshed over the side of the trough I was supposed to be filling, pooling on the concrete. Must have been overflowing for a good minute or two. I hastily tipped the watering can back, stopping the flow, feeling like a complete idiot.

"It's that girl, isn't it?" Heath's grin widened.

My stomach clenched. Surely no one saw us last night? We were careful climbing down, weren't we? I eyed Heath suspiciously, knowing his penchant for stirring the pot.

"You mean Megan," I corrected him, trying to sound casual.

"Christ, mate, it must be serious if you actually know her name!"

"Hey!" I shot back, stung by his words. Okay, maybe I wasn't exactly known for long-term relationships, but I wasn't the player Heath made me out to be. And Megan felt different.

Heath held up both hands in mock surrender.

"Just saying! Must have it bad if you can't even concentrate on filling a water trough. Pretty basic stuff, even for you."

"Just tired," I muttered defensively, turning away to check Bruce's trough. "Long week at the show." I hated feeling this exposed, like my thoughts were written all over my face.

"Right. Tired." Heath snorted. "And what was with the lovey-dovey tune you were whistling? Sounded like something out of a Disney movie. Mate, she's got you completely whipped and chained up by the balls."

"She certainly has," I mumbled, thinking of exactly *how* she had me, picturing her hands exploring...

"What?" Heath's eyes widened in disbelief.

I snapped back, catching his expression. "Gotcha." I laughed, trying to deflect.

He folded his arms, unconvinced. "So? You gonna invite her back to the farm, then?"

"Why would I do that?" I moved past him, grabbing the watering can again, needing something to do with my hands.

All these questions forced me to think about the future, about logistics, about potential complications, and my head started to ache. It was much easier, much more pleasant, to just think about Megan and seeing her soon, finding somewhere private, getting naked again.

"Seriously, mate? Are you really in denial?"

I just looked at him blankly, stalling.

Heath sighed dramatically. "It's obvious, Jackson. You're falling for her. Hard."

"It's only been a few days," I protested, though the words felt weak even to me.

"Days, weeks, months... doesn't matter when it hits you. You're hooked, mate. And if you want to keep her hooked, you'd better make a move. Invite her to Sunnydale. Show her you're serious. Once you find something good, you don't let it go."

"Where would she even stay?" The practical detail snagged in my brain, a convenient excuse to avoid the bigger issue.

"In your bedroom, you idiot!" Heath rolled his eyes. "Where else?"

I frowned. That was exactly where I wanted her, tangled up in my sheets every morning. But we barely knew each other.

What if we had a fight tomorrow? What if this whole thing fizzled out as quickly as it started? Then it really *would* just be another notch on the bedpost, and the thought felt surprisingly sour.

Heath, clearly exasperated, tried another tack. "Okay, fine. If you want to be all proper about it, maybe she could stay at Julie's old place? It's empty, right?"

I practically choked. "Julie's? Are you insane? No."

"Well, figure something out!" Heath slapped me on the back, jarring me. "Just ask her, mate. Tell her you want to see where this goes. You head back tomorrow night, right? Clock's ticking. Don't screw this up. You'll regret it if you walk away without even trying."

I shook my head, trying to process the onslaught of unsolicited advice. A tight knot formed in my gut. Heath was right about the time running out. But inviting her to the farm? She was a city girl, through and through. Would she genuinely want to spend time out there, miles from anywhere? It felt like a huge leap from a show fling to experiencing real farm life.

No. Too fast. Too much.

I put the watering can back in the corner with our gear and turned toward the members' stand for breakfast. My stomach churned, my mind a mess. Heath's words echoed, battling with my own anxieties.

Just enjoy the time you have left, I told myself firmly. *Keep it simple.*

"Can't believe these prices," I mumbled, standing in line with Megan at the members' dining room. The smell of bacon and coffee warred with the knot in my stomach.

"You don't have to pay, Jackson," Megan said softly beside me.

I automatically reached for her hand, lacing our fingers together. It felt natural, right. Like we were a couple.

But we're not. Not really. Not yet.

Could we be? We hadn't talked about it.

Heath's words from earlier pushed at me. *Ask her. Talk about it.*

But the fear of rejection, of ending this fragile, exciting thing between us kept the words tangled in my throat. I liked this. Liked holding her hand and the way she looked at me. Liked it way too much to risk screwing it up.

"No, I want to," I insisted, forcing a smile. "My treat. But seriously, show prices are robbery. Still shocks me every year." I leaned down and kissed her, a quick, sweet peck. Just tasting her settled me slightly, but also reminded me exactly what I *really* wanted to be doing instead of standing in a breakfast queue.

I pulled back before I got carried away, though I could already feel myself hardening. Damn it.

"What looks good?" I asked, trying to focus.

She hesitated, scanning the menu board.

"Don't pick the cheapest thing because of me," I urged. "Go on, get the full works?" This felt like a ridiculously inadequate date, especially with my parents sitting over in the corner, watching us like hawks.

I was pretty sure Mom had already spread the word that I was bringing 'the photographer girl' to breakfast. Every time I glanced their way, she was looking over, making me flush crimson.

And then there was Heath and Julie and the rest of the guys from the sheds, all clustered at another table, smirking. I felt like an exhibit myself. Maybe suggesting breakfast *here* hadn't been my smartest move. My ears burned like they were made of hot coals.

"Hmm, I don't think I could manage all that," Megan decided finally. "Just bacon and eggs on toast sounds perfect."

"Okay. Coffee, too, obviously. Though I'll warn you, it's nowhere near as good as the stuff over in the Ag tent." I stepped forward, placed our order, paid quickly, and stuffed my wallet back in my pocket. "Right, let's sit... over there." I steered her pointedly toward the far side of the room.

"Don't you want to sit near your mom and dad?" Megan teased, her eyes sparkling.

"Definitely not." I took her hand again, navigating past the round tables. "Or Julie. Or Heath. Or anyone else I've ever met in my entire life, preferably." I stopped at an empty table in the corner. "Just you."

I looked into her eyes, losing myself for a second in their warm brown depths. She had this way of looking at me that just ignited something. Lust, pure and simple, blasted through me.

Fuck it. Courage surged, fueled by desire. I leaned down and kissed her again, longer this time, ignoring the wolf whistle that came from Heath's table.

"Here okay?" I gestured to the chair that would put her back to my parents and the peanut gallery.

Megan grinned, seemingly unfazed. "Sure." She sat down. "You have quite the fan club over there."

"Yeah, well, apparently they've got nothing better

to do than watch my every move," I grumbled, shooting a glare over my shoulder. Heath blew me a kiss. "Bastards."

I slumped into the chair beside Megan. This was excruciating. And Heath's lecture about 'making a move' kept replaying in my head, messing with my already scrambled thoughts.

Did I want a future with her? Yes. Absolutely. Did I also just want to drag her back to the hayloft right now? Hell yes.

"Looks like they're certainly enjoying the show," Megan commented dryly, winking at me.

"Right then." I decided, throwing caution to the wind. "Let's give 'em something *real* to talk about." Fueled by a mix of defiance and pure want, I slid my arm around her shoulders, pulled her close, and crashed my lips down onto hers. Hard. Hot. A kiss that left no doubt about my intentions, about exactly what I wanted to do with her, to her.

I poured everything into it, focusing only on her, the taste of her, the softness of her lips yielding under mine. My tongue flicked against hers, exploring, demanding, wanting more. I only broke away when the need for air became desperate. Taking a deep breath, ready to dive back in, I was interrupted by the waitress.

"Bacon and eggs, and one with the lot."

"Here," I managed, slightly breathless. Miraculously, she put the plates down correctly. The aroma of bacon, eggs, mushrooms, and grilled tomato hit me, making my stomach rumble despite the turmoil in my head. "Thanks." The waitress vanished before I finished the word.

"I'll grab the coffees," Megan said quickly, her cheeks flushed, and escaped toward the counter. I watched her go, a pang of guilt hitting me.

Maybe that kiss was too much? Too public? Too possessive? I knew I'd gone too far, I felt the evidence straining against my jeans.

I fiddled with my fork, waiting for her return. Kissing like that in public wasn't my style, especially not with my parents fifty feet away.

What was I thinking? It was a kiss promising sex, pure and simple. A promise I fully intended to keep. Just later. I had commitments today. Meetings. Judging. Or maybe not.

Wicked thoughts started brewing, I could ditch the meetings, grab Megan, and find somewhere quiet. Just one more time. But even as the thought formed, I knew it was a lie.

One more time would never be enough. Not with Megan.

I wanted the everyday stuff too. Waking up next to her, arguing about who left the cap off the toothpaste, falling asleep tangled together. Shit. Heath was right. I was in deep.

Megan returned with two steaming mugs. "Hope you like it strong."

"Definitely," I said, grateful for the caffeine kick. "Didn't get much sleep last night." I watched with satisfaction as her blush deepened.

"Cheeky," she retorted, setting the coffees down and digging into her breakfast. "I'm starving."

"Been working out hard?" I couldn't resist.

Megan laughed, a sound that did ridiculous things to my insides. "Not nearly as much as I'd like to be."

"I know how to fix that," I said, raising an eyebrow suggestively.

"Oh, do you now?" she played along, her eyes sparkling.

"Yep." Here goes nothing. "Got plenty of work needs doing on the farm." The words tumbled out before I could second-guess them. An invitation. Sort of.

"I bet you do," she replied easily, taking another bite of bacon.

The knot in my stomach tightened again. She

didn't get it. Or she was deliberately ignoring the implied invitation. Disappointment warred with relief. Maybe it was better this way. Safer. I focused on my scrambled eggs, shoveling them in.

Can't move this fast. It'll scare her off.

"Was that... an invitation?" Megan asked suddenly, her fork hovering mid-air.

The eggs seemed to lodge in my throat. I couldn't speak, just managed a jerky nod. "Yeah," I finally croaked out. "If... if you wanted. If you don't think it's too soon, or too forward."

She didn't answer immediately, just slowly lowered her fork, her expression unreadable. Then she put the forkful of eggs into her mouth, chewing thoughtfully.

I watched her face, trying to decipher her reaction. She looked paler, or maybe shocked.

Shit.

I shouldn't have asked. I attacked my eggs again, unable to meet her eyes, bracing for the rejection I felt radiating across the small table.

"I... I hadn't really thought that far ahead," she said finally, her voice quiet.

"Right. No, of course not," I backtracked rapidly, relief warring with a fresh wave of disappointment. "Forget I said anything. It was just a suggestion. No pressure. Really." I couldn't look at her.

"I'll think about it, Jackson," she said softly. "Seriously. When... when do you go home?"

"Tomorrow night." The words felt like lead.

"Oh. That soon?" Her face fell, genuine disappointment clouding her features.

I nodded mutely. "Yeah. Harvest won't wait. Have to get back."

"Of course." She poked at the remaining eggs on her plate, pushing them around like she was herding sheep. "So... that's why you asked. About the farm."

The implication stung. "No! Well, yes, partly. But mostly..." The words rushed out, desperate now. "Look, I don't know how this long-distance thing works, or if it even *can* work, but I want to keep seeing you, Megan. Get to know you properly. I know it's only been a few days, but..." I trailed off, horrified.

God, I sound desperate. Which I was. Desperate not to lose her.

"I... I need to think," she stammered, looking overwhelmed.

I risked a glance up. Her hair tumbled around her shoulders in soft curls, her floral top was buttoned just low enough to offer a hint of cleavage.

My body reacted instantly, overriding the emotional turmoil. Waiting for her to 'think about it' felt like torture. What if she thought her way right out of seeing me again?

"I don't say stuff like this lightly," I added quickly, needing her to understand. "I really do want to keep seeing you."

"Excuse me." A throat cleared pointedly beside our table.

I looked up. Dad. Standing there, arms crossed, looking stern.

Great. Perfect timing.

Mom had probably sent him over. Or maybe Heath or Julie had helpfully filled him in on my pathetic attempt at asking Megan out.

"The breeders' meeting, Jackson," Dad said, his voice leaving no room for argument. "Starts in fifteen minutes. All the main breeders will be there."

"I know. I won't forget."

"See that you don't."

I nearly choked on my last mouthful of egg. Fifteen minutes? Shit. I hadn't even asked Megan how *she* felt, what *she* wanted from this, other than more mind-blowing sex, and that wasn't exactly a topic for discussion with my father hovering over us. Dad didn't move.

"Don't worry, Mr. Pearce, I'll make sure he gets there on time." Megan, bless her, smoothly intervened, holding out her hand. "I'm Megan, by the way."

"Mike." Dad shook her hand, his expression softening slightly. "Pleasure. Good. He needs someone to keep him on track."

I resisted the urge to slide under the table. *This cannot be happening.*

"Needs a strong hand, this one," Dad continued, grinning now. "To keep him in line."

Is the entire world conspiring against me today? I groaned aloud. "Dad!"

Megan actually laughed. "Good to know. I'll remember that."

"Hope we see more of you, Megan," Dad said, giving her a warm smile before turning back to me, his expression hardening again. "The meeting, Jackson. Don't be late."

"I *know*," I ground out, glaring at his retreating back.

"Gee, you really are Mr. Important at the show," Megan teased, taking a sip of her coffee. "We probably should head off soon. Don't want you to be late on my account."

"Not you too." I sighed, finishing my eggs.

Lowering my voice, I leaned closer. "Or... we could ditch the meeting and, you know..." I raised an eyebrow suggestively. Her cheeks instantly flushed pink. She knew exactly what I meant.

"You have commitments, Jackson," she replied, her voice firm but her eyes betraying a flicker of interest. "And actually, so do I. Need to check in with Helen."

I slumped back in my chair, the rejection sinking in, even though it was expected.

"It's not that I don't *want* to," she added quietly, leaning closer conspiratorially.

"No?" My head snapped up, hope flaring. God, she messed with my head. One minute I was convinced she was blowing me off, the next...

"Definitely not." She pursed her lips, thinking for a second. "But we can meet up later. After your meeting, and after I see Helen. I insist."

"Good." Relief washed over me. "Because I'm planning on seeing a *lot* more of you later."

Her response was a quick, promising kiss across the table. "Come on, Mr. Important. You'll be late. And I don't want to ruin the good impression I apparently just made on your dad."

The kiss, the easy acceptance, maybe her thinking about the farm invitation *was* a good sign.

"Right. You better make sure I actually get there, then," I said, standing up. "Because honestly, all I want to do right now is ditch everything and spend the rest of the morning with you."

Megan laughed again. "Let's go. Lead the way to this vital meeting."

"Okay, okay. But first…" I cupped her face, pulling her up slightly from her chair, and kissed her again. Long, slow, deep.

A kiss designed to make her dizzy, to make her forget about meetings and bosses, to make her think only of me, of us. I poured all the frustration, all the desire, all the desperate hope into it. I felt her respond, leaning into me, her lips crushing mine, her tongue meeting mine, bold and demanding. Heat flared, instant and urgent. My body pulsed, hardening impossibly fast.

I pulled back reluctantly, breathing hard. I stood up properly, holding out my hand. She placed hers in mine without hesitation, her skin warm and soft. The simple contact sent fire through my veins. I wanted those hands on me. Now.

"This way," I said, my voice husky, running my thumb over the back of her hand as we walked out of the dining room, away from the prying eyes to melt into the relative anonymity of the thickening crowds. I needed to give her something more to think about, something to convince her that coming to the farm, spending more time with me, was exactly what she wanted to do.

"Is this... really the way to the meeting?" Megan asked after a moment, suspicion lacing her voice as I steered her down a less crowded side path.

I grinned. "Busted." I stopped, turned, and before she could react, scooped her up into my arms, lifting her clean off the ground. I kissed her again, fiercely this time. "Just needed a more convincing argument for coming to the farm," I murmured against her lips.

"Oh yeah?" she breathed, clinging to me. "And how were you planning on doing that?"

I raised an eyebrow deliberately. "The best way I know how."

"But... the meeting. You don't have time."

"Trust me," I whispered, setting her back on her feet but keeping her pinned against me, my hands sliding around her waist. "I can make time." I kissed her again, needing more, feeling the urgency spike between us, sharp and demanding.

Her hands slid down my back, over my jeans, gripping my ass cheeks tightly. A low groan escaped me. I stiffened, pulsing against her, needing release, needing *her*.

Time was short. Fifteen minutes, maybe less now. But maybe that was the point. The thrill of the forbidden, the explosive satisfaction of a quick, desperate coupling.

Before I could start tearing at her clothes right there in the middle of the showgrounds, I forced myself to pull back, just an inch. "Up for a quickie?" I breathed, my eyes locked on hers.

Her eyes widened, then darkened with answering heat. "Hell, yeah."

CHAPTER 29

Megan

I couldn't quite believe I was doing this. Hurrying through the bustling showgrounds, practically glued to Jackson's back, heading for... a quickie in his locker room? The unresolved tension from breakfast with his clumsy invitation, my hesitant response, the looming deadline of his departure tomorrow night, had somehow combusted into this urgent, almost frantic need for physical connection.

It felt reckless, impulsive, and utterly necessary. If the future was uncertain, maybe grabbing hold of the present, however fleeting, was the only answer. Being with Jackson seemed to short-circuit my usual caution, turning me into someone I barely recognized, someone driven purely by want. A horny devil, indeed.

He glanced back, grinning, pulling me faster down a less crowded path toward the sheds. My heart hammered against my ribs, a frantic rhythm matching our hurried steps. We reached the small locker room door.

He fumbled with the key, glancing around quickly. I kept my eyes fixed on the door handle, avoiding eye contact with anyone who might pass by. The slightly illicit thrill of it all sent a fresh wave of heat through me.

The second the lock clicked open, he ushered me inside the cramped, windowless space. It smelled faintly of sweat, liniment, and maybe stale beer. He turned to lock the door behind us, shutting out the world. In that confined space, with the adrenaline singing in my veins and the raw need clawing at me, all pretense of patience vanished.

Before the lock even clicked shut, I pushed myself against his back, pressing my front fully against him, slipping my hands around his waist and down the front of his jeans. My fingers closed around his erection, already hard and hot, straining against the denim. Divine. A jolt went through me, pure electricity.

"Whoa, hang on a bit." He chuckled, still fumbling with the lock behind him.

"This is a quickie, remember?" I whispered against his back, my fingers working frantically at his button, then the zipper. I pushed the rough denim down over his hips, taking his boxers with them.

My hand closed around his bare shaft, slick with pre-come. I started stroking, fast and purposeful, glorying in the way he thickened further, pulsing hot against my palm.

The lock finally clicked. He turned, grabbed me, and pulled me into a crushing kiss. His mouth was hard, demanding, his tongue plunging inside, tangling with mine. It was a kiss that mirrored the urgency thrumming between us. There was no tenderness, just raw need. I kissed him back with equal fervor, grinding my hips forward, needing to feel him against me, *in* me.

My own jeans felt like an intolerable barrier. I reached down, fumbling with my button, trying to tug them down. His hands immediately went to my breasts, cupping them roughly through my top and bra, making it almost impossible to concentrate.

"What's this? Payback?" I gasped, struggling with

my jeans while his thumbs found my already hard nipples.

He laughed, a low, rough sound against my mouth. "Of course. You made it damn near impossible to lock that door. Started thinking you wanted an audience."

"Ha!" I finally managed to shove my jeans and knickers down, kicking them impatiently over my shoes, not caring where they landed on the dusty floor.

His fingers tightened, pinching both nipples simultaneously through the fabric. I inhaled sharply, arching against him, a confusing mix of sharp pleasure and almost-pain shooting through me. "Hmmm," I moaned against his lips. "Do that again."

"No way," he murmured, pulling back slightly, his eyes blazing into mine. That flash of connection, even in the midst of this frenzy. "Quickie, remember?" He reached into his discarded jeans pocket, pulling out a condom packet. "We've both got places to be."

"Are you sure?" I breathed, my mind completely fogged, all logic obliterated. "I don't remember anywhere I need to be right now." All that mattered was him, here, now. Job, Dad, the uncertain future, it all faded into insignificance.

He ripped the packet open with his teeth and rolled the condom on with practiced speed. "Ready?" he asked, his voice thick.

"You better check," I whispered, leaning back against the cool, rough wood of the locker room wall, spreading my legs slightly, offering myself to him. My own wetness trickled down my thigh, slick with anticipation.

His fingers danced over my mound, then slid down, parting my folds, dipping into the slick heat.

"Oh yeah," he confirmed, his voice rougher now. "Definitely ready." But he didn't stop touching me, his fingers starting a relentless circling motion against my clit.

I leaned my head back against the wall, no longer caring about noise, purely needing release. I gripped the back of his neck, pulling him closer, needing more.

He moved his fingers faster, more purposefully, then clamped his mouth over my breast, sucking hard through the fabric, finding my nipple instantly. The sudden, unexpected intensity sent shockwaves through me.

My muscles clenched violently. Sweet, helpless noises escaped my throat as he brought me crashing toward an orgasm with brutal efficiency. I rocked against his hand, riding the wave, until I tipped over the edge with a long, shuddering moan, my muscles contracting uncontrollably. I slumped forward, pressing my forehead against his shoulder, momentarily boneless.

Before I could fully recover, he scooped me up, my legs wrapping instinctively high around his waist. He positioned himself, and I lowered myself down onto him, gasping as he slid deep inside, filling me completely. We both groaned, a shared sound of pure, animal pleasure.

He braced me against the wall, keeping himself buried deep inside me for a moment, then pulled back almost completely before thrusting back in. Hard. Fast. Purposeful.

Each jarring impact sent jolts of sensation through my already sensitized body. I groaned again, arching into him, taking him deeper, chasing the friction, the building pressure.

Our breaths came in harsh, ragged gasps, echoing in the tiny space. The pace was frantic, almost punishing, a stark contrast to the lazy exploration in the hayloft. This was pure, urgent release.

The pressure built inside me again, impossibly fast, until my body simply took over, convulsing around him, tipping me into a second, shattering orgasm just as I felt him pulse deep inside me, his own release flooding through him.

He held me tight for a moment, burying his face in my neck, his body trembling slightly against mine as we both struggled to catch our breaths. He nuzzled against my hair, inhaling deeply.

"God, Megan," he breathed, his voice thick with spent passion. "I want you."

A shaky laugh escaped me. "Good," I whispered back, clinging to him, my arms tight around his neck. "Because I want you too."

He gently lowered my feet back to the floor, keeping me close, his forehead resting against mine. He kissed me then, soft and sweet this time, a stark contrast to the earlier frenzy. A moment of tenderness in the aftermath.

"Right." He sighed, pulling back slightly, reality intruding. "If I don't get to that meeting on time, Dad will know *exactly* why I'm late."

Jackson laughed, though it sounded a little strained. "Don't care about the meeting. But yeah, you mentioning it has definitely killed the mood."

My arms, still looped around his neck, dropped down to his waist. The urgency had passed, leaving behind a warm glow, but also the returning awareness of the clock ticking. "You'll see me later, though," I said, needing the reassurance.

He kissed me again, lingering this time. "Count on it," he murmured against my lips. "I'm not letting you go again today without *more*."

Heat flushed my cheeks. I leaned into his kiss, wanting to drown out the nagging voice reminding me that 'more' only lasted until tomorrow night.

"Good," I whispered back between kisses, clinging to the present moment, pushing the future away. "Because I want to see you again. And again. And again."

And I don't want you to leave. And I don't know what to do about the farm. And I'm scared.

But I didn't say any of that. Instead, I just kissed him back, focusing on the solid feel of him, the taste of him, the undeniable, intoxicating reality of him right now. That was all I could handle.

CHAPTER 30

Megan

"Okay, spill. What's kept you so busy all week? I feel like I've barely seen you." I took a long lick of my honey ice cream, double scoop, my usual show treat, as Kristie and I ambled toward the grandstand, seeking shade to watch the last of the horse events.

"Oh, you know. Lots of things," Kristie replied, a smug little smile playing on her lips. My friend wasn't usually the kiss-and-tell type, but I had my methods.

"It's a boy, isn't it?" I probed gently.

Kristie's cheeks instantly flushed bright red. Guilty as charged.

"Bingo!" I grinned, feeling rather proud of my deduction, even if it was the obvious conclusion.

"It's early stages," she mumbled defensively, focusing intently on her own ice cream. "I'm not getting carried away."

"The fact you even *had* to say that proves the exact opposite," I teased.

"Does not!"

"Totally does. And getting defensive isn't helping your case."

"Hmph," she grumbled, before turning the tables. "Anyway, what about *you*? Rumor has it Jackson Pearce is quite besotted with a certain city photographer." She raised a knowing eyebrow.

I promptly swallowed wrong, choking on a mouthful of ice cream and dissolving into a fit of coughing. *Me? Part of the showgrounds rumor mill? How?* When I finally caught my breath, Kristie was looking unbearably smug.

"Yeah, who's lost for words now?" she crowed. "Seriously though, Megan, Jackson's a really good catch."

I glanced at her, intrigued. "You know him well?"

"Know the family," she clarified. "They're good people. Really involved in the community, super supportive of each other. I guess..." her voice softened with sadness, "losing Erin probably brought them even closer."

"Right. Small world out here, I guess? Everyone knows everyone?" It felt both comforting and slightly intimidating.

"Pretty much," Kristie agreed. "Between field days, local shows, community stuff... you bump into the same people, share stories. It's not like the city, you know? Fewer distractions." She paused, licking her ice cream thoughtfully. "Keeps you focused on what matters."

I felt my cheeks getting hot as I sensed where this was going. "Are you suggesting...?"

"I'm just saying Jackson's a good catch," she repeated pointedly. "And you two seem... good together."

She wasn't wrong. There was so much I liked about Jackson. The obvious—his ridiculously good looks, the way my body responded to his touch—but also the less tangible things. The easy way he held my hand, the genuine concern in his eyes when I'd stumbled last night, even if he'd overreacted, the respect he showed me, even when teasing. The way he'd opened up about Erin, it all felt significant.

"So," Kristie pressed gently, "have you two actually talked about what happens *after* the show? When he goes back to the farm?"

I shook my head, squirming inwardly. She'd

zeroed in on the exact worry knotting my stomach. "It's... complicated."

Kristie rolled her eyes. "Complicated? Megan, honestly. You're both walking around looking like lovesick puppies. It's blindingly obvious you're crazy about each other. What's so complicated?"

"It's just... different worlds," I mumbled, the old anxieties surfacing. "He's a farmer. I'm... not. I have my dad in the city, my photography career is just starting to take off..."

The fears felt suddenly overwhelming. Could I really leave Dad alone, especially after Mom? Could I find fulfilling work miles from anywhere? Would I even fit in? Julie's spiteful words about me not lasting in the country echoed unpleasantly in my mind.

"Okay, stop right there," Kristie interrupted firmly. "Different worlds? Yes. Impossible? No. Megan, I honestly think you could love country life."

"How can you possibly know that?" I challenged, feeling defensive.

Kristie sighed, clearly frustrated. "Because I know *you*. You love exploring new things. You thrive on challenges. You're curious, you like learning." She ticked the points off on her fingers. "This is just another adventure, Megan. A potentially life-changing one."

"I don't know..." I trailed off, uncertainty swirling.

"So find out!" she urged, her gaze serious. "How about you just *try* it? Give it a real shot before you write it off. You always used to be the first one to jump into things, give anything a go. What happened to that girl?"

Her words stung because they were true. I *had* become more cautious, more afraid, since Mom died. "How?" I asked weakly, the practical obstacles looming large again. "My work... Dad..."

"Seriously, Megan?" She gave me a stern look that reminded me of my mother. "Think outside the box! Could you freelance from the country? Look for temporary work nearby? Maybe a short-term contract for a few months, just to test the waters? See if it works, see if *he's* worth it?" She raised a challenging eyebrow. "Isn't finding love worth taking a risk?"

I paused, the question hanging in the air.

Is he worth it? Looking back over the past week, the laughter, the challenges, the unexpected intimacy, the way he made me feel alive. The answer was immediate. Yes.

"You're right," I admitted, a sense of clarity cutting through the fog of fear.

"About bloody time!" Kristie grinned, relieved. "Promise me, Megan. Promise me you'll give it a real chance. Don't let fear make the decision for you." She held out her pinkie finger.

A small smile touched my lips. It felt childish, but also significant. A tangible commitment. "Promise," I said, linking my pinkie with hers.

"Good." She squeezed my finger. "Now, about *my* mysterious man... you're just going to have to move to the country so we can have that coffee catch-up I promised you."

I laughed, feeling lighter than I had all day. "Deal. But I still bet it involves a farmer."

"You worry about snagging your own farm boy first," she retorted playfully. "Then we'll talk."

CHAPTER 31

Megan

Later that evening, tucked under Jackson's arm in the chilly grandstand, the remnants of Kristie's advice and my pinkie promise echoed in my mind. We'd made good use of his locker again after the crowds thinned out, a frantic, necessary release that left me feeling both sated and slightly breathless. Now, watching the V8 Utes tear around the arena track below, a comfortable silence settled between us, but my thoughts were anything but quiet.

He shifted, pulling me closer against the cool spring air. I hadn't brought a jumper, and the warmth radiating from his body was welcome. He turned slightly, pressing a soft kiss to the top of my head. My hair smelled faintly of his shampoo, mingled with the sweet scent of hay.

"Think we might have spent a bit too much time in the hay," he murmured, his voice low and warm near my ear. He gently untangled a piece of straw from my hair, holding it up for me to see.

I laughed, leaning into him. "Or maybe not enough?" The playful words slipped out, but the contact, the intimacy of the moment, sent a familiar bolt of pleasure straight through me, momentarily overriding the anxieties.

He groaned softly, a sound that vibrated through his chest against my side. "God, I'm going to miss you," he said quietly, his arm tightening around me, pulling me securely against him.

My breath caught. His words were simple and heartfelt, but they landed with the weight of his impending departure.

I didn't respond, I couldn't. What was there to say?

I'll miss you too felt inadequate. *Don't go* felt impossible. *Come visit me* felt like putting the ball back in his court when I hadn't even decided if I could realistically catch it.

The silence stretched, heavy with unspoken things. He thought I wasn't interested, I realized with a pang. After his clumsy breakfast invitation and my hesitant response, my silence now probably felt like confirmation. But it wasn't disinterest, it was fear, uncertainty, the overwhelming weight of logistics, and potential heartbreak.

"What time do the fireworks start?" I asked finally, needing to break the tension, change the subject.

He didn't miss a beat. "Haven't I given you enough fireworks already?" he whispered, his breath warm against my ear.

Despite the underlying sadness, I giggled. "More than enough. But... I could always do with more." The lightness felt forced, but his answering chuckle eased some of the knots in my stomach.

"Good," he replied, his tone teasing again. "Hate for you to go away... displeased."

He kept his gaze fixed on the arena below, where small, train-like carriages loaded with fireworks were being positioned. He didn't risk looking at me, and I wondered if he was afraid of what he might see in my eyes, or afraid of revealing too much of his own disappointment.

"Not a hope of that happening," I murmured, leaning up to kiss his cheek gently. The warmth of his skin, the slight rasp of stubble sent a shiver of longing through me, a fierce desire to hold onto this, onto him.

Did he feel it too? I wanted to ask if he really meant it, if this week meant as much to him as it did to me, but the words stuck in my throat. Pushing him felt risky, fragile.

"Kids, we need you to scream really loud to turn off the lights for the fireworks!" The announcer's voice boomed over the speakers, shattering the intimate moment.

Jackson nudged me. "Standard procedure. You going to scream?"

"I'm not a kid," I retorted playfully.

"Oh, I know how to make you scream." He winked, his hand sliding down my thigh, dangerously close to my inner leg. The familiar heat flared instantly.

I clamped my hand over his, stopping his exploration. "All right, all right! I'll scream."

"Three... two... one..." The countdown echoed across the showgrounds.

On cue, I let out a loud, long, surprisingly piercing scream, joining the chorus around us.

Jackson jumped, pulling away slightly to cover his ears. "Bloody hell, Megan!" he exclaimed when I finally stopped, laughing. "Remind me not to underestimate your lung capacity. Maybe I haven't been working you hard enough."

I poked my tongue out at him. "Dare you."

His eyes darkened, the playful glint replaced by something more intense. "You'll have to come to my place for that, then," he said quietly, the challenge clear.

My heart stuttered. *Come to my place.*

Another invitation, less clumsy this time, more direct. The memory of my promise to Kristie, the thrill of possibility, warred with the lingering fear.

"Maybe I will," I replied softly, tilting my head, trying to convey interest without fully committing, buying myself more time. It felt like a fragile offering, a half-step forward.

"I hope so," he murmured, his voice low. He sounded hopeful, but also guarded. He reached forward then, capturing my mouth in a kiss that started slow and gentle, full of unspoken questions.

The first firework exploded overhead, showering the sky with glittering gold. He kept kissing me, deepening the pressure as if trying to memorize the feel of me, unwilling to let go. But the spectacle drew my attention. I pulled back reluctantly.

"Oh, wow! I love fireworks," I breathed, shimmying closer to him on the old wooden bench seat as the sky erupted in color. "Oooh!" Happiness, pure and simple, bubbled up inside me, momentarily eclipsing the worries. The bursts of light reflected in his eyes as he watched me, a soft, almost wistful expression on his face.

He squeezed me close again. *This could be our last night together.* The thought landed heavily. I pushed it away, focusing on the dazzling display above, on the solid warmth of Jackson beside me, determined to soak up every second of this fragile, beautiful moment. I would make new memories tonight, memories to keep me company long after he drove away tomorrow.

CHAPTER 32

Megan

The next morning, the final day of the show, felt heavy with impending departure. While waiting for Jackson near the cattle sheds, a crazy, impulsive idea took hold.

Acting on the momentum from my promise to Kristie, I pulled out my phone and opened the JobSeeker app. My fingers trembled slightly as I typed 'photographer' and 'Clare, South Australia' into the search fields.

Could I really do this? The thought of leaving Dad and stepping away from the city contacts I was just starting to build to throw myself into the unknown was terrifying. But the alternative, letting Jackson walk away tomorrow without even *trying* to bridge the distance felt even worse.

I scrolled through the limited results. Not much. My heart sank. Then I saw it.

Junior Photographer position, Clare Valley regional newspaper. Six-month contract.

My pulse leaped. Junior Photographer. I wasn't technically qualified, still had units to finish in my course. But maybe I could study externally? It felt like a long shot, fiercely competitive, no doubt.

But it was *something*. A possibility. A concrete step I could take, driven by Kristie's push and the undeniable pull I felt toward Jackson.

A six-month contract was long enough to know. Long enough to see if this feeling, this connection, was real and sustainable outside the bubble of the show.

My hand shook as I clicked the link and read through the criteria. Experience with community events? Check. Own equipment? Check. Willingness to travel within the region? Yes. The deadline for applications was the end of next week. Okay. Deep breath.

I can do this.

Daring to hope for a future that included both my passion and this man felt incredibly vulnerable. I wouldn't tell him yet. Not until I'd applied, maybe not even unless I got an interview.

This needed to be *my* decision, my risk, not just something I was doing *for* him. It was my safety net, my way of keeping some control. But knowing the possibility existed settled something within me. It made the thought of him leaving tomorrow slightly less devastating.

"READY?" Jackson asked, standing beside Bruce, holding out the thick lead rope.

My stomach plummeted. "Ready as I'll ever be," I mumbled, trying to project confidence I definitely didn't feel. Standing this close to the massive bull again brought back a surge of fear, a phantom throb where his hoof had connected with my head days ago. The sheer size and power of him, multiplied by the dozens of other cattle milling around us waiting for the Grand Parade to start, felt overwhelming, claustrophobic. My head started to ache with tension.

"It's easy," Jackson reassured me, his calm voice a stark contrast to my internal panic. "He knows the drill."

"Right. Easy." I didn't believe him for a second. Leading a one ton bull around a crowded arena felt about as easy as performing brain surgery. Should I tell him about the job application I was planning? No. Not yet. Too soon, too uncertain. First, survive this parade. Then, maybe.

He held the rope out insistently. "Come on, city girl. Show us what you're made of."

There was no backing out now. Taking a deep breath, I reached out and took the thick, slightly coarse rope. The weight of it felt immense. Butterflies erupted in my stomach, beating frantic wings against my ribs. Jackson stepped back, leaving me alone with the beast, a ridiculously trusting smile on his face.

"Hey! Don't go too far!" I hissed, my voice tight with panic. Bruce, thankfully, remained placid, occasionally swishing his tail, seemingly unfazed by the change in handler. But the potential energy simmering beneath his calm exterior terrified me. Could I really control him if he decided to bolt?

"You're fine," Jackson called back, infuriatingly calm. He didn't come closer. Instead, he pulled his phone from his back pocket. "Smile!"

"I wasn't ready!" I protested as the camera clicked, feeling exposed and ridiculous.

"You looked great." He grinned, showing me the photo. It was surprisingly okay with me looking slightly terrified but determined, standing beside the enormous, placid bull.

"Something to remember me by?" I asked, trying for lightness.

"Hope I get the real thing soon enough," he replied softly, wrapping an arm around my waist, pulling me close for a second. His strength, the solid warmth seeping through my jumper, momentarily steadied my nerves, sending a familiar fog through my brain. I inhaled sharply, forcing myself back to the present.

Focus, Megan. I wanted to visit him. I was *going* to visit him. I was certain now. That certainty gave me a sliver of courage.

The line of cattle ahead started moving. Jackson's hand slipped from my waist, the loss of contact sending a shiver down my spine despite the wool jumper.

My pulse kicked up again as the reality of the situation hit me. I held the rope tighter, my knuckles white. His country style, the crisp striped shirt, the pale moleskin jeans clinging to his thighs was ridiculously attractive. He radiated a calm competence that both reassured and intimidated me.

Everything about him screamed 'kiss me,' even as my brain screamed 'don't get trampled!'

I cleared my throat, forcing down the inappropriate thoughts. "Okay," I said, trying to sound composed. "How do I do this?"

"Just walk forward," he instructed, his blue eyes meeting mine, offering quiet encouragement. "He'll follow. Keep a steady pace, hold the rope firmly but not too tight."

"It can't be that simple."

"Try."

Taking another deep breath, channeling every ounce of courage I possessed, I stepped forward, giving the rope a gentle tug. To my astonishment, Bruce lumbered forward beside me, matching my pace. We fell into line, moving toward the main arena entrance.

It's like walking a very, very large, potentially dangerous dog, I thought, trying to suppress a hysterical giggle. It was hard to concentrate. Leading a bull that weighed more than my car, with the man I was rapidly falling for walking calmly beside me was surreal.

My mind kept flickering back to fantasies involving Jackson and unbuttoned shirts, contrasting sharply with the primal energy of the parade.

"He's very well-trained," I managed, needing to break the internal tension.

Jackson chuckled. "Doesn't take much. Besides, he's got his eye on his own prize today."

"What prize?" I glanced up at him. He looked impossibly handsome, relaxed, and in his element.

"Think he's sweet on the heifer walking in front of us," he confided with a wink.

Heat washed up my neck. I turned to the bull. "Is that right, Bruce? Got your eye on someone?" Bruce just snorted, continuing his steady plod.

"Teenage hormones," Jackson sighed dramatically. "Gets 'em every time."

I laughed, the sound slightly shaky but genuine. We entered the main arena, joining the swirling mass of livestock—cattle, sheep, horses, even alpacas—circling the track.

The noise, the smell, the sheer number of animals should have overwhelmed me, but strangely, it didn't. Walking beside Jackson, feeling the steady rhythm of Bruce beside me, a surprising sense of calm settled over me. The butterflies stopped fluttering.

I squared my shoulders, lifted my head, and actually started to enjoy it, soaking up the atmosphere, the energy, the feeling of being part of something ancient and vital. For a fleeting moment, surrounded by the sights and sounds of country life, with Jackson solid and reassuring at my side, I felt like I belonged.

The feeling stayed with me as we completed the circuit and made our way back toward the cattle sheds, Bruce lumbering on my right, Jackson on my left. The fear had receded, replaced by a quiet sense of accomplishment. I'd done it. I'd faced the fear, and it hadn't beaten me.

Now for the other fear. Telling Jackson.

"So," I began, my voice steadier than I expected. "I was looking at jobs earlier..."

"Yeah? Good for you," he replied, scuffing his boot on the ground, his tone carefully neutral. I could sense his disappointment, his assumption that this was my way of confirming I wasn't coming. It made me feel guilty for letting him hang, but I needed to do this my way.

"It's... it's up near Clare," I continued, plunging ahead before I lost my nerve. "Junior photographer role. Probably a long shot, I'm a bit under-qualified, but..."

"Clare?" He stopped walking, looking up sharply, surprise flickering across his face. "Wait. Does that mean...?"

"Yes," I confirmed, meeting his hopeful gaze directly. The nervousness was still there but overlaid with a thrill of anticipation. "Yes, Jackson. I'm coming to visit you, that's if I get the job."

His face broke into a wide, dazzling smile, pure relief and happiness radiating from him. "Really? Megan, that's... that's great. Really great. Well, I'm sure you'll get the job, but you're welcome to visit... I mean..."

"We'll see where it leads, right?" I added, needing to temper the intensity of his enthusiasm and to keep expectations realistic, both his and mine.

"Exactly," he breathed, stepping closer. He dipped his head and kissed me, right there between the cattle sheds. It wasn't frantic like the locker room kiss, or possessive like the breakfast kiss. This one was full of promise, relief, and soaring hope.

I closed my eyes, melting into him, wishing with everything I had that the job application would work out, that visiting the farm would work out, that *we* would work out. It was a huge leap into the unknown, but for the first time, it felt less like falling and more like flying.

CHAPTER 33

My phone rang, its cheerful, upbeat tone dragging me from my current chaos of the cardboard-and-tape-scented ruins of my apartment, trying to decide if the single, chipped mug in my hand belonged in the 'Kitchen' box or the 'Deal With Later' box.

I couldn't find my phone. Fuck, had I packed it? I all but nose-dived into the box in front of me in a flurry of panic, then I saw the light, the name lit up, and my nerves eased a little.

It was Dad. Of course, it was Dad. My stomach immediately clenched with a familiar, low-grade guilt.

"Hey, Dad! How are you?" I chirped, injecting a

level of enthusiasm into my voice that I absolutely did not feel.

"I'm good, love. Just getting my fishing gear sorted for the weekend. Say, you haven't seen my lucky lure, have you? The little silver one with the red feather? Can't seem to put my hands on it."

I froze, the chipped mug still in my hand. The silver lure. The one Mom gave him for their twentieth anniversary. The one I'd borrowed a month ago for a still-life photography project and had sworn I'd put back in his tackle box.

"Um," I said, my brain frantically scanning the disaster zone around me. "I think... I think I might have it here somewhere, Dad. I'll have a look and bring it over."

"No rush, love. Just don't lose it, eh?"

We hung up, and the full weight of my failure as a daughter crashed down on me. I hadn't just packed the milk. I had packed my father's most cherished possession and was now, apparently, planning to lose it in a cross-country move.

Excellent work, I thought. *You've officially graduated from 'thoughtless' to 'actively destructive'. He's probably at home right now, eating canned soup for dinner and talking to the dog for company, and you've just stolen his only source of joy.*

I tore open a box labelled 'Studio Crap.' Nothing but old lenses and a truly frightening number of USB cables for electronics that no longer exist. I moved on to 'Bathroom' where there was definitely no fishing lures, then 'Important Docs' and my will to live.

Nothing.

My panic escalated. I was a terrible daughter. A monster. I was abandoning my lonely, widowed father and taking his lucky lure with me as a sick trophy. I finally spotted it, a small, unassuming box tucked by the door, labelled in my neatest, most optimistic pre-move handwriting: 'Donate to Charity.'

My blood ran cold. I ripped it open, and there, nestled between a questionable self-help book and a scarf I'd convinced myself I'd learn to knit, was a small, Ziploc bag containing one very sentimental, very nearly-donated-to-the-needy, fishing lure.

This was my life now. A state of limbo so profound, I was fundamentally misunderstanding the concept of treasured family heirlooms. My worldly possessions were currently divided into two distinct categories. Pile A, Stuff for Dad's spare room, assuming he still loves me after this, and Pile B, Exhibits for the Museum of Poor Life Choices, should this whole farmer thing go spectacularly wrong. My entire future hinged on an email that still hadn't arrived.

It had been a week. Seven days since I'd watched the red taillights of Jackson's Ute disappear, taking my sanity with them. Seven days of existing in a weird, restless twilight zone where my phone was a permanent, and permanently disappointing, extension of my hand.

Every night, he'd call. His voice, rumbling and warm, would be a balm on my frayed nerves for the first five minutes, and then pure torture for the next fifty. He'd talk about the harvest, the frustration of a broken-down header, the specific golden light that hit the western paddock at dusk. And I'd sit in my sterile apartment, surrounded by the scent of packing tape and anxiety, feeling the hundreds of kilometers between us like a physical chasm.

Our texts were a stilted minefield of longing and restraint.

Jackson: *Just saw a ute that looked like your car. Heart did a stupid jump. Miss you.*

My fingers would tremble as I typed and deleted a dozen replies. My thoughts tangled between what I wanted to write and what I thought I should write. *I miss his hands on my body... No, too slutty. I want to climb him like a tree... No, too desper-ate. Tell him you miss his... personality. Yeah, that's believable.*

In the end, I went for a safe option.

Me: *Careful, Farmer. Don't want you crashing your tractor while daydreaming.*

It was a flirtatious shield, a way to keep things light when everything inside me felt heavy, momen-tous, and terrifying.

The truth was, I was terrified. This thing with Jackson had been born in the hyper-real, intoxi-cating bubble of the show. It was a week of stolen moments, of hayloft encounters and locker-room quickies. The lust was undeniable.

My body was apparently ready to sign a thirty-year mortgage with this man, while my brain was still trying to figure out if he was a good idea or just a really, really good-looking bad one. Could a relation-ship be built on that much heat survive the cold, hard reality of distance?

My phone buzzed on the counter, Kristie's name flashing.

"Please tell me you've heard something," she said, skipping the pleasantries. "Because you sound like you're about to start cataloging your dust bunnies for entertainment."

"Worse." I sighed. "I almost donated Dad's lucky fishing lure to Vinnies."

There was a pause, then a snort of laughter. "Oh, honey. You've got it bad. That's not just lovesick, that's certifiable."

"It's not funny! My lease is up, my apartment is a disaster zone, and my entire future is in the hands of some editor who probably took one look at my application and used it for hamster-cage lining."

"Or," Kristie said, her voice infuriatingly reasonable, "they're a regional newspaper with a small HR department and they're taking their time. You're talented, Megs. They'd be idiots not to interview you."

"But what if they don't?" The words tumbled out. "What do I do? Move back in with Dad? Pretend I don't have a semi-permanent ache in my chest every time my phone doesn't ring?"

"Okay, deep breaths," she said softly. "First, you're not moving back in with your dad. Second, I have news. You know that little stone cottage on the edge of town I told you about? The one with the blue door?"

"Vaguely."

"Well, it's coming up for rent. Six-month lease.

The agent owes my dad a favor. I could probably get you first refusal if you wanted it."

My heart squeezed painfully. A cottage. A real, tangible place. "Kris, I can't commit to that. I don't even have the job."

"It's not a commitment, it's an option. It's better than staying with Jackson right off the bat, isn't it?"

She had a point. Jackson had offered, of course. 'Just stay with us at the farm,' he'd said easily. But the thought of moving straight into his life, his family's home, with the ghost of Erin and the weight of their history was too much. I needed my own space. A place to lick my wounds if I discovered this was all a huge, catastrophic mistake.

"What if it is a mistake, Kris?" I whispered. "What if all we had was lust? That can't sustain a relationship."

"Can't it?" Kristie asked cheekily. "Sounds like a pretty good foundation to me. Look, you two couldn't keep your hands off each other. But you also talked. You laughed. He made you feel safe enough to lead a one ton bull that had previously tried to rearrange your skull. That's not just lust, Megan. That's... something."

I thought of him sitting on the concrete floor of the cattle shed, his face etched with grief. I thought of the surprising tenderness in his touch after the frantic urgency of our lovemaking. She was right. It was something.

"You just have to be brave enough to find out what that something is," Kristie finished gently.

After we hung up, I felt a renewed sense of resolve. I made myself a black coffee and got back to packing. I was methodically taping up a box of books when my laptop, sitting open on the dining table, chimed with a new email notification.

My whole body froze. My heart started to pound.

I sat down, my hand trembling as I reached for the trackpad. My inbox was full of junk. And there, sitting at the very top, in bold, unread text, was a line that made the air leave my lungs in a rush.

From: Margaret Bishop

Subject: Your Application for Junior Photographer

This was it. My finger hovered over the trackpad, a millimeter from knowing. I squeezed my eyes shut, took a deep breath, and clicked.

The email was short, professional.

Dear Ms. Lyall,

Thank you for your application. We were very impressed with your portfolio, particularly your work from the Royal Adelaide Show. We would like to invite you for a video interview this Friday at 10 a.m. to discuss the position further.

I read it once. Twice. A third time. The words swam, refusing to sink in. *Impressed with your portfolio... invite you for an interview...*

A wild, disbelieving laugh bubbled up out of me, a sound of pure, unadulterated shock. It wasn't a yes, not yet. But it was a chance.

I was still staring at the screen, a giddy, half-hysterical grin plastered on my face, when my phone started ringing, its cheerful tone making me jump a foot in the air. I snatched it up, my hands still shaking, not even looking at the caller ID.

"Hello?" I breathed, my voice shaking, knowing it was Jackson.

"Hey, you."

His voice, warm and low and so incredibly real, washed over me, a grounding wire in the middle of my emotional hurricane.

"Hi," I managed, my own voice barely a whisper.

"Sorry to call out of the blue," he said. "Just... I was thinking about you. Actually, that's a lie. I'm always thinking about you." He chuckled softly. "But I was just looking at that photo you sent me, the one of me and Bruce. And I was thinking... I really hate that we're only talking on the phone."

He paused, and I held my breath, my grip on the phone tightening.

"So, I know it's soon, and I know you've got stuff to figure out," he continued, his voice dropping, becoming more serious, more intense. "But I have to ask. Have you made a decision yet, Megan? About coming up here? Because this waiting... it's killing me. I need to know if I'm going to see you again."

I stared at the email on my laptop screen, the words of the invitation glowing like a beacon. I looked around at the chaos of my half-packed life. I thought of the blue door of the cottage, of his arms around me, of the terrifying, exhilarating precipice I was standing on. He needed to know.

And suddenly, so did I.

CHAPTER 34

Jackson

"Everything okay?" I ask, my voice tight with suspense.

There's a pause, just a beat of silence on the line.

The inside of this tractor cab is my own personal circle of hell. A very slow, very dusty, very boring circle. For six hours, my entire world has been the low rumble of the diesel engine, the relentless hiss of the spray boom, and the acrid, chemical tang of herbicide that clings to the back of your throat.

It's a job that requires just enough concentration to stop you from driving into a fence post, but not nearly enough to stop your mind from wandering.

And my mind has only one destination these days, a city apartment hundreds of kilometers away, occupied by a woman who has apparently stolen my brain.

Then I hear a half-sob, half-laugh. "I got it, Jackson."

I frown, my mind blanking. "Got what?"

"The job!" she squeals, and the sound is pure, unadulterated joy. It shoots through the phone, straight into my chest, and blows every last bit of worry and tension clean out of me. "I got the job! The interview was a disaster. I was wearing cat pajamas, but they offered it to me! I'm coming to Clare!"

For a second, I can't speak. The rumble of the tractor fades. The hiss of the spray boom disappears. The whole world just... stops.

"Jackson? Are you there?"

A grin splits my face, wide and uncontrolled. A whoop of pure, primal joy erupts from my chest, echoing in the small cab. I punch the air with my free hand. "You got it? You really got it? Holy shit, Megan!"

"I really got it! I start in two weeks! I've found this little cottage to rent, Kristie helped me..."

She's still talking, her words tumbling out in a rush of excitement, but I'm barely listening. Two weeks. She's coming. She's really, truly coming. The relief is so potent, so overwhelming, it feels like I could float right out of the tractor seat. I'm laughing, just laughing into the phone like a complete idiot.

It's only when she says my name again, a questioning note in her voice, that I snap back to reality.

"Sorry," I say, still grinning like a fool. "I'm just... fuck, Megan. I'm so happy. I can't wait to see you."

"Me too," she whispers, and I can hear the smile in her voice now, the same dizzying happiness that's making my own head spin.

We talk for a few more minutes, making vague, ridiculously exciting plans. I'll help her move her boxes. We'll go out for dinner at the best pub in town. I'll show her the sunset from the west paddock.

"I have to go," she says finally. "I have to call my dad and tell him I'm officially abandoning him."

"Go," I say, my voice soft. "Call me back after."

"I will."

I hang up the phone, my face aching from smiling. I feel ten feet tall, bulletproof. I glance in the rearview mirror, intending to check my spray line.

And my heart stops.

Instead of a neat, precise line of green turning to a faint, dying brown, there's a massive, dark, overlapping swath of destruction. In my euphoric state, I'd completely forgotten to shut off the boom on my last turn. I'd double-dosed, maybe even triple-dosed, a fifty-meter stretch of healthy, promising-looking wheat. It's scorched earth.

"Fuck." Dad is going to kill me.

As if on cue, the CB radio crackles to life, his voice sharp and laced with disbelief.

"Jackson, what in the blue hell are you doing out there? From the house, it looks like you're trying to write your girlfriend's name in bloody herbicide! Get your head out of your ass and pay attention!"

I slump back in my seat, the phone still clutched in my hand. I stare at the scorched patch of crop, a testament to my distraction. My dad is yelling, I've just ruined thousands of dollars' worth of wheat, and I'm in for a lecture of biblical proportions.

And I couldn't be happier.

She's coming. In two weeks, Megan Lyall will be here. And this time, I'm not letting her go. How the hell am I going to survive the next month?

CHAPTER 35

Megan

I was currently in what I'd dubbed Stage Four of Moving, Utter Despair. My official residence was now the floor, where I was using a roll of bubble wrap as a pillow and contemplating a new life as a minimalist hermit. It seemed easier than figuring out which of my seventeen mismatched mugs to keep.

The Five Stages of Moving, as I'd discovered, were a cruel joke. Stage One, Euphoria, lasted four hours. Stage Two, The Reckoning, revealed I was a hoarder of sentimental junk. Stage Three, Bargaining, involved promising my future self I'd never buy another decorative cushion. And now, here I was at despair.

My phone buzzed, the sound muffled by yet another cushion. I burrowed through the debris field that was once my living room to find it.

Jackson: How's the packing going?

I typed back with one thumb.

Me: *Currently questioning every life choice I've ever made. I think my kettle just judged me for owning it.*

A few seconds later, three dots appeared. I couldn't wait for his response.

Jackson: *Just tell me which box the bed is in. It's the only one that matters.*

A jolt, hot, immediate, and entirely inconvenient when you're surrounded by your own filth, shot through me. My fingers hovered over the keyboard.

All that heat and nowhere to put it. I moved my life for a man who primarily saw me as a mattress.

The doorbell rang, saving me from having to craft a reply. I scrambled to my feet, tripping spectacularly over a box labelled 'Crap I Don't Know Where To Put'.

It was Dad. He stood in the doorway holding two cups of coffee and a bag of pastries, a worried frown creasing his forehead as he surveyed the disaster zone.

"I thought you might need reinforcements," he said, navigating the box-strewn landscape.

"You brought caffeine and sugar," I said, kissing his cheek. "You're not reinforcements, you're a one-man army."

He settled himself on the one dining chair that wasn't draped in my underwear and handed me a coffee. "Looks like you're making progress." It was a kind lie. He watched me for a moment, his gaze soft. "You're sure about this, Megan?"

The question was gentle, but it landed with the force of a physical blow. "I got the job, Dad. It's a huge opportunity."

"I know, I know. I'm so proud of you. It's just... it's a long way." What he meant was, *It's a long way from me.*

"I'll come back all the time," I said, the words feeling flimsy.

"Of course," he said, forcing a bright smile. "Right, where do you want me?"

For the next hour, he helped with taping up boxes. I left him carefully wrapping the photo frames from the mantelpiece while I tackled the kitchen. A few minutes later, he walked in holding a sealed box.

"Done with these," he said, looking pleased with himself. He placed the box neatly on a stack by the door. "Just fit them all in that one. Saved you some space."

"Thanks, Dad. You're a lifesaver."

He beamed, then headed back to the living room. I finished packing a box of plates, then went to retrieve the last of the photos. I picked up a frame of me and my sister, then looked at the now-empty mantelpiece. Wait. Where was it?

My heart stuttered. The big silver frame. The one of him and Mom on their wedding day, both impossibly young and beaming.

"Dad?" I called out, my voice tight. "Where's the wedding photo?"

"In the box, love! All wrapped up safe and sound."

I walked over to the stack of boxes he'd been working on. None were labelled 'Photos.' My eyes scanned the room, landing on the box he'd just carried out. The one he'd looked so pleased with. My marker-pen scrawl on the side was stark and clear, 'Donate.'

"No," I whispered. My blood ran cold.

I lunged for the box, my fingers tearing at the packing tape. "Dad! Which box?"

He appeared in the doorway, his face etched with confusion. "That one, I think. What's wrong?"

"Dad, this is the donation box! For the op shop!" I ripped the flaps open, my hands shaking, and started pulling out bubble-wrapped shapes with frantic energy. A vase I hated. A set of placemats. And then, finally, the cool, familiar weight of the silver frame.

I sank to the floor, clutching it to my chest, my breath coming in ragged sobs. The relief was so intense it felt like pain.

"Oh, Megan. Oh, God, I'm so sorry." Dad knelt beside me, his face pale with horror. "I didn't even look at the label. I just saw a box with space in it. I'm so sorry, love."

"It's okay," I choked out, wiping my eyes with the back of my hand. "It's my fault. I shouldn't have... everything's a mess."

Guilt, thick and suffocating, coated the back of my throat. It would have been easier if he'd begged me to stay. But this, him trying to help and me being so lost in my own chaos that I almost threw away our most precious memory? It was a thousand times worse. It made me feel like the world's most selfish daughter.

"Don't you worry about me," he said softly, his hand warm and solid on my shoulder. He'd read my mind. "I'll be fine. I've got the dog. And my golf buddies are threatening to make me their permanent fourth. It's your turn to be happy, Megan. Go get it." He pulled a worn, floral-patterned book from his back pocket. It was Mom's recipe book. "I found this in the kitchen box. Thought you'd want to keep it safe."

I took it from him, my fingers tracing the faded cover. I opened it to a random page. A recipe for lamb stew, with a note scrawled in the margin: *Robert's favorite! Make on a cold night.*

Tears pricked my eyes again, but this time they were different. "Thanks, Dad."

After he left, I stood in the middle of the room, holding my mom's recipe book to my chest. Was I doing the right thing? Was this insane? Uprooting my life for a man I'd known for a handful of days, leaving the one person who needed me most?

My phone buzzed again.

Jackson: *You never answered. Should I be worried?*

I took a shaky breath. I could text him back something safe. Or I could choose. I could choose the terrifying, thrilling future over the quiet, lonely past.

My fingers flew across the screen.

Me: *Never. Just trying to decide if I should pack the lingerie or just wear it for the drive.*

It wasn't just a text. It was a promise. A leap.

The three dots appeared instantly.

Jackson: *Wear it. And drive fast.*

A hysterical laugh bubbled up out of me, half-sob, half-giggle. I sank down onto a box labelled 'Winter Coats' the tension in my chest easing just a fraction. I was leaving my past in a stack of cardboard boxes and driving toward a future I knew only by the sound of his voice and the memory of his hands on my skin. And for the first time, I admitted to myself just how terrifying, and how thrilling, that really was.

CHAPTER 36

Megan

The woman on my phone was a liar.

A calm, British, pathological liar. For the last twenty minutes, she'd been telling me to "Proceed on the current road," a road that had devolved from a respectable two-lane bitumen highway into a dusty, one-lane track that was now little more than a suggestion. And for the last ten minutes, since the screen had frozen on a pixelated map of nowhere, she'd gone completely silent.

So had my phone. No bars. No signal. No hope.

"Recalculating," I muttered to the dead screen, my voice mocking the cheerful tone that had led me to my doom. "Recalculate this, you digital Judas."

I was officially, unequivocally, lost. My little

hatchback, packed to the gills with every worldly possession I hadn't trusted to the removalist truck, was coated in a layer of fine red dust so thick it looked like it had been spray-tanned. The endless expanse of pale, parched grass and skeletal-looking gum trees stretched in every direction, mocking my city-girl naivety.

I'd had a plan. A simple plan. Drive north. Follow the signs. Arrive at the cute stone cottage Kristie had found for me, unpack a few essentials, and wait for Jackson to finish work. Maybe I'd even have a shower and pretend I was the kind of effortlessly cool woman who could move her entire life two hundred kilometers without breaking a sweat or a nail.

Instead, I was on the verge of becoming a cautionary tale for a true-crime podcast.

My only saving grace was a sliver of common sense I'd absorbed from years of watching survival shows with Dad. Clare was north of Adelaide. The sun, currently blazing in the cloudless sky, was my only compass. Keeping it roughly behind my right shoulder should, in theory, be taking me in the right general direction. It was a flimsy, desperate piece of logic, but it was all I had.

The road, and I use that term loosely, was getting

worse. The corrugations were so bad my teeth rattled in my skull, and every so often I'd hit a patch of deep, loose gravel that felt like driving on marbles. I gripped the steering wheel, my knuckles white, my focus narrowed to a tiny pinpoint. Just keep the car straight. Just keep moving.

It happened in a split second. One moment I was crawling along at a sensible twenty kilometers an hour, the next, the steering wheel went terrifyingly light in my hands. The back end of the car swung out, a sickening, graceful slide into chaos. A strangled scream tore from my throat as I wrestled with the wheel, my foot hovering uselessly over the brake, remembering a panicked driving lesson from my dad years ago: *Never brake in a skid, Megs, just steer into it.*

Steer into what? The ditch? Or the fence line made of rusty wire and sheer optimism?

The car fishtailed violently, once, twice, before the tires finally bit into a firmer patch of dirt, lurching me to a stop sideways across the track. I sat there, frozen, my heart hammering against my ribs like a trapped bird. My entire body trembled, a fine, uncontrollable tremor of pure adrenaline and terror.

I switched off the engine. The sudden, absolute silence was deafening, broken only by the frantic thumping of my pulse in my ears. I dropped my forehead against the steering wheel, the plastic warm and sticky beneath my skin. And the tears came. Hot, frustrated, terrified tears.

What in the hell was I doing?

I'd uprooted my entire life. I'd left my dad, my friends, the city I knew like the back of my hand. For what? A six-month job I was probably under-qualified for and a man I'd met during the show. A man whose relationship with me was built on a foundation of hayloft groping, frantic locker-room quickies, and a handful of stilted phone calls.

The doubt, which had been a quiet hum in the back of my mind, now roared to life. This was insane. Real relationships weren't like this. Real relationships were built on shared experiences, on quiet Sunday mornings and arguments about what to have for dinner. They weren't forged in the high-octane, hormone-fueled bubble of a country show. What if I got there and it was all gone? What if, away from the adrenaline and the competition, we looked at each other and realized all we had was a fleeting, powerful blast of lust?

I could turn around. I could limp back to the main road, head south, and be at Dad's place by nightfall. I could call the newspaper and make up some excuse. I could undo all of it.

I wiped my eyes with the back of my dusty hand, leaving a muddy streak on my cheek. No. I'd made a promise to Kristie. I'd made a promise to myself. I had to see this through. Even if it ended in disaster, I had to know.

Taking a deep, shuddering breath, I started the car, carefully maneuvered it back onto the track, and kept driving.

Ten minutes later, like a mirage in the desert, I saw it. A solid, black ribbon of bitumen. A real road. I could have wept with relief. I pulled up to the inter-section, a simple T-junction with no signs, no indica-tion of which way led to civilization. Left or right. It felt like a decision of cosmic importance.

"Eeny, meeny, miny, moe," I whispered, closing my eyes and pointing. My finger landed somewhere to the left. Left it was.

I pulled out onto the smooth, sealed road, the quiet hum of the tires a beautiful, welcome sound. I'd been driving for less than a minute when my phone, sitting silently on the passenger seat, suddenly pinged to life, a cascade of notifications flooding the screen. And then it started ringing, Kristie's face lighting up the display.

"Where have you been?" she demanded, her voice a mix of relief and exasperation. "I've been calling for the last hour! Are you there yet? Do you like the cottage? Did you take a detour via Mars?"

A hysterical laugh bubbled up out of me. "Worse. I took a detour via Satan's back paddock. Kris, I was so lost. My sat nav died, there was no signal, I nearly wrote my car off on some godforsaken dirt track..." The words tumbled out, the near-hysteria of the last hour finally finding a release.

"Oh, honey," she said, her tone softening. "Welcome to the country. Never trust a GPS. You should have just stuck to the main highway."

"You think?" I deadpanned, the familiar banter a comforting balm. "I'm a mess. I'm covered in dust, I probably smell like fear, and I was genuinely considering making a life for myself as a hermit in the wilderness."

"Well, you look like you've found your way out," she said. "The agent left the key under the pot plant by the front door. The blue one. You can't miss it. And she said the power's on and the removalists came yesterday, so everything should be there. Just try not to have a complete meltdown before your farm boy gets there, okay?"

"No promises," I said, but I was smiling. I

followed her directions, and a few minutes later, I saw it.

It was perfect. A tiny, ancient cottage made of warm, honey-colored sandstone, nestled on the very edge of town with paddocks stretching out behind it. It had a wraparound verandah, a chimney, and a front door painted a cheerful, vibrant blue. It looked like something out of a fairy tale. My fairy tale, maybe.

I pulled into the gravel driveway, my legs feeling like Jell-O as I climbed out of the car. The air was different here. It smelled of dry grass, eucalyptus, and clean, open space. I walked up the path, found the key exactly where Kristie said it would be, and was about to put it in the lock when I heard it.

The low rumble of a diesel engine.

I turned, my heart giving a familiar, painful lurch. A dusty, dark blue Ute was pulling up behind my car. He was here. Jackson swung himself out of the driver's seat, and for a second, we just stared at each other across the driveway.

He looked even better than I remembered. He wore a faded work shirt with the sleeves rolled up to his elbows, revealing strong, tanned forearms. His jeans were worn and dusty, and his boots were scuffed. He took off his cap, running a hand through his hair, and his eyes—God, his eyes—were fixed on me, a look of pure, unadulterated relief on his face.

I didn't walk. I ran.

I crashed into him, my arms wrapping around his neck, burying my face in the crook of his shoulder. He smelled of diesel, sunshine, and him.

He staggered back a step, his arms coming around me, holding me so tight it was hard to breathe. I clung to him, the last of the day's terror finally draining away, leaving me weak and shaky in his arms.

"Hey," he murmured into my hair, his voice a low vibration against my ear. "You're shaking."

"I got lost," I whispered into his shirt, the words muffled. "I thought I was going to die out there."

He pulled back just enough to look at me, his hands framing my face, his thumbs gently wiping away the tear tracks and dust from my cheeks. "You're here now," he said softly, his gaze tender and full of a warmth that melted the last of my fear. "You're safe."

And then he kissed me.

It started gently, a soft, reassuring press of his lips to mine. A promise. A welcome. But then the tenderness deepened into hunger and need. I moaned, my hands tangling in his hair, pulling him closer. This wasn't a gentle reunion anymore. This was a reclaiming.

His tongue swept into my mouth, and I met it with my own, the kiss turning frantic, desperate. We hadn't seen each other for over two months, two months of longing and uncertainty, and it all came pouring out in that single, desperate point of contact.

"Inside," I gasped, breaking the kiss to fumble for the key still clutched in my hand. "Let's go inside."

We stumbled up the path together, a tangle of limbs and mouths, his hands already sliding under my shirt to find the bare skin of my back. I finally managed to get the key in the lock, shoving the door open and pulling him into the cool, dim hallway.

The cottage was beautiful. The removalists had done their job. My sofa was against one wall, and my boxes were stacked neatly. It was fully furnished, ready for me. But I barely registered it. All I could see, all I could feel, was him.

He kicked the door shut behind us, pinning me against it, his mouth devouring mine. My keys and bag dropped to the floor with a clatter.

I ripped at the buttons on his work shirt, needing to feel his skin against mine. One of them popped off, skittering across the wooden floorboards. I didn't care.

His hands were at the waistband of my jeans, unfastening them with a rough, impatient tug. We were a mess of frantic, fumbling hands and ragged breaths, shedding clothes as fast as we could.

He lifted me, my back pressed against the cool wood of the door, and my legs wrapped around his waist without a second thought. There was no fumbling for a condom this time, he was already prepared, the wrapper ripped open with his teeth. He entered me in one smooth, powerful thrust, and we both cried out, a shared, guttural sound of homecoming.

It was frantic, almost brutal. There was no tenderness now, only a raw, desperate need to erase the distance, to close the gap that had been between us for the duration of the show.

He moved with a driving, relentless rhythm, and I met him thrust for thrust, my head thrown back, my nails digging into the hard muscle of his shoulders. It was everything I remembered and more, a wildfire of pure sensation that consumed all thought, all doubt, all fear.

The pressure built impossibly fast, a blinding, white-hot supernova, and I shattered, my name a ragged cry on his lips as he followed me over the edge, his own release a hot, pulsing flood deep inside me.

We slumped against the door, our bodies slick with sweat, our breaths coming in harsh, shuddering gasps. He rested his forehead against mine, his eyes closed, his weight a solid, grounding presence.

After a long moment, he gently lowered me until my feet touched the floor, though his arms stayed wrapped around me, holding me up. He kissed my forehead, my eyelids, the tip of my nose, his lips soft and full of a tenderness that was a stark contrast to the storm we'd just unleashed.

I leaned my head on his chest, listening to the frantic beat of his heart gradually slowing to match my own, my arms looped around his waist. We were here. Together. In the hallway of my new home.

Well, I thought, a slow, satisfied smile spreading across my face as I snuggled deeper into his embrace. *Whatever else this is, the passion is definitely still spicy.*

CHAPTER 37

Megan

I woke to the unfamiliar sound of magpies warbling outside my window and the distinctly familiar feeling of a man's leg thrown possessively over mine. For a disorienting second, I had no idea where I was. The light was different, the air smelled of dust and old stone, and there was a large, warm, and decidedly naked farm boy drooling softly onto the pillow next to me.

Then it all came flooding back. The terrifying drive. The tearful reunion. The frantic, desperate collision in the hallway that had left my back imprinted with the grain of the hundred-year-old front door.

A slow smile spread across my face. I was here. He was here. We were here.

I carefully extricated myself from his octopus-like embrace, my movements slow and deliberate. The floorboards were cool beneath my bare feet as I tiptoed around the battlefield of our discarded clothes, my jeans in a heap by the door, his shirt lying forlornly near the fireplace, a single button missing in action. I found my overnight bag and pulled on a pair of shorts and a clean T-shirt, feeling marginally more human.

When I returned from the bathroom, he was awake, propped up on one elbow, his hair a mess, a sleepy, ridiculously handsome grin on his face. The sheet was pooled low around his hips, revealing a very pleasant expanse of tanned, muscular torso. My stomach did a little flip.

"Morning," he murmured, his voice thick with sleep.

"Morning," I replied, trying for casual. "Did you sleep okay?"

His grin widened. "Like a man who just had every ounce of stress and sexual frustration exorcised from his body. You?"

"Pretty much the same," I admitted, a hot blush creeping up my neck. I busied myself by picking up his shirt from the floor. I held it up, pointing to the gap where a button used to be. "Casualty of war."

He laughed, a low, rumbling sound that vibrated through the quiet room. "My dad's going to ask about that. I'll tell him I was wrestling a particularly feisty city photographer."

I tossed the shirt at him, my blush deepening. "Tell him she won."

"Oh, he'll know that already," he said, catching it with one hand. "I haven't been this relaxed in months." He swung his legs out of bed, completely unselfconscious in his nakedness, and started pulling on his dusty jeans. I tried very hard not to stare. I failed. Spectacularly.

"So," he said, zipping up. "As the official, self-appointed welcoming committee for the greater Clare region, I feel it's my duty to give you the grand tour, before you decide to flee back to the city."

"Is it always this quiet?" I asked, following him out into the main living area. The silence was profound. On a Sunday morning in my old neighborhood, I'd be hearing traffic, sirens, and the distant roar of a coffee grinder from the cafe on the corner. Here, there was just the warbling of birds and the faint rustling of leaves.

"Pretty much," he said, pulling on his boots. "Come on. I'll show you the metropolis."

Walking down the main street of Clare was like stepping onto a film set after the crew had all gone home. The wide street was practically deserted. Beautiful old stone buildings stood shoulder-to-shoulder, their verandahs shading empty footpaths. A few cars were parked here and there, but the overwhelming impression was one of stillness.

My city-girl brain was short-circuiting. Where was everyone? Was there a zombie apocalypse and no one told me? The quiet I'd found so charming last night now felt unsettling. A little bit lonely.

Jackson must have sensed my unease because he nudged me gently with his elbow. "Don't look so worried. It's Sunday. People are at home, at church, or nursing a hangover." He gestured with a sweep of his arm. "See? We have everything. A chemist for your headaches, a bank for your millions, a mechanic for when you inevitably hit a kangaroo..."

"Is that a legitimate concern?" I asked, my eyes wide.

"Absolutely," he said with a completely straight face. "And most importantly," he pointed across the street, "not one, not two, but three pubs. We're practically Las Vegas." He turned to me, his expression softening. "It's not a bustling place, Megs. But it's solid. We've got more here than a lot of small towns that are struggling. We're lucky."

He said it with a quiet pride that was surprisingly touching. He loved this place. I looked around again, trying to see it through his eyes. The solid stone buildings. The wide, clean street. The backdrop of rolling hills, just visible at the end of the road.

"And wineries," I added, a smirk playing on my lips. "You forgot to mention the metric ton of wineries. A girl could get used to that."

He laughed, the sound echoing in the quiet street. "See? You're fitting in already."

We found the one pizza place that was open and ordered a large supreme, eating it straight from the box on a bench in a small, manicured park. It was a simple, domestic act that felt more intimate than anything we'd done so far.

"That's you, by the way," he said, pointing with a crust of pizza.

I followed his gaze to a two-story stone building on the corner. It had large, multi-paned windows and looked like it had been standing there since the dawn of time. A simple, elegant sign read, *The Clare Valley Chronicle.*

My stomach did a nervous flip-flop. It was real. Tomorrow, I would walk through that door. Tomorrow, I had to be a professional, I would be there new photographer.

My phone buzzed in my pocket, startling me. Dad. My heart sank. I'd completely forgotten to call him.

"Hey, Dad," I said, trying to sound breezy.

"Megan! Thank God! You were supposed to call when you arrived! I was about to ring the police, send out a search party! Are you okay? Did you get there?" His voice was a torrent of frantic, paternal worry.

"I'm fine, Dad, I'm so sorry," I said, twisting a loose thread on my shorts. "I got here safe. I just... got caught up."

"Caught up? What does that mean? Is the cottage okay? Did the car break down?"

I took a deep breath, glancing at Jackson, who was watching me with a curious, gentle expression. "No, everything's fine. I'm fine, Dad, really. I'm with Jackson."

The name hung in the air between us, a quiet declaration. It was the first time I'd said it to him. The first time I'd linked my new life here, in this town, with him.

Jackson's reaction was almost imperceptible. A slight softening around his eyes, the corner of his mouth twitching into a half-smile before he looked away, giving me my privacy. But he'd heard. And I knew, somehow, that it meant something.

Back at the cottage, as the sun began to dip below the hills, painting the sky in fiery strokes of orange and pink, the mood shifted. The easy, playful energy of the day settled into something deeper, quieter. He followed me inside, and when I turned to face him, he reached out, his hand cupping my jaw.

The kiss wasn't like the frantic collision from the day before. It was slow, deep, and searching. It was a question and an answer all at once. It spoke of relief, of longing, and of a tenderness that made my knees weak.

He led me to the bedroom, our hands linked. The need from before spiked inside me, a sharp memory of our bodies joined at the show, of him rocking me to bliss. But as he spun me to face him, something was different.

The frantic urgency was gone, replaced by a deep, possessive heat in his eyes. He cupped my face in his hands, and his lips met mine, slow and searing. I nearly exploded with desire right there.

My hands roamed his muscular frame, slipping

under his shirt to feel the heat of his skin before moving over his hips and up the hard wall of his chest. This wasn't enough. I needed his shirt off, his bare chest crushing mine. I worked the buttons free, pushed the fabric off his powerful shoulders, and immediately pressed my mouth to his toned muscle, kissing my way downwards.

Stopping at the waistband of his jeans, I unfastened the button, my gaze locking with his as I licked my lips. I pushed the heavy material down his thighs, taking his briefs with them. His hard, thick cock sprang free, already slick and ready.

A sharp contraction of need pulsed between my own legs. I wanted him inside me, right now. But first, I wanted to pleasure him, to know his body more intimately despite the fire raging inside me.

I knelt, taking his full length into my mouth, sucking gently on the swollen tip before pulling back. He groaned heavily, his hands tangling in my hair with a desperate urgency. I played my tongue over his head, enjoying the salty juices that beaded at the tip with every touch.

Then, breathing slow, I took him deep, giving him the full depth of my throat before sucking harder and pulling back again. He wobbled on his feet, his hands gripping my head to keep his balance as I repeated the movement, increasing the pressure from my mouth. Just when I didn't think he could get any harder, he did, growing hotter and thicker against my tongue.

He eased himself from my mouth, his breath ragged. Reaching down, he helped me to my feet. He made quick work of my shirt and bra, then took his time, using his mouth to harden my nipples, flicking his tongue over the tightening nubs until I groaned his name. His hand slipped down between my legs, his fingers finding the moisture that had pooled there as he stripped my jeans and now-damp panties away.

With a grace that took my breath away, he pushed me back onto the bed. He lowered his hot, ready body onto mine, crushing my breasts against his chest with a pressure that sent a bolt of pure pleasure through me. My legs wrapped around his hips, guiding his hard cock to my entrance, where the tip slipped and slid along the length of me in the juices he'd coaxed out.

With a single, powerful tip of his hips, he thrust into me. I groaned as a bolt of heat rushed through me, my intimate muscles pulsing rapidly, demanding more of him. He rocked back and forth, a steady, relentless rhythm pushing me higher and higher toward my peak.

I tumbled out of control as bliss took me to heights I never thought possible, my body convulsing around him. My climax sent him over the edge. He let go completely, his own release a long, shuddering orgasm that seemed to last an eternity as we were joined as one.

Later, tangled in the sheets of my new bed in my new house, the silence felt different. It wasn't empty anymore. It was peaceful, filled with the shared warmth of our bodies and the soft sound of our breathing.

"I should go," he murmured against my hair after a long, comfortable silence.

I pulled back, a protest already forming on my lips.

"You've got your first day tomorrow," he said, stroking my cheek. "You need a proper night's sleep, not me distracting you."

The gesture was so thoughtful, so mature, it caught me off-guard. He was thinking about me, about my career. It wasn't just about the heat between us. A wave of affection, so potent it almost hurt, washed over me.

He kissed me one last time at the door, a long,

sweet, lingering kiss that promised more. Then he was gone, his Ute rumbling softly as it disappeared down the street.

I was alone. Alone in my cottage, in my new town. I walked through the quiet rooms, touching the furniture, my furniture. I laid out my clothes for the morning. A crisp white blouse, smart black trousers, and my favorite boots, hoping it would portray a professional look and show I was capable.

I caught my reflection in the dark glass of the living room window. The terrified woman from the dirt road was gone. In her place was someone calmer, someone who looked content.

Okay, I thought, a small, satisfied smile touching my lips. I survived the drive. I survived the boy. The chemistry is definitely not a problem.

I smoothed down the front of the blouse I'd laid out on the sofa, the smile fading slightly as a familiar knot of anxiety tightened in my stomach.

Now for the hard part, I thought. Tomorrow, I have to prove I belong here.

CHAPTER 38

Megan

Come on, Megan. You are a professional. You are a competent adult. You are not going to throw up from nerves before you even walk in the door.

This was the mantra I'd been repeating for the last ten minutes, my knuckles white on the steering wheel. I was parked a block away from the *Clare Valley Chronicle* office, giving myself a pep talk that wasn't working.

Before leaving the house, I'd changed my outfit three times, finally settling on what I hoped was a "creative but serious" look that probably just screamed "new girl trying too hard."

My camera bag, sitting on the passenger seat, felt like it weighed a thousand kilos.

"Okay," I breathed, finally putting the car in gear. "Showtime."

There was a single, tight-looking parallel park right outside the office. Perfect. Nothing says "I'm a confident local" like flawlessly executing a reverse park under pressure.

I took a deep breath, checked my mirrors, and began to maneuver the car. It was going well. I was a leaf on the wind. I was a parking goddess. I was also, apparently, an idiot who forgot which pedal was the brake.

In a moment of flustered panic, my foot slipped, hitting the accelerator. The car lurched forward onto the pavement, stopping with a gut-wrenching jolt mere inches from a woman who looked old enough to have personally witnessed the town's founding. She was moving with the aid of a metal walker, and she froze, her hand clutching the front of her floral dress. She turned her head, her movements slow and deliberate, and fixed me with a death stare so potent I felt my soul wither.

My hands, slick with sweat, gripped the steering wheel as I sat in the car for a full five minutes, engine off, just staring at the front door of the *Clare*

Valley Chronicle. It looked harmless enough, a simple glass door with the newspaper's name in fading gold letters.

But my stomach twisted into a tight, agonizing knot, churning with a litany of worst-case scenarios: what if they hated me, what if they saw me as just another city girl playing make-believe in their world?

Taking a shaky breath, I decided that stewing in my own anxiety was no longer an option. *Action. You need action.* I turned the key, the engine rumbling to life, and noticed my parking job was crooked as a dog's hind leg, taking up nearly two spaces. A perfect metaphor for how out of place I felt.

Determined to at least *look* like I had my life together, I put the car in reverse to straighten up. Glancing over my shoulder, I saw the coast was clear and began to ease back, only to have my foot slam onto the brake pedal with a force that sent my handbag flying off the passenger seat. The car lurched to a halt mere inches from a woman who had appeared out of thin air, clutching a reusable shopping bag.

A tidal wave of heat surged up my neck and flooded my face. My brain short-circuited. I could only throw my hands up in a gesture of frantic apology, mouthing "I'm so sorry!" through the windscreen. The woman's eyes widened in surprise, but then her expression softened into a soft, crinkling smile that I placed a half-second too late.

Oh god, it was Kim, Jackson's mom.

Mortification, hot and absolute, threatened to swallow me whole. Of all the people in the entire valley to nearly run down on my first day of work, it had to be her. Scrambling out of the car, I fumbled with the locks and grabbed my bag, my movements clumsy with panic.

"Kim! Oh my god, I am so, so sorry! I didn't see you, I was just trying to fix my parking, and I..." I trailed off, gesturing vaguely, my face burning so intensely I was sure it was visible from space.

Kim let out a warm, musical laugh that immediately sliced through my frantic apology. "Well, that's one way to make an entrance," she said, her eyes sparkling with amusement, not anger. She gently placed a hand on my arm, a steadying and profoundly kind gesture. "Deep breaths, love. No harm done. If you're this nervous about your parking, I can only imagine how you feel about walking through that door."

Her perception was so accurate it startled me

into silence. She saw right through the clumsy driving to the terrified woman underneath.

"First-day jitters are a bugger, aren't they?" she continued, her tone conspiratorial and comforting. "Listen to me. Margaret is no fool; she hired you because you're brilliant. You walk in there, you be yourself, and you show them what you can do. Country folk have a nose for nonsense, but they respect someone who's genuine. And you, my dear, are genuine." She gave my arm a final, reassuring squeeze. "We're all so glad you're here."

The knot in my stomach didn't just loosen; it dissolved, washed away by her unexpected and unconditional kindness. I managed a real smile, feeling the blush on my cheeks finally begin to recede. "Thank you, Kim."

"You've got this," she said firmly, before winking. "Now, go on. Knock 'em dead. Just try not to do it literally in the car park."

Laughing, feeling lighter than I had all morning, I turned and walked toward the office, my grand entrance not what I had planned at all.

The inside of the *Clare Valley Chronicle* was a chaotic jumble of desks, paper, and the smell of old coffee. A woman with sharp, intelligent eyes and a salt-and-pepper bob looked up from a computer screen. "Can I help you?"

"Hi, I'm Megan Lyall," I stammered. "The new photographer."

"Megan, good. You're here," Margaret Bishop, the editor, bustled towards me from a side office, she was older, sharp and had a tone that was brisk and all business. "No time for the grand tour. David needs a photographer. A winery just won the national gold medal for their Shiraz, and we need a cover story for the weekend edition. Grab your gear."

Before I could even process what was happening, a man in his late forties with a kind, lived-in face and a rumpled shirt stood up from a nearby desk. He had a wedding ring on his finger and a friendly smile that immediately put me at ease.

"David Pritchard," he said, extending a hand. "Ready to be thrown in the deep end?"

"Ready as I'll ever be," I said, shaking his hand, grateful for his warmth.

Moments later, I was in the passenger seat of his car, my camera bag on my lap, heading out of town. The near-miss with the grandmother was still playing on a loop in my head.

"So, what brings you to Clare? Aside from the

thrilling world of regional journalism," David asked, his eyes twinkling.

"A change of scenery," I said, which wasn't a lie. "And the job, of course."

"Good, good." He nodded. Then he dropped the bomb. "So," he said, his tone casual, "Margaret mentioned you know Jackson Pearce. He's quite the catch around here. Salt of the earth, that one."

Of course. Of course, he knows. A wave of heat rushed up my neck. Welcome to small-town life, Megan, where your dating profile is public knowledge and probably discussed over scones.

"Uh, yeah. I know him," I managed, trying to sound nonchalant.

"Good family, the Pearces," David continued, oblivious to my internal meltdown. "Been farming that land for generations."

Thankfully, we arrived at the winery before I had to elaborate on just *how* I knew the local salt-of-the-earth farm boy. The place was stunning. A seamless blend of modern architecture, all glass and sharp, clean lines of steel, built around the bones of an old stone tasting room.

Massive oak barrels stood like ancient sentinels behind a sleek, polished concrete bar. My photographer brain immediately kicked into gear, the nerves replaced by a familiar hum of creative energy. I saw angles, light, and shadow. I was in my element.

The owner, a man named Julian, was as polished as his winery. He was handsome, charismatic, and spoke about his grapes with the passion of a poet. As he and David talked, I moved around them, snapping photos, losing myself in the satisfying click of the shutter.

"And this," Julian said, his eyes gleaming with pride, "is the champion." He produced a bottle of deep, dark red wine and uncorked it with a flourish. "A celebratory taste is mandatory."

He poured three glasses. My heart sank a little. I wasn't a red wine drinker. To me, it mostly tasted like angry grape juice with a hint of furniture. But I was the new girl. I couldn't refuse.

"To the gold medal," David toasted.

I smiled, clinked my glass against theirs, and took a polite sip. And then I paused. It wasn't angry at all. It was smooth, velvety, and tasted of dark cherries and something warm and spicy. It was delicious.

"Wow," I said, genuinely surprised.

Julian beamed. "Another sip," he insisted.

And so I had another polite sip. And then another as he showed us the barrel rooms. And maybe one more back at the bar. The combination of first-day nerves, an empty stomach, and wine that was dangerously easy to drink was a potent one. By the time we were packing up to leave, the world had taken on a soft, fuzzy edge.

Back at the office, I felt giddy and triumphant. I'd survived. I'd taken good photos, and I hadn't mentioned the near-vehicular homicide to my new colleagues. A successful day. I grabbed my car keys, ready to head home and bask in my glory.

"Whoa there, Speedy," David said, putting a gentle hand on my arm. He peered at my face. "You're a bit flushed. How many 'sips' did you have?"

"Just a few," I said, probably a little too brightly.

He held out his hand. "Keys."

"I'm fine, really," I protested, my cheeks burning for a whole new reason.

"Rules of the road," he said kindly but firmly. "And rules of not letting the new girl wrap her car around a tree on her first day. I'm not having that on my conscience. Who can I call? Jackson?"

The mortification was absolute. My new, kind, middle-aged colleague was calling my new farm-boy boyfriend to come and pick me up from work like I was a teenager who'd had too many ciders at a party. I wanted the floor to swallow me whole.

I nodded mutely, handing over my phone.

Jackson arrived less than ten minutes later. He appeared in the office doorway, leaning against the frame with his arms crossed. He was covered in a fine layer of dust, his work boots were scuffed, and he looked tired. He took in the scene of me, red-faced and wobbly, with David, looking like a concerned parent, and a slow, exasperated smile spread across his face.

"Megan," he said, his voice a dry, amused rumble. "It's been twenty-four hours. Are you trying to set a record?"

The ride home was quiet. I sat staring out the window, replaying every mortifying second of the day. He didn't say anything, just drove, the corner of his mouth twitching every so often.

He walked me to the door of the cottage. The wine was still buzzing through my veins, and now that the acute embarrassment was fading, it was being replaced by something else. Something warm and needy. He was here. He smelled of dust and sunshine and hard work.

I unlocked the door and turned to him, grabbing the front of his shirt. "You could come in," I said, my voice a little husky. I pulled him closer, rising on my tiptoes to kiss him.

He met my kiss, his lips firm and warm. For a

moment, he kissed me back, a deep, thorough kiss that made my head spin even more. But then, he gently pulled away, his hands holding my shoulders to steady me.

"As much as I want to stay," he murmured, his eyes full of a warmth that was both frustrating and incredibly endearing, "I've got a water pump that needs fixing and two hundred sheep that don't care if you're cute when you're drunk. Get some water and go to bed, Megan."

He kissed my forehead, a soft, lingering press of his lips. "I'll see you tomorrow."

And then he left. I stood in the doorway and watched his Ute's taillights disappear down the street. I was alone in my quiet cottage, feeling a dizzying cocktail of emotions from the wine's lingering buzz, the deep, cringing embarrassment from work, and a profound, melting warmth from being so thoroughly and responsibly taken care of.

A slow smile spread across my face.

Okay, so getting drunk on my first day wasn't my finest hour, I thought, closing the door and leaning against it. But being rescued by a handsome farmer who smells like sunshine and responsibility? Maybe that's a new kind of foreplay.

CHAPTER 39

Jackson

The Clare Agricultural Co-op has a unique smell. It's a mix of grain dust, fertilizer, and the burnt coffee that's been stewing in the pot since 6:00 a.m. It's the smell of my entire life. I was grabbing a new filter for the water pump when a heavy hand slapped me on the back, nearly sending me into a display of sheep shears.

"Jackson, my boy!"

I turned to meet Barry Douglas. A man whose voice was as loud as his floral-patterned work shirts.

"Barry," I said with a nod.

"Heard you had to rescue your new city girl-friend from the *Chronicle* office yesterday," he boomed, a grin splitting his sun-weathered face. A couple of other farmers looked over from the counter, their expressions a mixture of curiosity and amusement. "David Pritchard was in here this morning. Said she was three sheets to the wind after tasting Julian's new Shiraz. Can't blame her, it's good stuff!"

I felt a familiar knot tighten in my gut. News in this town traveled faster than a fire in a dry paddock. I forced a dry smile. "She's just enthusiastic about supporting local business, Barry."

"That's one word for it!" He laughed, slapping his knee. "Keep an eye on that one, son. The city ones can be delicate."

I just nodded, paid for my filter, and walked out into the bright morning sun. It wasn't the teasing that bothered me. It was the speed. The efficiency of the grapevine. The story was already out, the narrative already being written, *Megan Lyall, the flighty city girl who gets drunk on the job.* It wasn't true, but truth didn't always matter much around here. I thought of her, trying so hard, and felt a protective anger flare in my chest.

An hour later, I was on the tractor, the familiar rumble of the diesel engine a steady rhythm beneath me. The rhythmic hiss of the sprayers was usually enough to let my mind go blank, but today it was just background noise. My thoughts kept drifting back to Megan.

I couldn't help but smile, picturing her face, flushed with wine and embarrassment. *Cute when she's drunk.* The thought was immediate, followed by a deeper, more complicated pang of worry. I wanted this to work. I wanted *us* to work. And for that to happen, she needed to find her footing here, to earn her own place, her own respect.

This town could be welcoming, but it was also wary. It had a long memory. An incident like that on her very first day, just made the hill she had to climb that much steeper.

Then I thought of last night, and the worry was consumed by a different kind of heat.

Leaving her at that cottage door had been one of the hardest things I'd ever done. The memory was branded on the inside of my eyelids. The way she'd grabbed my shirt, her eyes dark and hazy with wine and want. The taste of her kiss. My own self-control had been stretched thinner than old fencing wire. If I had stayed, I wouldn't have left. I would have wrecked her for her second day of work and then felt like a bastard for it in the morning.

It was a constant war inside my own skin. The responsible man who knew she needed to succeed on her own, versus the man who just wanted to throw her over his shoulder and keep her in his bed for a week. The desire for her wasn't just a spark, it was a full-blown scrub fire, and it was getting harder and harder to keep it contained.

I was so lost in thought that I barely registered the sound of the quad bike pulling up at the end of the row. It was Dad. He cut the engine and watched me finish the pass, his expression unreadable. He was a man carved from the same dry earth we farmed, and he didn't waste words.

"Barry was talking in the co-op," he said, not as a question. "About your girl."

I cut the engine on the tractor, the sudden silence deafening. "He talks a lot, Dad."

"He does," Dad agreed, his gaze fixed on the horizon. "Jackson, a life out here is hard. It takes backbone. A woman who gets sideways on her first day... you just need to be sure she's got what it takes. Before you get in too deep."

He said it with the quiet, practical concern of a man who'd seen too many people try and fail to make a life out here. But it hit me harder than Barry's booming laugh. This wasn't just town gossip anymore. This was a direct question about my judgment.

His words solidified something in my gut. A plan. I'd finish up, shower off the day's grime, and drive into town. I'd pick up dinner from the pub, something solid and comforting, and take it to her. It wasn't a grand gesture. It was just a quiet way of saying, *I'm here. You're not alone in this.* A way to check in, to offer support without making a big deal out of it.

I was on the last row, the sun dipping low and painting the hills in strokes of orange and gold. I felt a sense of purpose settle over me. I could do this. I could be the man she needed and the man I wanted to be.

Then came a violent lurch, a sound like a gunshot, and the sickening, explosive hiss of escaping air.

I climbed down from the cab and stared. The rear tractor tire had blown, and a piece of rubber the size of a small car, was completely, irrevocably flat. Changing it wasn't a matter of a jack and a tire iron. It was a two-hour, grease-covered, back-breaking job involving blocks, chains, and a whole lot of swearing.

The sun was bleeding out of the sky, the warm day turning cool. I was stuck. I couldn't leave the tractor here. I wouldn't make it to town. I pulled my phone from my pocket, my hands already black with grease from checking the damage. I opened my messages and stared at her name. A wave of pure, hot frustration washed over me.

I typed out the only thing I could. Five words that said nothing and everything.

Me: *Can't make it tonight. Flat tire.*

CHAPTER 40

Megan

A woman cannot live on shame and Honey Nut Cheerios alone.

I came to this profound conclusion on my second night in a row of dining on cereal eaten straight from the box while standing in my kitchen. Jackson's 'flat tire' text from the night before had been followed by a morning text that read:

Jackson: *Still fixing it. This thing is fighting me. Sorry, Meg.*

The rational part of my brain accepted this. Tractors are complex. Tires are big. Life happens.

The insecure thoughts in my head, however, were now convinced that 'flat tire' was a complex agricultural metaphor for 'I've realized you're an embarrassing disaster-human and I need to create some distance.'

The silence in the cottage was starting to get a personality. It was a smug, judgmental silence that seemed to say, *See? We told you this was a bad idea.*

"Fine," I said to the empty room, startling myself. "I'll cook. I'll be a functional adult who buys vegetables and everything."

This is how I found myself, twenty minutes later, pushing a shopping trolley with one squeaky wheel around the Clare Valley Foodland. The squeak was the perfect soundtrack for my mortification, announcing my awkward presence with every rotation.

The place was the social hub of the universe. In the ten minutes I'd been there, I'd seen more air-kissing and over-the-aisle gossiping than at a fashion week after-party. On the other hand, I felt like I was wearing an invisibility cloak made of city-girl awkwardness.

I was staring at a wall of pasta sauces, para-lyzed by choice, when a voice, dry as dust and sharp as broken glass, spoke from directly behind me.

"You don't want that one. It's all sugar."

I jumped so hard I nearly took out a pyramid of

canned tomatoes. My blood didn't just run cold, it flash-froze.

It was her. The woman I'd nearly sent to the great beyond with my car. She was even more terrifying up close. Her eyes were a pale, piercing blue, and they were fixed on me with an unnerving intensity. Her walker was parked beside her, a silent, metallic accusation.

"Oh! Hi," I squeaked, my heart attempting to exit my body via my throat. "I'm so, so sorry about the other day. With the car. I'm still getting used to..."

She waved a dismissive, bird-like hand, cutting me off. "You're the new girl. At the paper." It wasn't a question. "You look like you don't know how to choose a pasta sauce."

I was being judged on my grocery skills by the woman I almost flattened. This was my life now.

"I was just..." I began, but she wasn't listening.

She pointed a surprisingly steady, wrinkled finger at the bottom shelf. "That one," she commanded. "The one in the plain jar. It's made by a woman over in Armagh. Tastes like real tomatoes, not all sugar." She peered at me, her head tilted. "You're Jackson Pearce's girl, aren't you?"

The question, coming from her, felt like an interrogation. I nodded mutely.

"Hmph," she grunted, a sound that could have meant anything. Approval. Disdain. A sudden medical event. "His mom, Kim makes a decent sauce. From scratch, of course."

She gave me one last, long, assessing look, from my fashionable but impractical boots to my probably anxious face. Then, with another noncommittal "Hmph," she turned her walker with surprising agility and squeaked away down the biscuit aisle.

I stood there for a full minute, my heart rate slowly returning to normal. I grabbed the sauce she had indicated and proceeded to the checkout, feeling like I'd just survived a final exam I didn't know I was taking.

The girl at the register was young and cheerful, her name tag reading 'Chloe'. "Find everything okay today?" she asked, scanning my items.

"Yep, thanks," I said.

"Oh, you're the new photographer!" she chirped. "My cousin's wife is David Pritchard's sister-in-law. He said you were lovely." The small-town grapevine was not only real, it was apparently more efficient than fiber-optic internet. "And you're with Jackson Pearce! He's such a sweetie. We went to school together. He was always so serious."

She smiled at me, a genuine, welcoming smile.

But all I felt was the crushing weight of being known but not *known*. I was a collection of labels. The New Photographer. The Girl Who Can't Park. Jackson's Girl.

I paid for my groceries and walked back to my car, the bag feeling heavy in my arms. The sun was setting, casting a golden light over the beautiful stone buildings. It was lovely. It was peaceful. And I had never felt more profoundly alone.

Back in the cottage, I cooked the pasta and ate it at my tiny table, the silence pressing in. The sauce was delicious. The old woman was right. Of course, she was. Which was somehow even more annoying. But it didn't matter. I wasn't invisible anymore. I was an exhibit, an interesting new specimen in the town's terrarium.

As I washed my single plate in the sink, I knew with a sudden, burning clarity that Margaret's assignment for the Spring Fair wasn't just a job, it was a chance. A chance to stop being a label and start being a person.

If I was going to be seen, I wanted to be seen on my own terms. I had to get under the skin of this place because if I didn't, it was going to swallow me whole.

CHAPTER 41

Megan

The next day at the office was no better, made worse since I hadn't heard from Jackson since the trouble with his tire. Had coming here to Clair been a waste of time?

The normal hum of keyboards and low chatter felt different, charged. Every time a head popped up over a cubicle wall, I was sure it was to get a look at the new town drunk. My mortification had its own gravitational pull, and I felt like I was walking around in a little cloud of shame. David Pritchard gave me a sympathetic look as I passed his desk.

"You doing okay, champ?" he asked, his voice full of a kindness that felt horribly like pity.

"Fine," I said, forcing a smile that felt like it might crack my face.

Just before lunch, Margaret's voice cut through the air. "Megan. My office."

I walked the green mile to her glass-walled office, my stomach doing nervous backflips. This was it. The 'it's not working out' speech.

I sat down, and she slid a contact sheet of my winery photos across the desk. My heart hammered against my ribs.

"These are fantastic," she said, her tone brisk. "You see the story, not just the subject."

"Thank you." The knots in my stomach eased, maybe I could do this job in the country after all.

"You'll be fine then at the annual Clare Valley Spring Fair is this weekend. Every year we run the same boring photos of smiling politicians cutting ribbons and prize-winning scones. I don't want that." She tapped a finger on the desk for emphasis. "I want a photo essay. I want you to capture the character of this place. The faces, the hands, the life behind the scenes. Get under its skin."

Get under its skin. The one thing I desperately wanted to do. It was more than an assignment, it was a lifeline.

That afternoon, my phone buzzed with a text from Jackson. A long, rambling, deeply apologetic message about the tire, the time it took, and how sorry he was. He asked if he could come over tonight to make it up to me.

A surge of relief, so potent it made me dizzy, washed over me. I felt a sudden need to take back some control, to create the normal, easy date night I was craving.

I quickly sent a reply.

Me: *No, let me make it up to you. You fix the tractor, I'll fix the food. Come over around 7?*

His reply was immediate.

Jackson: *Deal.*

For the next few hours, I was a woman on a mission. I was a domestic goddess. I was the picture of a cool, capable girlfriend who could whip up a delicious meal at a moment's notice. In reality, I was a woman who bought expensive pasta and the jar of sauce the terrifying old woman had pointed out, but the fantasy was what mattered.

He arrived at seven on the dot. And he looked wrecked. It was the only word for it. He'd showered, but he looked like he'd been wrestling with a truck engine, and the truck had won. An aura of diesel and honest-to-God dirt clung to him like a second skin, and there was a deep, bone-deep exhaustion in his eyes.

"Hey," he said, his voice rough. He gave me a tired smile that still managed to make my stomach flutter.

We ate at my tiny kitchen table. The conversation was stilted, full of holes that I tried, and failed, to fill. After a few bites, he mostly just pushed the pasta around his plate.

"Let's go sit on the couch," I said, taking his plate.

He followed me, sinking into the cushions with a heavy sigh. This was it. The moment I'd been waiting for. He put his arm around me, pulling me in close so my head rested on his shoulder. The familiar, solid feel of him was intoxicating.

"I'm so sorry, Megan," he murmured, his voice a low rumble against my hair. "I really wanted to..."

His voice trailed off. His breathing, which had been shallow, suddenly deepened into a slow, steady rhythm. His arm, which had been holding me firmly, went slack. His whole body went heavy against mine.

He was asleep.

He had fallen asleep. Mid-sentence.

For a full minute, I didn't move. A hot flash of pure, undiluted annoyance surged through me.

Are you kidding me? I thought. *I cook, I wait, I get my hopes up, and you fall asleep?* I had a primal urge to poke him in the ribs.

But then, the anger fizzled out. I shifted just enough to look at him. His face, usually set in a line of quiet competence, was completely slack. His jaw was unclenched, the small lines of stress around his eyes smoothed out. He was totally, utterly gone. This wasn't a rejection. It was a surrender. He felt safe enough with me to let his guard down so completely that his body just quit.

And that's when a new feeling, a profound and aching loneliness I hadn't let myself acknowledge, finally settled into my bones. It wasn't the loneliness of being alone in the cottage. It was the loneliness of being with someone and realizing you were worlds apart.

The farm wasn't just his job, it was a vast, needy creature that demanded all of his energy, all of his strength. He was right here, my head on his chest, and he was a million miles away, lost in a world of broken machinery and endless work I couldn't even begin to comprehend.

I must have drifted off myself, because I woke with a start to the sound of a groan from the couch. The first pale light of dawn was filtering through the windows. Jackson was stirring, stretching his long limbs and blinking in confusion.

A floorboard creaked in the lounge. I sat up, my heart giving a slow, heavy thud. In the pale pre-dawn light filtering through the window, I saw him. He was standing there, rumpled and lost, and as he took in his surroundings, a look of such absolute mortification bloomed on his face it was like watching a physical blow land.

"Oh, God," he whispered, burying his face in his hands. "Megan I didn't mean to fall asleep."

"It's fine," I said, my voice husky with sleep.

"No, it's not fine," he said, scrambling to his feet. He looked rumpled and lost. "I fell asleep on you. On our date." He couldn't seem to look me in the eye. He started gathering his things, his boots, his keys, with a frantic energy. "I have to go. The stock..."

"Jackson, it's okay," I said, standing up.

He finally looked at me, and his eyes were full of an apology so deep it hurt. He crossed the room in two strides, gave me a quick, clumsy kiss that was more of a collision than a caress, and then he was gone. The front door clicked shut behind him, leaving me alone in the quiet, gray light.

The awkwardness of that morning set the tone for the rest of the week. At work, I felt like a tourist.

I'd hear David and Margaret talking about people I didn't know about events that had happened years ago, about the upcoming fair. I was an observer, a satellite in a fixed orbit around a world I couldn't quite enter.

I'd come home to the cottage, and the silence would press in. I tried to unpack another box, this one filled with old photo albums. I opened one and saw a picture of me and my friends from the city, laughing, arms slung around each other at a crowded bar. A pang of homesickness, sharp and painful, hit me so hard I had to sit down.

On Thursday afternoon, I couldn't take it anymore. I pulled out my phone, my thumb hovering over his name.

Me: *Hey. Are we still on for the fair on Saturday? No pressure if you're swamped.*

The "no pressure" was a lie. The pressure was immense. It felt like everything was riding on his answer. The three dots of doom appeared and disappeared twice before a reply came through.

Jackson: *Absolutely. Wouldn't miss it. I want to show you a proper country show. I'll even win you a stuffed animal.*

The relief was so sudden and so complete that it felt like I could breathe again. The hope, bright and buoyant, flooded my chest. This was it. A real date. A chance to be a part of his world, not just a spectator in it.

Margaret's words echoed in my head. *Get under its skin.*

The Spring Fair wasn't just an assignment anymore. And after his promise, it wasn't just about winning a stuffed animal. It was my way in.

If I couldn't pull him into my world, I had to find a way to enter his. I had to understand the life that made this strong, capable man so tired. It wasn't just about getting under the town's skin anymore. It was about finding a way under his.

CHAPTER 42

Megan

THE PHONE CALL came just after eight, as I was trying to decide if wearing pristine white sneakers to a country show was a rookie mistake of catastrophic proportions.

"Megan," Jackson's voice crackled down the line. He sounded like he'd been gargling gravel. "I'm so sorry."

My stomach dropped. This was it. The blow-off. My brain, a seasoned connoisseur of rejection, immediately started cataloging the possibilities. *His prize-winning sheep has anxiety. A rogue cloud looks threatening. He's remembered he's a rugged farmer, and I'm a girl who is used to a concrete jungle and lights and the heaviest thing I lift is my camera.*

"Jackson? Are you okay?" I asked, my voice impressively steady.

There was a heavy sigh on the other end. "The calf is sick. A new one. I can't leave her." There was a low, mournful moo in the background as if for dramatic effect. "She's not taking milk, and her temperature's up. I've been up with her all night. I really wanted to go with you, Meg. I'm so sorry."

He sounded so genuinely gutted, so completely frustrated, that the balloon of my own disappointment deflated with a sad little hiss. This wasn't a convenient excuse. This was his life. A life that involved sick baby cows, sleepless nights, and responsibilities I couldn't even work out.

"Don't be sorry," I said, and I meant it. Mostly. "Is she going to be okay?"

"I hope so. Dad and I are doing everything we can. I just... dammit. Today was supposed to be for us."

"It's okay," I said again, my voice softer this time. "You do what you have to do. I'll hold down the fort at the scone stand."

We hung up, and I stood in the middle of my little cottage. Okay. Pep talk time. I was a big girl. I was a professional photographer on a mission. I did not need a handsome farmer to hold my hand while I navigated a crowd of people comparing the size of their pumpkins.

I grabbed my camera bag, put on the white sneakers anyway as a small act of defiance, and headed out the door.

The Clare Spring Fair was a full-body assault on the senses: the air thick with sizzling onions, spun sugar, and a potent livestock perfume I chose not to identify. The entire population of the valley must have been crammed into the dusty paddock, a complex social web woven from decades of shared history and gossip. Among them, I was a Roomba with a broken sensor, bumping aimlessly into the legs of a world that wasn't mapped for me.

I took a deep breath and pulled out my camera. Work. Focus on work.

I pushed through the crowd, letting my lens do the talking. I found the story in the details. The gnarled, dirt-caked hands of a shearer, resting on a fence post. The laser-focused gaze of a teenager in the poultry pavilion, her entire world narrowed down to the prize-winning hen she was cradling like a Fabergé egg. I captured the organized chaos of the wood-chopping competition, all flying splinters and straining muscles.

The photos were good. I knew they were. But I felt like I was in a glass box, observing life through a viewfinder. I was documenting the skin of this place, but I was nowhere near getting under it.

And then, just as I was lining up a shot of two old-timers in a heated debate over a prize-winning rose, my camera battery died. Of course it did. The universe, it seemed, had decided my observation period was over.

Frustrated and needing a break, I wandered toward a large marquee with a sign that read 'CWA'. The air inside was warm and sweet, smelling of strong tea and baked goods. I got in line and ordered a scone and a cup of tea from a woman with kind eyes and a fine dusting of flour on her apron.

She passed me the plate. "That's a serious-looking camera you've got there, dear."

"I'm the new photographer for the *Chronicle*," I explained.

Instead of a polite nod, her eyes twinkled. "Ah," she said, her voice full of a knowing, cheeky warmth.

"So, you're the one who got sideways on Julian's Shiraz. And you must be Jackson's girl."

Was I ever going to live down drinking too much shiraz?

But the shame never came. The woman, whose name tag read 'Evelyn', simply patted my hand.

"Don't you worry about that," she said with a conspiratorial wink. "Anyone who appreciates good wine is all right in my book. Jackson's a good boy. Stubborn as his father, but he's got his mother's heart."

What could I possibly say to that? *Thanks, I hope I'm worthy of his good heart?*

Her casual warmth only made it worse, highlighting how much I felt like an outsider playing a part. Every kind word felt like another line in a job description I wasn't qualified for, and the doubt coiled cold and heavy in my stomach.

Evelyn's smile turned knowing, as if she could read my mind. "Oh, Kim's a dear. Kim makes the best sponge cake in the valley. She'll be so happy to see him with a lovely girl like you. He was always such a serious little boy. I remember one year at this very fair, he must have been seven or eight, he spent his entire pocket money, two whole dollars, at the ring toss, trying to win a little glass horse for her. He never did win it, but he stood there for hours, determined."

Evelyn's story settled in my chest, a warm little ember glowing through the last hours of the fair and all the way back to the cottage. For the first time all afternoon, a genuine smile found its way to my lips. The ugly scene with Julie from the show finally began to fade, replaced by a much clearer image: a small, serious boy with dusty knees, spending his every last cent to win a glass horse for his mom. It was more than a cute anecdote; it was a window into his character, a piece of him that was real and solid, untouched by all the recent drama and hurt.

When I pulled up to my cottage, a small cooler bag was sitting on the doorstep. My heart gave a hopeful little leap. I picked it up and carried it inside, setting it on the kitchen counter. Inside was a glass bottle of fresh milk, condensation beading on its sides, and a jar of dark red jam. A simple, hand-written label was tied to the jar with a piece of twine.

Jackson: From Mom's recipe. Sorry about today.

I'd been checking my phone all afternoon, waiting for a text, an excuse, anything. But this was better. The gesture was so incredibly thoughtful it made my chest ache.

I ran my thumb over the cool, beaded glass of the

milk bottle. The jam, made from his mother's recipe, felt like a peace offering. An invitation. But the silence of my empty kitchen was a loud reply, and for a moment, the sweetness of the gift only made the loneliness feel sharper.

CHAPTER 43

Jackson

The barn was quiet except for the soft rustle of hay and the occasional, healthy bleat from the pen. The calf, now full of milk and no longer radiating heat like a furnace, was finally asleep. I leaned against a support beam, the exhaustion so deep it felt like it had settled in my bones. It was a good exhaustion, the kind that comes after a win. But it was hollowed out by guilt.

I'd spent the whole day picturing Megan at the fair. Picturing her wandering through the crowds alone, a city girl in a sea of unfamiliar faces, probably wearing shoes that were totally wrong for the terrain. I'd let her down again. It was becoming a pattern.

The farm would demand its pound of flesh, and I'd offer up our plans as a sacrifice. Dropping the jam and milk on her doorstep felt less like a romantic gesture and more like leaving supplies for a castaway I'd marooned. I was failing some fundamental test of being a boyfriend, constantly showing up with an apology instead of just showing up.

The heavy scrape of boots on concrete pulled me from my thoughts. I turned to see dad walking over to the pen and looked down at the sleeping calf, his expression giving nothing away.

"She'll make it," he said. It was the highest praise he was likely to give.

"Yeah. She's a fighter."

He nodded, his gaze drifting toward the open barn door. "Saw your girl at the show today, but not you."

"Yeah, well. Work doesn't do itself," I said, gesturing vaguely toward the barn's interior. I'd wanted to go, but Dad had been running himself ragged lately. Letting him and mom have the fair to himself felt like the right thing to do.

"Yep." He paused, rubbing the back of his neck. "Saw her talking to Evelyn for a good long while."

I waited. There was more coming.

He finally looked at me, a flicker of something,

surprise maybe, in his eyes. "Evelyn doesn't suffer fools gladly."

And that was it. He clapped me on the shoulder, a rare gesture, and walked out of the barn. But that one sentence landed like a thunderclap in the quiet of my mind.

It was my dad's version of a glowing five-star review. Evelyn was a cornerstone of this town, a woman whose quiet approval meant more than the mayor's. And Megan had earned it. On her own. While I was here wrestling a sick animal, she was out there, navigating my world without me.

A fierce, unfamiliar surge of pride washed through me, so potent it pushed back the exhaustion. Megan wasn't fragile. She wasn't waiting for me to rescue her. She was diving in headfirst.

The guilt didn't disappear, but it changed shape. It became a motivator.

I pulled my phone out of my pocket, my fingers clumsy with dirt and fatigue. I scrolled through my contacts, past 'Barry Co-op' and 'Dave Fencing', until I found the number I was looking for. I'd driven past the place a hundred times: The Vintner's Table. The only restaurant in the valley with linen tablecloths.

My call was answered by a woman with a voice

smoother than the Shiraz they served. I booked a table for two for the following night, feeling like I was trying to order a spare part for a machine I didn't know how to operate. A proper date. No tractors, no emergencies, no excuses.

The next evening, I scrubbed every last trace of the farm from under my fingernails, put on my good shirt, the one without a faded machinery logo on the pocket, and drove to her cottage feeling a level of optimism that was borderline reckless.

She opened the door, and her smile hit me like a physical force. "You're here! And you're awake!" she teased.

"For now." I grinned, stepping inside. "You look amazing."

"You clean up nice, farmer Jackson." She was practically vibrating with excitement. "Before we go, you have to see these. I spent all morning editing."

She pulled me over to her laptop. "Okay, so this is what I got from the fair..."

She started clicking through the photos. And they were incredible. She'd captured it all. The raw, unvarnished truth of the place. I saw Barry's son, grinning like an idiot after winning the woodchop, sawdust clinging to his sweaty brow. I saw the gnarled, arthritic hands of old Mr. Henderson, the man who taught me how to fish, cradling a prize-winning tomato.

I felt that same surge of pride from the night before. "Meg, these are... wow."

"Right?" she said, her voice full of passion. "I just love the honesty of it all. The reality."

She kept clicking. And then I saw it. A photo of Evelyn. She was looking at something off-camera—at Megan, I realized—with that warm, knowing smile. She was framed by her stall of prize-winning jams and cakes, a quiet queen in her kingdom of sugar and flour. It was a beautiful shot. Perfect.

But seeing it, seeing all of them, stirred something else inside me. A confusing, unsettling feeling. This wasn't just a collection of anonymous, rustic faces to me. This was my life. These were my people. And seeing it all laid out, captured and framed and turned into art felt intimate. Too intimate. Like she'd walked through my house, my history, and taken souvenirs.

A surge of pride in her talent brought with it a strange, protective defensiveness. Then came the awareness, sharp and sudden: I was being observed. Studied. The attention was invasive, and I instinctively recoiled from it.

CHAPTER 44

Megan

The Vintner's Table was exactly as advertised. It had linen tablecloths so blindingly white I was worried they might be sterile, and a tactical array of forks laid out beside my plate. I was immediately confronted with a tiny one that looked like it was designed for Barbie's first seafood platter. This was it. A real date. A grown-up, no-chance-of-falling-asleep-on-the-couch date, and my first challenge was not to accidentally spear a bread roll with the wrong utensil.

Jackson, in his good shirt, looked handsome and solid and about as comfortable as a cat in a car wash. He kept shifting in his chair, a beautifully carved wooden thing that was probably a local artisan's masterpiece, as if it were actively trying to bite him. On the other hand, I was practically levitating.

The waiter, a man who moved with the silent, unnerving grace of a ninja, brought us a basket of bread that was still warm and poured us wine. I was buzzing, riding the wave of hope that had started in the CWA tent and crested when I'd seen the jam on my doorstep.

"I'm so excited about this photo series," I said, leaning forward after the waiter vanished into the shadows. "Margaret is going to lose her mind. I was talking to Evelyn, the woman from the CWA tent, the one who knew your mom, and she was telling me all these stories. It just clicked for me. I don't want to just take pictures of the town, I want to capture its *life*."

Jackson nodded, taking a sip of his wine. He was listening, but his eyes had that same distant look I'd seen when he was looking at the photos on my laptop. It was the thousand-yard stare of a man who spends his days looking at, well, a thousand yards of wheat.

"I just want to capture the reality of it all," I said, my voice full of the passion I was feeling. "The struggle is part of the beauty. It's so real, so honest."

The word hung in the air between us, suddenly heavy and awkward. *Struggle.*

Jackson's posture changed. It was subtle, just a stiffening of his shoulders, but I felt it like a drop in barometric pressure. He slowly placed his fork down on his plate. The small clink of metal on ceramic was deafening in the whisper-quiet restaurant.

He looked at me, his gaze flat. "It's easy to find the 'beauty' in the struggle when you get to go home to your quiet cottage, Megan. It's different when you're the one living it."

And there it was. The slap. Not a physical one, but an emotional one, delivered with the quiet precision of a surgeon.

My face burned. The fancy restaurant suddenly felt like a stage, and I was the star of a one-act play titled *Girl Makes a Complete Fool of Herself.*

"Is that what you think this is?" I asked, my voice a low, trembling thing I barely recognized. My hands were shaking under the table, so I clasped them together, trying to stop. "That your life is just a quaint little photo project for me?"

The hurt was so sharp, so unexpected, it morphed into something else. Something hot and furious.

"I was trying to understand you," I said, my voice

rising, forgetting to whisper. A woman at the next table glanced over, her expression disapproving. "To understand this place because I'm falling for you, you idiot!"

Oh, God. Did I just say that out loud? In a restaurant where people use different forks for fish and feelings?

The dam didn't just break, it exploded. Every frustration, every lonely night, every moment I'd felt like an outsider came pouring out of me in a torrent.

"I am so lonely here, Jackson! I feel like a ghost half the time. And when I finally make a connection, when I finally feel like I'm starting to get it, you throw it in my face! You cancel plans, you fall asleep on me, you make me feel like I'm a million miles away even when I'm in your arms!"

His face was a mask of shock, then pain, then a frustration that mirrored my own.

"I was up for thirty-six hours with a sick animal that my family's livelihood depends on!" he shot back, his voice louder now, definitely drawing glances. The ninja-waiter materialized near the kitchen door, his face a perfect mask of professional neutrality, but his eyes were wide. He was enjoying the show. "What do you want from me? I'm not some guy from the city who can just clock out at five p.m.

This is my life! And I'm terrified that you'll get tired of it and leave because you don't understand that the 'struggle' isn't beautiful when it's three a.m. and something is dying!"

His words sucked all the air out of my lungs. Because there it was. His biggest fear. And it was terrifyingly close to my own. *He's right,* I thought. *I would barely handle a dead phone battery. How was I going to handle a dead cow?*

The fight was over. There was nothing left to say. The anger was gone, leaving behind a wasteland of hurt. Our fancy appetizers sat between us, completely forgotten. The waiter approached our table, took one look at our faces, and retreated without a word, a true master of his craft.

The drive home was a special kind of torture. The silence in the cab of his Ute was thick and suffocating, broken only by the crunch of gravel under the tires. My thoughts were having a party, replaying every single horrible word in my head, and providing helpful color commentary.

You idiot! Really, Megan? Eloquent. And when he mentioned the sick calf, you could have shown a little empathy. But no, you made it all about your lonely little feelings. I stared out the passenger window, watching the dark vineyards streak by, my own reflection a ghostly, miserable stranger. Jackson gripped the steering wheel, his knuckles white.

He pulled up outside my cottage and killed the engine. The sudden, absolute silence was heavier than the noise of the argument. It was a weighted blanket made of regret and unspoken accusations.

Neither of us moved or spoke. We just sat there in the dark, separated by a few feet of vinyl and a gulf so wide I had no idea how we could ever cross it. He smelled of soap and frustration. I probably smelled of expensive wine and failure.

CHAPTER 45

Megan

The silence in the Ute had been a cold, heavy passenger sitting between us. The silence in my cottage, after the click of the front door, was a living thing. It was a predator, circling me in the dark, its teeth bared.

I stood in the middle of the living room, still wearing my fancy date-night dress. It felt like a Halloween costume for a character I was no longer qualified to play: Happy, Hopeful Girlfriend. I'd been so sure, so ridiculously, naively sure that tonight was the turning point.

Turns out, it was. Just not in the direction I'd planned.

My hands trembled. I reached behind my back to unzip the dress, but my fingers were clumsy, shaking too hard to get a grip on the tiny, delicate zipper. It was stuck. Of course, it was stuck. I was literally trapped in the uniform of my own failure. A hysterical little laugh bubbled up in my throat. I yanked harder, twisting my arm at an unnatural angle, and the zipper gave way with a sharp, tearing sound. Great. I'd not only destroyed the relationship, but I'd probably destroyed the dress, too.

I ripped it off, my movements awkward and frantic and threw it in a heap on the floor. I pulled on the oldest, softest T-shirt I owned, a faded band tee from a concert I went to when I was nineteen, seeking a comfort that wasn't there.

My laptop was still on the kitchen table, open to the photos from the fair. I sank into the chair, my body feeling like it weighed a thousand kilos, and forced myself to look.

I saw them through his eyes now.

The photo of Evelyn, which had felt like a connection, a gift, now looked like an invasion. I hadn't captured a quiet queen in her kingdom. I'd stolen a piece of her for my own artistic vanity. I hadn't earned the right to be in her kingdom, and I'd barged in anyway with a camera, like some kind of digital colonist.

I clicked to the next one. The gnarled, arthritic hands of old Mr. Henderson, cradling his prize-winning tomato. Before, I'd seen the honesty. The reality. Now, I saw a man's pain, a life of hard labor etched into his knuckles, and I'd called it beautiful. I'd turned his struggle into an aesthetic.

Jackson was right. My God, he was so right.

A wave of nausea washed over me. I slammed the laptop shut, the clack of plastic echoing the final, definitive sound of the fork hitting the plate in the restaurant. The sound of it all ending.

My phone, lying on the counter, buzzed. Jackson's name lit up the screen.

Jackson: *Meg. I'm so sorry. That's not what I meant.*

I stared at the words, my vision blurring with tears I refused to let fall. *But it is what you meant,* I thought. It was the truest thing he'd ever said to me.

I didn't reply. A minute later, the phone started ringing, his face appearing on the screen. My hand shot out and slapped the silence button so hard the phone skittered across the counter. I couldn't talk to him. What would I even say? *Hi, sorry for being a shallow parasite who tried to turn your generational trauma into a pretty picture for my portfolio?*

I switched the phone to silent and left it on the counter, a blinking, accusing light in the darkness.

Sleep was a joke. I tossed and turned, the fight playing on a loop in my head. His face, a mask of hurt and frustration. My own voice, high and shrill with a loneliness I'd finally confessed, only to have it thrown back at me as proof of my own weakness.

The next morning, I felt like I'd been run over by a tractor. A really big one. With a flat tire.

I had to go to work. I had to face people. I put on my emotional armor in the form of black trousers, a black blouse, and a face of makeup so carefully applied it could have survived a hurricane. The foundation was a little too thick, the eyeliner a little too severe.

The office was a discord of normal life that felt like a personal attack. Keyboards clattered. Phones rang. David was laughing about something with Margaret. I ducked my head and made a beeline for my desk, desperate to become invisible.

It didn't work.

"Morning, champ," David said as I passed, his voice gentle.

"Morning," I mumbled, not meeting his eye.

He appeared at my desk a few minutes later, holding a cup of coffee. He placed it down beside my keyboard. I stared at it as if it were a venomous snake.

"You okay?" he asked quietly.

I couldn't look at him. If I looked at his kind, concerned, fatherly face, I would shatter into a million pieces right here, all over my desk. Kindness was a weapon I was not equipped to handle right now.

"Just tired," I said, my voice a brittle whisper.

He was silent for a long moment. I could feel his gaze on me, full of a pity that felt like acid on my raw nerves. "All right," he said softly, and I heard the unspoken words hanging in the air between us. *If you need anything.* He squeezed my shoulder gently before walking away.

I stared at the coffee, a perfect, thoughtful gesture that only made the ache in my chest worse. The tears I'd been holding back all night finally won. One hot, traitorous tear slipped down my cheek. It hit my carefully applied 'waterproof' mascara, which immediately betrayed me, creating a gray, muddy track down my face. My armor had failed.

I had left my dad, my friends, my entire life. I had driven down a godforsaken dirt track and into the arms of a man who I thought saw me, a man whose world I was desperate to understand.

And in one night, in one fight, I had lost it all. I wasn't just a ghost in this town anymore. I was a ghost in my own life, with smudged eyeliner and a broken heart, and I had absolutely no idea what to do next.

CHAPTER 46

Jackson

There's a specific, hollow ring a spanner makes when you throw it against the concrete floor of a silent shed at two in the morning. It's not a satisfying crash. It's a thin, metallic shriek that says, *You're an idiot, and now you've got to bend over and pick me up.*

I bent over and picked it up.

My hands shook, from the replay reel spinning behind my eyes. The look on her face when the words left my mouth. It wasn't anger, not at first. It was a look of pure, unadulterated shock as if I'd reached across the table and slapped her. Then the shock had curdled into a deep, shimmering hurt that had knocked all the air out of the room.

I'd taken her loneliness, something she'd

confessed to me, trusted me with, and I'd sharpened it into a weapon. I'd used it to stab her. All because she saw beauty in a life I only saw as a struggle. I'm a real fucking idiot.

I leaned my forehead against the cold metal of the tractor, the smell of diesel and grease filling my lungs. I'd been trying to fix the seized bolt on the hydraulic arm for three hours, a simple job that had turned into a war. Every time I put my weight on the wrench, the metal groaned but didn't give. It was a perfect metaphor for my entire bloody life. Applying brute force to a problem that needed a different touch, and just making everything tighter, more broken.

You broke it, a quiet voice in my head stated, calm and final. *And you can't fix this one with a wrench.*

I'd proven my own worst fear correct. I wasn't the guy who could make the city girl happy. I was just the farmer who would inevitably drag her down into the mud with him.

My phone was a dead weight in my pocket. I'd pulled it out a dozen times. Stared at her name. I'd texted the word 'sorry' but it looked piss-weak and pathetic on the screen, so I'd deleted it. I'd typed, *That came out wrong,* but then deleted that, too. How do you explain, in a text message, that you're so terrified of someone leaving that you create the very reason for them to leave? It was insane.

I'd called. Twice. It went straight to voicemail, a digital abyss that felt more final than a slammed door. The silence on the other end was louder than any argument. It was a solid wall I had no idea how to break through.

I didn't go to bed. I just stayed in the shed until the first hint of gray lightened the sky, my gut churning with a toxic cocktail of shame and regret.

When I finally walked into the kitchen, Mom was there, nursing a mug of tea. She took one look at my face and her calm expression sharpened with concern, her posture straightening. She didn't ask what was wrong. She knew.

She set her mug down on the counter with a firm *clink*, the sound cutting through the quiet morning air. "I know that look. Don't you start down that road."

Her tone wasn't weary or sad; it was bracing, like a splash of cold water. "That girl has more grit in her little finger than some people have in their whole body. This life isn't easy, but don't you dare mistake a tough day for a weak spirit. Megan is a fighter."

It wasn't a soft comfort. It wasn't a gentle platitude. It was a direct order, a shot of steel delivered with the unwavering conviction that only she possessed. Where my father might have offered sympathy for a struggle, my mother demanded respect for the person struggling. She wasn't preparing me for failure; she was reminding me of Megan's strength, and in doing so, challenging me to find my own.

Her certainty caught me off guard. "I know she is, Mom," I managed, my voice rough. "But..."

She cut me off before I could finish, her gaze unwavering. "But nothing. This life tests everyone. It tested me, it tested your father. Now it's testing her. The question isn't whether *she's* tough enough. The question is whether you're going to stand there feeling sorry for yourselves or get back out there and be the partner she deserves."

Later that day, I had to go into town for that hydraulic fitting. I drove the Ute on autopilot, my brain numb, replaying the fight, my dad's words, the silence on the phone. I was halfway down the main street when I saw it.

Her car.

The little white hatchback, parked neatly in front of the Clare *Valley Chronicle's* office. It looked so out of place, so clean and small against the dusty Utes and farm trucks that lined the rest of the street. It was her. A little piece of her world, sitting right there in the middle of mine.

A physical ache, sharp and sudden, shot through my chest. It felt like one of my ribs had cracked. I had to grip the steering wheel to keep my hands steady, my knuckles turning white.

For a wild, stupid second, I thought about stopping. Just parking the Ute, walking into that office, and... and what? What the hell would I say? *Sorry I'm a sleep-deprived asshole who doesn't know how to handle a good thing? Sorry I blew up our relationship because you took a nice picture of a tomato?*

I couldn't. I'd just be proving her point all over again. The needy farmer, interrupting her work, and making his problems her problems.

I pushed my foot down onto the accelerator and drove past, my eyes fixed on the road ahead. But in my rearview mirror, I watched her car shrink until it was just a tiny white speck, and then it was gone.

The silence from her phone wasn't just silence anymore. It was an answer. It was the sound of a door being quietly, firmly, locked. And I was the one who had handed her the key.

CHAPTER 47

Megan

I had just finished scrubbing my keyboard with an alcohol wipe—a desperate, futile attempt to erase the physical evidence of my meltdown—when the dreaded summons cut through the office hum.

"Megan. My office."

My spine went rigid. Oh, God. This was it. I'd been in a holding pattern of misery all morning, and the air traffic controller of my doom had finally cleared me for landing. David had probably told Margaret I was leaking fluid at my desk, and now I was being called in for a formal review of my emotional instability. I considered asking if I should bring a lawyer. Or a helmet.

I stood up, my legs feeling about as sturdy as

overcooked spaghetti, and began the walk of shame toward the glass-walled office. Every head in the room seemed to turn as I passed. Brenda from accounts, a woman whose face was a permanent mask of mild disapproval, was definitely taking bets on whether I would cry or spontaneously combust. I was no longer the new girl. I was the new girl who was *clearly going through something.*

Showtime, I thought. *Time to get fired for being both a bad photographer and emotionally unstable. I've hit the failure jackpot!*

I sat in the chair opposite Margaret, my hands clasped so tightly in my lap that my knuckles were white. On her desk, laid out like evidence at a murder trial, were the contact sheets from the Spring Fair.

My stomach didn't just plummet, it went into a full-on, gravity-defying freefall. This was worse than a pity-talk. She'd seen them. She'd seen the intrusive, superficial, touristy garbage I'd produced. She was going to tell me I'd failed the assignment. That I hadn't gotten under the town's skin. I'd just photographed its surface like a cheap postcard.

"I've been looking at these all morning," she said, her tone as unreadable as a doctor's prescription. She tapped a finger on the photo of Evelyn.

I braced for impact. *Here it comes. She's going to tell me that I have the artistic sensitivity of a house brick.*

"This is it, Megan," Margaret said, her voice quiet but ringing with a strange intensity. "This is the honesty I was talking about."

I blinked. My brain, which had been preparing for a category five hurricane of criticism, short-circuited. It was like expecting a charging rhino and getting a fluffy kitten instead. It didn't compute.

"What?" I managed to choke out, the word sounding small and stupid in the quiet office.

She looked up from the photos and met my eyes. The usual briskness was gone, replaced by a look of profound, professional respect that was more shocking than any insult.

"You see these people," she said, her gaze sweeping over the images. The weathered hands on the tomato. The teenager, trying to look cool while holding a prize-winning chook. "You haven't just captured them, you've *honored* them. There's no judgment here. There's no agenda. There's just... them. Their dignity. Their exhaustion. Their pride. This," she tapped the photo of Evelyn again, her finger landing right on the woman's quiet, knowing smile, "isn't just a picture of an old woman with a scone. It's a portrait of a matriarch. It's art."

Art.

The word hung in the air between us. It was the last word I expected to hear. It was the opposite of intrusion. The opposite of tourism.

My gaze dropped back to the photos, but I was seeing them through a new filter. Not Jackson's. Not even my own, shame-filled one. I was seeing them through Margaret's. I saw the trust in Evelyn's eyes. She hadn't felt invaded, she had felt seen. I saw the pride in Mr. Henderson's hands, not just the pain. He wasn't a victim of his labor, he was a testament to it.

Jackson's words had felt like the absolute truth. The gospel of my own failure. But Margaret was my boss. She was a journalist, a woman who had built her life and career on seeing things clearly, without sentiment. She was the most respected, neutral party I could imagine. And she was telling me I wasn't a fraud.

I wasn't a tourist taking happy snaps of the quaint locals.

I was a photographer. An artist. And I had done my job.

The knot of shame in my chest didn't disappear, but it loosened its death grip. The fight wasn't about my work. Not really. The fight was about two different worlds colliding. It was about his exhaustion and my loneliness. It was about him feeling trapped by a life I was trying to romanticize because I desperately wanted to find a way inside it.

I hadn't been wrong. But that didn't mean he was wrong, either.

"Thank you," I whispered, the words feeling ridiculously small.

I walked out of her office and back to my desk, the contact sheets clutched in my hand like a shield. The coffee David had given me sat cold and forgotten. I didn't need it. A different kind of warmth was spreading through my chest.

My gaze fell on one image in particular, Jackson, silhouetted against the dawn, his shoulders squared against the vast, unforgiving landscape.

It wasn't his hardship I'd found beautiful. It was his resilience. The quiet dignity in his fight. The stubborn hope etched into the lines around his eyes. These weren't photos of a man's struggle; they were photos of his strength.

And in that difference, I found my own.

CHAPTER 48

Jackson

The co-op is a place of quiet routine and familiar smells—grain dust, fertilizer, and the faint, earthy scent of damp soil. Usually, it grounds me. Today, it just felt like a big shed full of things I had to lift.

I was hefting a bag of sheep feed onto my shoulder, my muscles screaming in protest from a night spent throwing spanners and regret around my workshop. Every physical ache was a dull echo of the bigger, sharper ache in my chest. I was on autopilot, my body going through the motions of a life I'd apparently decided to set on fire. I grabbed another bag, the rough hessian scraping against my neck, and threw it onto the Ute's tray.

The thud was unsatisfying. It didn't drown out the voice in my head, the one that had been on a constant loop since the fight.

Idiot. You had one good thing, and you broke it.

"Jackson."

A familiar voice cut through the low hum of the store's fluorescent lights, and my shoulders tightened instinctively. I turned, my movements feeling heavy and slow, planting my hands on my hips to brace myself.

My breath was a ragged thing in my chest. It was David Pritchard, standing by a pallet of fencing wire. There was no judgment in his eyes, only a quiet, steady concern that felt far more piercing than any accusation.

A wall went up inside me. The last person on earth I wanted to face was someone from Megan's world. It felt like he could see everything—the venom of our fight, the hollow ache of a sleepless night, and the ghost of the spanner still lying on the cold concrete floor.

"David," I grunted, turning back to the pallet of feed as if the bags were the most fascinating thing in the world. My plan was to load them so fast he wouldn't have time for a conversation.

"Heard you two had a rough night," he said, his voice low.

Of course, he had. The Clare Valley grapevine wasn't just efficient, it was psychic. I imagined I was the lead story for the way I treated Megan.

"Something like that," I muttered, grabbing another bag and swinging it up.

My grip was slick with sweat, and the bag slipped, crashing back onto the pallet with a dull whump, sending up a puff of dust that made me cough. Perfect. Now I couldn't even lift things properly. I looked like a teenager on his first day of work experience.

David leaned against the side of my Ute, crossing his arms. He wasn't going anywhere. "For what it's worth," he began, and I braced myself for a lecture. "Margaret showed me the photos this morning. The ones from the fair."

I stiffened, my jaw tightening. "And?"

"And," he said, looking me straight in the eye, "they're something special. I mean, truly special."

I gave a short, bitter laugh. "Special? Or a nice collection of quaint country folk for the city paper?" The words tasted like acid. They were my words, my accusation, and hearing a version of them now was bad enough.

David didn't even flinch. "I saw the one she took of old man Henderson. With his prize tomato."

A vicious, silent argument erupted in my head, one voice demanding I tell him to get lost, the other pleading for the quiet shame of being left alone.

"You know Hendo," David continued quietly. "You know how he complains about his arthritis, about his back, about the price of everything. But you also know how damn proud he is of that tomato. He's been trying to win that ribbon for twenty years. And somehow, she got that. In one picture. She got the pain, sure. But she got the pride, too. She sees us, Jackson."

He pushed himself off the Ute, his point made.

"She sees the real us. Not the caricature people drive through and see on their way to the wineries. Not many people who aren't from here ever get that. Or even try."

He gave me a short, final nod and walked back into the co-op, leaving me standing alone in the dust and the silence, one hand still resting on the bag I'd dropped.

His words knock around in my head threatening to set up camp. I tried to dismiss them.

He works with Megan, of course, he'd say that.

I straightened up and successfully loaded the

next bag, then another, the rhythm of the work a familiar, hollow comfort. But the words were still there.

She sees us.

I stopped, leaning against the Ute's tray, the sun hot on the back of my neck. I thought about the photo of Evelyn. I had seen it as an intrusion. But David saw it as an honor.

An image of James from down the road flashed in my mind, his shoulders slumped at the pub a few years back, nursing a beer after his city girlfriend had packed her bags and left without a word. I'd been waiting for Megan to do the same. To see the rust and the dirt as the hardship it was and then run.

But that wasn't what her lens captured. She hadn't just snapped a picture of a broken gate. She'd spent an hour there, waiting for the light to hit it just right. She wasn't documenting decay. She was searching for endurance.

The cynical bastard on my shoulder had told me she was judging, but he was wrong. She was learning. She was translating my world of dirt, rust, struggle, and pride into a language she could comprehend. Her art was her way of listening.

And I had told her she was wrong to even try. I hadn't just gotten angry. I had taken her genuine attempt to connect, to see my world, and I had thrown it back in her face as an insult. The problem wasn't that she saw beauty in the struggle. The problem was that I was so terrified she wouldn't be able to handle the reality of it that I attacked the beauty first, as a preemptive strike. I'd made my own fear her fault.

The weight of the feed bags was nothing compared to the weight that settled in my gut. I had two more bags to load, but I just stood there, staring at the co-op entrance, long after David had disappeared inside.

I finished loading the Ute on autopilot, the movements mechanical, my mind churning. The drive home was a blur of dusty roads and fence posts. I parked by the machinery shed and was just starting to unload when Dad walked out, wiping his hands on a rag.

"You've been wound tighter than a two-dollar watch since she got here, Jackson."

His words, so simple and true, broke something open in me. The bag of feed suddenly felt impossibly heavy. I set it down carefully on the tray of the Ute and finally turned to face him, the fight draining out of me, replaced by a profound weariness.

"I pushed her away, Dad." The admission came

out quiet, tasting like rust. "I kept waiting for her to break. Kept waiting for her to decide this life was too hard, that I was too hard, and run back to the city."

Dad raised an eyebrow, a flicker of surprise in his eyes, but he stayed silent, letting me find the words.

"I told myself she was delicate," I continued, the words finding their own rhythm now. "But she's not. She got kicked by a bull and was back on her feet in hours. She sees things in this place, things I've stopped letting myself see. She finds the strength in it, not just the struggle."

I took a breath, the truth of it settling deep in my bones. I met Dad's steady gaze. "The problem was never her. It was me. I was so scared she wasn't tough enough for this life, I never stopped to ask if I was brave enough to let her in."

Dad was silent for a long moment, his eyes searching my face. He pushed himself off the fence post and walked over. He just looked at me, a flicker of something like respect in his gaze.

"Well," he said, his voice gruff. "Sounds like you've got some fixing to do, then. And I'm not talking about the tractor."

He turned and walked back toward the house, leaving me standing by the Ute. The weight in my gut hadn't disappeared, but it had changed. It wasn't the leaden weight of regret anymore. It was the heavy, solid weight of purpose. He was right. I had some fixing to do.

CHAPTER 49

Megan

The four-page proof of my photo essay was spread across the coffee table like a patient on an operating table. The faces of the Clare Valley stared back at me. Evelyn. Mr. Henderson. They looked proud.

Margaret's words had stirred something in me, but the loneliness remained. The professional validation felt good, but it was like winning a shiny trophy for a race you ran with a broken leg. You still had a broken leg.

That's when I heard the knock.

It wasn't a loud knock. It was hesitant. Unsure. Three soft raps that seemed to apologize for their own existence.

My heart did a complicated maneuver that was part lurch, part flutter, part brace-for-impact. I froze, a half-eaten biscuit hovering near my mouth. There was only one person it could be.

I scrambled off the couch, my mismatched socks skidding on the floorboards. In my haste, my knee caught the edge of the coffee table. The proofs, my beautiful, validated, four-page spread, went flying, scattering across the floor in a cascade of artistic dignity and professional pride. "Oh, for—" I hissed, dropping to my hands and knees. This was me. A woman who couldn't even handle a surprise visitor without creating a scene of light-paperwork-based carnage.

The knock came again, even softer this time.

I took a deep breath and pulled myself to my feet. I walked to the door, my hand hovering over the doorknob. I was wearing a paint-stained T-shirt and leggings with a small hole in the knee. My hair was in a bun so messy it could have been mistaken for a bird's nest. I looked like the 'before' picture in a self-help ad. I opened the door.

And there he was.

He looked wrecked, like he hadn't slept in two days, and the lines of stress around his eyes were carved deeper than I'd ever seen them. He wore a clean shirt, but it was rumpled, like he'd put it on and then spent an hour pacing and running his hands through his hair.

He wasn't empty-handed. In his arms, held against his chest like a shield, was a worn, dusty, leather-bound photo album.

We just stood there for a second, the cool night air flowing between us, thick with everything we hadn't said. My eyes flickered from his face to the album, then back.

"Hey," he finally said, his voice rough.

"Hey," I replied, my voice barely a whisper. I instinctively crossed my arms, hiding the paint stain on my shirt.

He lifted the album slightly. "You... you said you wanted to get under my skin. To understand." He took a shaky breath. "This is the only way I know how to show you. The real way. Not just through a lens."

My heart hammered against my ribs. This wasn't an apology. Not yet. It was an offering. An invitation.

I stepped back, opening the door wider. "You should... come in."

He walked in, bringing the scent of fresh air and something else that was raw, undisguised vulnerability, into my little cottage. His eyes landed on the scattered proofs on the floor. His face fell. "Did I...?"

"No! No, that was me," I said quickly, bending down and frantically gathering the pages. "I'm just... clumsy."

He knelt down to help, and for a moment, we were just two people awkwardly picking up paper, our hands brushing as we both reached for the photo of Evelyn. The static shock was so sudden, we both pulled back.

Once the mess was contained, he walked over to the coffee table and carefully placed the album down. The old, worn leather, next to the glossy, modern paper. His history, next to my interpretation of it.

He sank onto the couch, not looking at me, but at the album. "Meg, what I said at the restaurant... there's no excuse. It was cruel." He finally looked up, and his eyes were full of a shame so profound it hurt to look at. "You showed me something beautiful, and I told you it was ugly. I took your passion, the very thing that makes you *you*, and I threw it back in your face."

I sat down in the armchair opposite him, pulling my knees to my chest. I didn't say anything. I just listened.

"The truth is," he continued, his voice cracking slightly, "I was terrified. I was terrified that you'd see the reality of it all, the debt, the dirt, the sheer bloody exhaustion of it, and you'd run. And you wouldn't be wrong to run. So I did the stupidest thing I could think of. I pushed you away first. I used your art as a weapon because I was scared, you'd eventually see my life as a cage. The same way I see it sometimes."

I finally found my voice. "It's not a cage, Jackson."

"Isn't it?" He gestured around the room. "You have this. You have your work. You can go anywhere. I have... that." He pointed out the window, into the vast, dark expanse of the valley. "It's not beautiful when a piece of machinery you can't afford to replace breaks down in the middle of harvest. It's not beautiful when you're staring at a sick animal, knowing its life is in your hands. That's my reality. And I was so afraid you wouldn't want it."

My turn.

"I was naive," I said softly. He looked up, surprised. "I saw the poetry of it all. I saw the light, the texture, and the history. But I didn't feel the weight of it. Not really. I was so wrapped up in my own loneliness, so desperate to find my place here, that I didn't stop to think about what it must feel like to be chained to it."

He opened the old album. The first page had a single, black-and-white photo of a young woman with a kind smile and eyes exactly like his, standing proudly next to a much smaller, shinier tractor.

"My mom," he said quietly. "She was a town girl. A nurse from Adelaide. She saw the beauty in it, too."

He slowly turned the pages, and I saw his whole life. Jackson as a gap-toothed kid on his dad's shoulders. A surly teenager covered in grease. A young man standing with his parents, the farm stretching out behind them like a kingdom. It wasn't a collection of photos. It was a life. A hard, beautiful, complicated life.

He was right. I hadn't understood the weight. But he was also wrong. I wasn't afraid of it.

"I don't want you to stop seeing the beauty," he whispered, looking at my proofs on the table. "I think... maybe I need you to help me see it again."

That was it. That was everything.

I slid off the armchair and knelt on the floor in front of him, closing the space between us. I placed my hand over his on the open album. He flinched, then relaxed, his fingers lacing with mine.

"I'm not going anywhere, you idiot," I murmured.

"Good," he breathed out, a wave of relief washing over his face.

He leaned in, and I met him halfway. The kiss was a quiet, desperate collision of apology and forgiveness. It was the feeling of coming home after being lost for a very long time. It was him letting me in, and me promising to stay.

CHAPTER 50

It was a perfect Saturday morning, the kind that felt like a reward for surviving the week. I was sitting on the backstep of Jackson's farmhouse, a mug of coffee warming my hands, watching the world wake up. Jackson was in the machinery shed, the clang of metal on metal a surprisingly comforting soundtrack.

In the two months since I'd moved to Clare, these weekends at the farm had become my anchor. I was slowly learning the rhythms of his life. The pre-dawn starts, the endless cycle of feeding and fixing, the profound, bone-deep quiet of the nights.

The Gremlin in my head still made appearances, of course. It had become a connoisseur of my anxieties. *You know, he hasn't actually said 'I love you' yet,* it pointed out yesterday while I was trying to photograph a particularly uncooperative goat for the paper. *Probably keeping his options open. In case a girl who knows how to drive a tractor shows up.* I'd told it to shut up. Mostly.

Jackson emerged from the shed, wiping grease from his hands on a rag. He saw me, and his face broke into that slow, easy smile that still made my stomach do a complicated little dance.

"Morning," he said, dropping a kiss on the top of my head as he passed. "Coffee ready?"

"On the counter."

He disappeared inside, and I took another sip of my own, feeling a sense of peace so deep it was almost unnerving. This felt real. This felt like it could be a life.

The peace lasted for approximately four more minutes. It was shattered by the screech of tires on the gravel driveway as Jackson's dad, Mike, skidded his Ute to a halt. He jumped out before the dust had even settled, his face a mask of grim frustration.

"Fence is down on the back paddock," he said, not as a greeting, but as a declaration of war. "Bloody roos knocked it flat. Half the new lambs are gone."

Jackson was out the door in a second, his coffee forgotten. "How many?"

"Counted at least fifty missing. They'll be halfway to bloody Adelaide by now if we don't move fast."

The atmosphere changed instantly. The lazy morning peace evaporated, replaced by a tense, focused energy. Jackson was already pulling on his boots, his movements sharp and efficient. He was in farmer mode.

"I'll take the quad, do a sweep of the north boundary," he said to his dad. "You take the Ute and check the creek line." He was already moving, grabbing keys, his mind a thousand miles away.

I stood there, feeling utterly, completely useless. The Gremlin cleared its throat. *Well, look at you,* it said. *The decorative girlfriend. Can't ride a quad bike. Probably thinks a ewe is a type of tree. Best stay out of the way and try not to sit in any more manure.*

For a moment, I listened to it. I watched them, this father-son team, a well-oiled machine of shared knowledge and experience, and I felt like a tourist again. An observer.

Then, something snapped. No. I wasn't that girl anymore.

"Wait!" I called out, my voice sharp enough to make them both turn.

Jackson looked at me, his expression a mixture of stress and impatience. "Meg, I don't have time right now."

"I can help," I said.

His dad gave me a look that was kind but deeply skeptical.

"I have my drone in the car," I said, the idea hitting me with the force of a lightning strike. "The one I use for aerial shots. It has a high-res camera. I can launch it from here and cover a huge area in minutes. It'll be faster than you two driving around."

They stared at me. I could see the cogs turning in Jackson's head. The skepticism warred with logic.

"It's worth a shot, isn't it?" I pressed, my confidence growing. "What have you got to lose?"

Jackson looked at his dad, who gave a slight, almost imperceptible nod.

"All right," Jackson said, his focus shifting entirely to me. "Show me."

Five minutes later, we were standing in the middle of a paddock, the drone whirring to life at my feet. I held the controller, my fingers moving with a familiar, confident speed. This was my machinery. This, I knew how to fix.

"Okay, it's up," I said, my eyes fixed on the screen that showed the drone's-eye view. The world flattened into a patchwork of green and brown. "Where am I looking?"

"Follow that tree line east," Jackson directed, leaning over my shoulder, his hand resting on my arm. "They like to shelter in the scrub."

I sent the drone skimming over the landscape, my thumb expertly guiding its path. The silence stretched, broken only by the high-pitched whine of the drone's motors. And then I saw them. A cluster of small, white dots, huddled in the shade of a cluster of gums nearly a kilometer away.

"There," I said, my voice tight with excitement. I zoomed the camera in. "Got them. Looks like the whole lot of them."

A rough sound, half-laugh, half-exhale of pure relief, escaped Jackson. "Holy shit," he breathed, his grip tightening on my arm. "I don't believe it."

He looked at me, and the pride in his eyes was so potent it almost knocked me over. It wasn't the look he gave me after sex. It wasn't the look of a man admiring his girlfriend. It was the look of a man seeing his partner.

He didn't say anything else. He just leaned down

and kissed me, a hard, dusty, grateful kiss right there in the middle of the paddock. And it was, without a doubt, the sexiest kiss he'd ever given me.

CHAPTER 51

Megan

My dad arrived on a Saturday, bringing with him a gust of city air and a cooler bag full of his own pre-made spaghetti Bolognese as if he suspected I was living on a diet of foraged berries and raw wheat. His hug was tight, a little too long, and full of the unspoken worry of a parent letting go.

"It's... quiet," he said, standing in the middle of my living room, looking around as if he expected a tumbleweed to roll past.

"It's Sunday, Dad." I laughed, taking the cooler bag. "The town is resting."

"Right," he said, though he looked unconvinced.

I'd been dreading this visit. Not because I didn't want to see him, but because I knew what it represented. It was an inspection. A wellness check. A father's quiet reconnaissance mission to determine if his daughter had made a catastrophic life choice. I worried all morning.

Jackson was coming for dinner. A proper, meet-the-parent dinner. The thought filled me with a level of anxiety usually reserved for tax audits and dental surgery.

He arrived right on time, holding a bottle of local Riesling and looking so clean and handsome in a button-down shirt that it made my heart ache. He shook my dad's hand, his grip firm, his gaze direct.

"Good to finally meet you, sir," he said.

"Robert, please," Dad replied, sizing him up.

The dinner was a masterclass in awkwardness. Dad, trying to be helpful, asked Jackson about the farm. The conversation immediately veered into a foreign language of rainfall averages, soil composition, and the market price of wool. I sat there, smiling like a flight attendant during turbulence, offering more wine and trying to remember how to breathe.

"It's a tough life," Dad said, his tone laced with concern as Jackson described the brutal hours of harvest. "You sure you're up for this, Megs?" he asked, turning to me.

And there it was. The question. The doubt.

Before I could answer, Jackson spoke, his voice calm and steady. "She's tougher than she looks, Robert."

Dad raised an eyebrow.

"A few weeks ago, we had a fence down, lost fifty lambs," Jackson continued, looking at my dad, not me. "We were looking at hours of searching, maybe losing some. Megan got her drone out, found them in ten minutes. She thinks differently. She sees things we don't. We wouldn't have found them all without her."

He said it so simply, so matter-of-factly. It wasn't a grand declaration. It was a statement of fact. A testament.

I stared at him, my throat tight. He wasn't just defending me. He was validating me. He was telling my dad that I wasn't a liability here, I was an asset.

My dad was silent for a long moment, studying Jackson over the rim of his wine glass. He looked from Jackson to me, and I saw the worry in his eyes finally, finally begin to recede. He saw it too. He saw that Jackson wasn't just some farm boy I was having a fling with. He was a man who saw me, who respected me. A man who would have my back.

"Well," Dad said, clearing his throat. He raised his glass. "To new ways of thinking."

It was a truce. An acceptance. A blessing.

Later, after Dad had left for his motel room in town, I stood with Jackson by the front door. The weight that had been sitting on my chest for months felt like it had finally lifted.

"Thank you," I said softly, wrapping my arms around his waist.

"For what?"

"For seeing me."

He smiled, that slow, heart-melting smile. "Always," he murmured, and he leaned down to kiss me. It wasn't a kiss of frantic passion or grateful respect. It was a kiss of quiet certainty. A kiss that felt like the start of a whole new future together.

EPILOGUE

Megan

The lead singer of the local band, a man who bore a startling resemblance to a garden gnome, was belting out a cover of a Cold Chisel song. It was just different enough, melody-wise, to be legally distinct from the original, but close enough that everyone could still shout along. This, apparently, was the pinnacle of live entertainment at the Clare Valley Harvest Festival. And honestly? It was glorious.

Six months ago, my camera would have been a shield. Now, it just felt like a part of my arm. I wasn't hunting for a story. I was just in it.

"Megan, love! Get a photo of this monster!"

I turned to see Evelyn, beaming, holding up a

pumpkin so enormous it looked like a small, orange planetoid.

"That's a prize-winner for sure, Ev." I laughed, snapping the shot. "Are you sure you didn't feed it steroids?"

She winked. "Just good soil and a lot of stern talking-tos. You and Jackson coming over for Sunday roast?"

"Wouldn't miss it," I said, and the words felt as natural as breathing. This was my life now. A life with standing Sunday dinner invitations and an encyclopedic knowledge of prize-winning vegetables. The loneliness that had once felt like a physical presence was gone.

Margaret had called last week, after the weekend edition with my photos had sold out. She'd offered me a permanent position as the paper's regional correspondent, a job I could do from anywhere in the valley.

A familiar arm slid around my waist, and the scent of sunshine and Jackson filled my senses.

"Trying to give me a heart attack, Farmer?" I grumbled, leaning back against his solid frame.

"Everything all right?" he asked, his voice a low rumble against my ear.

"Perfect," I said, watching David try to teach his toddler how to throw a hoop over a bottle of wine.

I looked at Jackson. He wasn't watching the crowd. He was watching me. The look on his face wasn't worry or confusion. It was pride. Pure, simple, uncomplicated pride. He wasn't just looking at the city girl he'd fallen for; he was looking at his partner, a part of his world, standing confidently in the heart of it all.

He seemed to sense my thoughts. "You fit here, you know," he said quietly, his thumb tracing a slow circle on my hip. "Like you were always meant to be here."

My heart squeezed. He'd spent so long afraid I wouldn't fit, and now he was the one pointing out that I belonged.

"Come on," he murmured, tugging my hand. "Let's get out of here for a minute."

He led me away from the noise, toward the edge of the oval where the darkness was gathering. We stopped under the sprawling branches of an old gum tree, the music softening to a distant, thrumming beat.

He turned to face me, pulling me close. "You're really here," he said, his voice thick with emotion. It wasn't a question. It was a marvel.

I smiled, my heart so full I thought it might burst. I thought of the terrified woman who had taken a wrong turn down a dirt road. She had been looking for a home.

I reached up and placed my hands over his. "I'm not going anywhere," I replied, my voice steady and sure. "Margaret offered me a permanent job. And besides," I added, my voice dropping to a conspiratorial whisper, "I hear there's some prime real estate opening up near the north pasture with a pretty great view."

His face broke into a slow, brilliant smile as he understood. The plans for the cottage were still just lines on paper, but they felt more real than any apartment I'd ever leased. He leaned down and kissed me, that held the promise of a thousand more sunsets over the paddocks, a lifetime of quiet moments, and noisy festivals. It was him, and it was me, right here.

Home. It wasn't just a feeling anymore. It was a way of life, and it was with Jackson.

The End

Enjoy more rural romances by Lilliana Rose

Chasing Dust Clouds

A Dusty Christmas

The Royal Show Affair
A Farmer's Christmas

Best in Show
A Country Christmas

Like urban paranormal romance?
Check out these books by Lilliana Rose

Protector Wolf Shifter Series
Bk1: Shadow Wolf
Bk2: Marked Wolf
Bk3: Rogue Wolf

Ochre Dragon Shifter Series
Dragon Bond
Dragon Reborn
Dragon Desire
Dragon Defiance
Dragon Law

Witch Moon Series
Bk1: Dark Moon Secrets

ACKNOWLEDGMENTS

Thank you, Kaylene, for always making time to offer your unwavering support and thoughtful advice—I'm truly grateful.

A heartfelt thanks to my dog, Sprinkles, for reminding me when it's time to eat, take a break, and call it a night. Your quiet presence, whether lying next to me or at my feet, brings comfort and companionship, making the writing journey feel far less lonely.

And to my growing boy, you're an invaluable part of my writing process, thank you for being my constant inspiration and joy.

ABOUT THE AUTHOR

Lilliana Rose writes heartwarming rural romances filled with love, resilience, and the charm of country life. Growing up on a sheep farm in Australia, she draws inspiration from her roots to create authentic stories where characters overcome challenges, navigate misunderstandings, and find their happily-ever-afters. Whether it's trading city heels for country work boots or embracing the simplicity of rural living, her stories celebrate love and the enduring spirit of the countryside. In addition to her romance novels, Lilliana has also published poetry, middle-grade fiction, picture books, and novellas under various pen names.

Check out more of her work at www.lillianarose.com.

Connect with her on social media.